To enjoy :

STRONG ENOUGH

MELANIE HARLOW
DAVID ROMANOV

Melanie Harlow

MH PUBLISHING

To Avery!
Enjoy!

Melanie Harlow

I want to dedicate this story to my husband, who is the coolest guy in the universe and my everything, forever.
D.R.

What he said.
M.H.

Cover Design: Letitia Hasser, Romantic Book Affairs

http://designs.romanticbookaffairs.com/

Cover Photography: Vitaly Dorokhov

http://instagram.com/vitalydorokhovphoto

Editing: Nancy Smay

http://www.evidentink.com/

Publicity: Social Butterfly PR

http://www.socialbutterflypr.net/

He was my secret conduit to myself—like a catalyst that allows us to become who we are, the foreign body, the pacer, the graft, the patch that sends all the right impulses, the steel pin that keeps a soldier's bone together, the other man's heart that makes us more us than we were before the transplant.

ANDRE ACIMAN, CALL ME BY YOUR NAME

ONE

DEREK

HER NAME WAS CAROLYN, and she was damn near perfect.

"Thank you very much for dinner," she said as I pulled up in front of her house. "I had a great time tonight, as usual,"

Beautiful. Sweet. Intelligent. Twenty-nine years old. Divorced from her high school sweetheart, no children, but wanted them in the future. Taught college algebra. Loved to travel. Volunteered for UNICEF. Ran marathons.

"Me too." I put the Range Rover in park. "Let me walk you to the door. Stay right there."

We'd been on six dates—one coffee, two lunches, and three dinners—and I'd enjoyed every one of them. She was exactly the kind of woman I'd envisioned for myself. Nothing about her turned me off.

The problem? Nothing about her turned me on, either.

She unbuckled her seatbelt and waited for me to walk

around and open the passenger door before getting out. I offered her a hand and she took it. "Thank you."

You're not trying hard enough.

Keeping her slender hand in mine, I shut the car door and escorted her up the front walk. The June night air was warm and balmy and smelled like orange blossoms. Everything about the evening whispered romance.

"Such a gentleman," Carolyn teased. "It's good to know that chivalry isn't dead."

"Not at all." I liked the idea of chivalry, that a man could be governed by a code of conduct based on tradition, honor, and nobility despite being a warrior at heart. That he buried his propensity for violence or his darker urges in order to preserve social morality, or at least the appearance of it. I understood that.

We stepped onto her front porch and she turned to face me. "Would you like to come in for a drink?" Her eyes glittered in the dark as her body swayed closer to mine. "And maybe stop being such a gentleman?" She ran her hands up my chest.

I slid my arms around her waist and pulled her against me, lowering my mouth to hers, praying to feel something. Anything.

But I felt nothing. No quickening pulse, no rush of heat, no stirring in my blood. (Or my pants.)

Shyly, she slipped her tongue between my lips, and I met it with mine, opening wider to deepen the kiss.

Nothing.

Frustrated, I clutched the material of her shirt in one fist and grabbed a handful of her hair with the other, hoping some aggression and resistance was what I needed to get turned on. For me, sex was best when it was a little antagonistic. A little combative. A power play. And it had been so long...

"Ouch!" Carolyn cried.

Immediately I let go of her and stepped back. "I'm sorry. I'm sorry. Are you okay?"

"Yes. I'm fine." She rubbed the back of her head and laughed nervously. "Don't be sorry. I'm the one who said the thing about not being a gentleman. It just surprised me." She softened her voice. "Could we maybe try again? Go a little easier this time?"

What's the fucking point?

"I'm sorry, Carolyn. I'm a little out of it tonight. Another time?"

"Oh, okay. Sure." She sounded let down, her eyes dropping to our feet. Then she looked up again. "Are we still on for tomorrow night?"

"Of course."

She beamed, clearly relieved. "Great. I'll bring dessert. I'm excited to meet your friends."

"They're excited to meet you."

Her smile widened. "Night."

"Night." Shoving my hands in my pockets, I watched her go in and shut the front door.

Fuck.

What the hell was my problem?

TWENTY MINUTES LATER, I let myself into the beautiful three-bedroom brick house I'd purchased a few years ago when I'd been about to propose to my then-girlfriend. I thought we'd be married by now. I thought we'd have a family by now. I thought I'd feel complete by now.

None of it had happened.

I turned off all the lights and trudged upstairs, feeling every one of my thirty-six years. In my bathroom, I frowned at my reflection in the mirror, running a hand over my slightly scruffy jaw. *Jesus, look at all the gray coming in.* For a while, it had only been a couple of spots, but now I was solidly salt-and-pepper. At the temples, too. Was it normal to go gray at this age? And what the hell was with those lines between my eyebrows? Was that from frowning? I quickly relaxed my face, and they mostly disappeared. But not entirely.

Goddamn, I was getting old.

At least I was still in good shape. I slipped my coat off and hung it and my shirt in my closet, tossed my T-shirt into the laundry basket, then stood in front of the full-length mirror on the bathroom door, eyeing myself critically.

No paunch yet. No flab. No "handles" anywhere. My stomach was still hard and flat, my six-pack still lingered, my chest and arms were still muscular. I might not have all the sculpted lines and bulges I'd had ten years ago, but I worked hard to maintain my physique. I liked working out. It made me feel strong and powerful and in control of my body. I commanded it to do something, and it obeyed. Run those miles. Lift that weight. Punch that bag.

Easy.

Same reason I kept my house so immaculate. My family and friends teased me endlessly about what they called my "obsession" with neatness. I didn't get it—who wouldn't want to come home to a house where everything was clean and organized? It wasn't a germ thing; it was just an aversion to chaos and mess. No clutter on the counters, no dirty laundry piled up anywhere, no dishes left in the sink. And I always knew exactly where a thing was because after I used it, I fucking put it away. What was so weird about that?

I got ready for bed and turned out the light, feeling a little pathetic since it wasn't even ten o'clock on a Friday night, but telling myself I'd get a good night's sleep and hit the gym early. I hadn't even closed my eyes when my phone buzzed on the nightstand. Picking it up, I squinted at the screen in the dark. My sister, Ellen.

"Hello?"

"Hey, it's me."

In the background, I could hear muffled bar noise—music, voices, the clanking of plates and glasses. "What's up?"

"I need a favor."

TWO

MAXIM

FOR THE FIRST time since jumping on a plane in Moscow, I started to wonder if I'd made a mistake.

It wasn't like me at all. I tended to make decisions quickly, but afterward I wasn't the type to agonize over whether I'd made the right one or not. I trusted my gut.

So last week, when my gut told me to stop dreaming about moving to the U.S. and make it happen already, I went with it. Booked a ticket, quit my job, packed a bag.

In hindsight, I *probably* should have planned it out a little better.

A friend of a friend—some guy named Jake—was supposed to be here at the airport to pick me up, but I'd been standing outside the international terminal at LAX for two hours already, and he still hadn't shown. I hoped nothing was wrong, but I was starting to think I might have to go to Plan B.

Not that I had a Plan B.

Pretty much everything hinged on Jake. He'd found me an apartment, and I'd already wired him the money for one month's rent. I hadn't liked the idea of paying for something without seeing it, but Jake said if I didn't grab it, somebody else would, and he didn't know of any other place I could rent that cheap, especially on such short notice. I told him I'd take it and sent the money. I hadn't asked for the address, though.

That was a mistake.

I checked my phone again, like somehow it might have magically charged itself in my pocket. Still dead. Unfortunately, in my excitement to leave, I'd forgotten to throw my charger into my bag.

Another mistake.

Unable to stand still any longer, I crossed the street and jumped in a taxi.

"Where to?" the driver asked.

Well, fuck.

"Downtown," I decided, figuring I'd grab some food somewhere, maybe see if I could charge my phone. Hopefully Jake would get in touch in the next couple hours. If he didn't, I'd have to get a hotel tonight. It would be ridiculously expensive and I didn't want to waste that kind of money on one night, but I didn't see any way around it.

It took a long time to get downtown—traffic was terrible. I was nodding off for the third time when the driver spoke.

"What's the address?" He glanced back at me, and I blinked a few times.

"Uh, no particular address. Any suggestions for a bar or restaurant around here?"

He scratched the top of his head with his thumb. "The Blind Pig is pretty popular."

"Blind Pig?" I repeated, a little confused. Maybe the

words had different meanings than what I thought. My English was pretty good, but far from perfect.

"It's another name they used for illegal speakeasies during Prohibition."

"Ah." Quickly I pulled my notebook from my bag and scribbled that down. I wanted to be a screenwriter, so not only did I have to improve my English, but I needed to learn all those little cultural details that would make a script authentic.

My friends made fun of me for it, but I always carried a notebook with me so I'd have somewhere to take notes and write down all the ideas that came to me at random times during the day or night. I'd learned the hard way that I wouldn't necessarily remember them later. And since I'd sold my laptop last week to pad my savings a little, a notebook was all I had. As soon as I could afford it, I'd have to get a new computer.

But that would take a while.

A few minutes later, the driver pulled over and switched off the meter. "It's just up ahead there on the right."

I thanked him, paid him with some of the cash I'd gotten from the airport ATM, and jumped out. Even though I wasn't sure where I'd sleep tonight, it was hard not to feel excited as I walked up the street. Before today, I'd only seen places like this on a screen, but this was *real*. I was actually here. It made me feel invincible, like anything was possible.

A moment later, I pulled open The Blind Pig's heavy wooden door and stepped inside. The light was low, the atmosphere warm, and the music upbeat. It was crowded, but I managed to find an empty seat at the long wooden bar.

"Hi there." The bartender smiled at me as I set my bag

on the floor. She had dark hair pulled into a ponytail and big brown eyes. "I'm Ellen. What can I get for you?"

"Could I look at a menu, please?"

"Of course." She brought me a menu and I looked it over, deciding to order the most American thing I could think of.

"I'll have a burger. And a beer."

"Great. Can I see your ID?"

"Sure." I pulled out the travel wallet where I kept all my important documents, handed her my passport, and dropped the wallet back into my bag.

"Russia, huh?" Ellen smiled at me again. "Are you here for work or just visiting?"

"Just visiting." I didn't want to jinx myself by announcing my intention to try to stay here for good. Technically, I could only stay for six months on my tourist visa, but I had no intention of using my return flight.

"Having a good time so far?"

"Well, I've only been here for about three hours, and I spent two of them waiting for my friend to pick me up from the airport, but he never showed."

The bartender gave me a sympathetic look. "L.A. traffic can be awful. Have you called him?" She handed my passport back to me, and I tucked it inside my coat pocket.

"I can't. My phone is dead. And I forgot to pack my charger." I gave her a smile intended to charm. I wasn't into women and never intentionally led them on, but I won't lie, sometimes being attractive to them was helpful. "Do you think anyone has one here I could use?"

It worked—or she was just nice, because she smiled back warmly. "I can check. Let me get you that beer— sounds like you need it. What kind would you like?"

"Corona, please."

She nodded, and a moment later, she set it in front of me. "This one's on me. I'll put your food order in. You're probably super hungry after that long trip."

"Yes. Thank you."

After a long drink from the bottle, I pulled my notebook from my bag again, and a school photo of my eight-year-old sister Liliya fell out from the front pages. She'd given it to me right before I left, and on the back she'd written, **To Maxim. Don't forget about me. Love, Liliya.** I set it on the bar as a woman slid onto the empty seat next to me. "Hi there."

She was about my age and dressed professionally, like maybe she worked in an office, but she was the kind of American blonde I pictured more like a lifeguard on TV or a dancer in a beach movie. Her grin was confident and flirty. American women were *so* different from Russian.

"Hello," I said.

She glanced at the photo of Liliya and gasped. "Oh my God, she's so beautiful! And she looks just like you. Is that your...daughter?" she asked tentatively, wrinkling her nose like she hoped that was not the case.

"No, that's my little sister. But we do look alike." Although we had different fathers, Liliya and I both had our mother's wide blue eyes, dark blond hair, and dimpled chin.

She smiled and held out her hand. "I'm Amy."

I shook it. "Maxim."

"Maxim." She repeated my name as I'd said it, complete with the accent. After giving my palm a suggestive squeeze and holding onto it way too long, she swiveled to face me, crossing her legs in a way that put them on display. "I've never seen you here before."

"I've never been here before."

"I like your accent. Where are you from?" She leaned a little closer to me, so close I could smell her flowery perfume.

"Russia."

"I was going to guess that!" She looked pleased with herself and slapped me lightly on the leg. "What brings you to L.A.?"

"Just visiting."

"Traveling alone?" She widened her eyes and batted her lashes.

"Uh, yeah."

"So you're single?"

It was strange to me the way Americans asked such personal questions. I'd have to get used to it. "Yes, but..."

"Yes, but what? You don't like American girls?" she teased.

Evasive words were on the tip of my tongue when a voice spoke up in my head. *There's no reason to hide here.*

"Yes, but I'm gay," I told her, meeting her eyes directly. It was the first time I'd said the words out loud to anyone. I wasn't ashamed or anything, but growing up where I had, sexuality simply wasn't talked about, whether you were gay or straight. Clearly, the boundaries here were different.

Amy sighed, centering herself on her chair, her body slouched. "Figures. I knew you were too good looking to be straight." She picked up her wine glass and took a long, long drink. "Sorry if I bothered you."

I smiled. "You didn't. It's okay."

"Somehow I always pick out the gay ones. It's like a curse."

I wasn't sure what to say. "Um. I'm sorry?"

She sighed and shook her head. "Anyway, welcome to

America. Cheers." She held up her wine glass. "Hey, how do you say cheers in Russian?"

"*Na zdorovie.*"

She blinked. "Yeah, I'm not gonna attempt it." But she clinked her glass against my bottle, and we both drank as Ellen appeared with a plate heaped with food—a thick, juicy hamburger and French fries.

My mouth watered. "That looks delicious."

"It is," she said confidently. "And I wasn't able to find a charger yet, but I'm still looking."

I picked up the notebook, sticking the photo of Liliya back inside the pages, so she could set the plate down in front of me. "Thank you so much. I can't believe I—"

I stopped speaking and looked down by my feet, where I was reaching around for my bag but felt nothing.

It was gone.

"AGAIN, I'm *so* sorry. Nothing like this has ever happened here before." Ellen leaned over the bar and touched my arm. She was the bar owner and felt personally responsible for the theft—she'd apologized a thousand times, even breaking down in tears. "I feel sick about it."

"It's not your fault," I told her. "It was very crowded. Even I didn't see it happen, and it was right at my feet."

The police officer who'd responded to her frantic call had asked everyone in the bar if they'd seen anyone leave with the bag, or anything suspicious at all, but no one had. He'd been nice, but hadn't seemed too hopeful that my bag would be found.

At least I still had my passport. Thankfully, I'd stuck it in my coat pocket rather than back in my bag after showing it to Ellen. Replacing it in the U.S. would have been a nightmare. My biggest problem was that my wallet had been in my bag, so my cash and my bank card were gone. Now buying a hotel room for tonight wasn't even an option. Neither was paying for my food and drink, not that I'd gotten to eat anything. And I was *starving*. But what could I do?

"God, you're so nice. I feel like any other guy would be freaking out."

"Wouldn't do me much good."

"But what will you do tonight?" Her brown eyes were wide and sad. "Where will you go?"

I shrugged. "I'll find somewhere."

Ellen threw her hands in the air, her voice rising in anguish. "How? You don't even know anyone here! And someone took your wallet, so you have no money!"

"I'll be okay. Really. I just have to charge my phone so I can find my friend." I tried to sound more confident than I felt.

A determined look replaced Ellen's tortured expression. "You know what? I'm going to help you. I believe in fate, and there must be a reason why you came in here tonight and all this happened."

I shook my head. "I believe in fate too, but this was probably just random bad luck."

She flattened both palms on the bar. "Nope. Nothing is random. Now it's getting late, and I can see how exhausted you are, so I'm going to find you a place to stay and charge your phone tonight. And then tomorrow, I'll help you find your friend."

"That's not necessary," I protested, stifling a yawn.

"Maxim. Look at you. You're about to fall over, you're so tired. And my mind is made up." Ellen nodded once, and her tone told me she wouldn't be argued with. "I'll be right back, I just have to make a phone call. You wait here." She brought me another Corona before disappearing through the kitchen door, leaving me to wonder who on earth she was going to call.

THREE

DEREK

OF COURSE my sister needed a favor. Did she ever call me when she didn't?

"I'm not fostering another rescue puppy, Ellen. I'm still trying to get the stains out from the last one I took in."

"It's not a puppy this time." She lowered her voice. "It's a person."

"A person?" I propped myself up on one elbow. "What kind of person?"

"A Russian person."

I frowned. "Ellen, what the hell? Is this another one of your friends from circus school?"

"I *told* you, it's not circus school. It's aerial arts class. And anyway, no, he's not from there. He was a customer whose bag was stolen while he was sitting at the bar tonight."

"His *bag*?"

"Like his carry-on bag. He'd literally just gotten off the

plane from Moscow a few hours earlier. And the friend who was supposed to pick him up at the airport didn't show."

"How'd he end up at the bar?"

"He got in a cab and told the driver to take him some-place downtown. The driver brought him here. It was fate!"

I ignored that. Ellen was always droning on about fate and stars and mystical crap. "And then his bag was stolen?"

"Yes. Right under everyone's noses while he was sitting at the bar. And no one saw a thing."

"Yeah, those guys are good. Probably saw him get out of a cab with a bag and pegged him as a tourist. Easy mark. You call the police?"

"Yes. They came and made a report, but they don't think they'll find it. And the poor guy was *so nice* about it. But now he's stranded here with nothing because someone at *my* bar stole everything he had. I feel responsible! I have to help him!"

I rolled my eyes. Ellen never saw a stray puppy or wounded bird or kitten up a tree she didn't want to rescue. She'd been like that all her life. I didn't fault her for having a big heart, but she had so much going on and so many room-mates, somehow I always ended up with random animals at my house until she figured out where to take them.

"First of all, El, it's not your fault. It could have happened anywhere."

"But it didn't. It happened right here."

I ignored her stubborn tone. "Second, why is he your responsibility? Where's his friend?"

"He doesn't know."

"Can't he call him?"

"His phone is dead."

"So charge it." For fuck's sake. My sister was thirty. Why did it feel like I was talking to a first grader?

"He forgot his charger in Moscow. And I can't find one here."

"Oh, Jesus." I pinched the bridge of my nose, feeling a headache coming on.

"Please, Derek. It's only for one night. And you have an extra bedroom and bathroom at your house."

"What about your house?"

"Come on, I've got three roommates. And one of them has her brother visiting, so he's taking up the couch. You live all alone in that nice big house."

It probably wasn't a dig at me, but it sort of felt like one.

"I bet that extra bedroom is all made up already, isn't it?" Ellen went on. "Clean sheets on the bed, no dust on the furniture, no throw pillows out of place. I bet even the bathroom is sparkling clean and has big, fluffy towels all folded up and ready to go."

"You know, making fun of me isn't the best way to get what you want."

"Okay, okay, I'm sorry. But it's true, right?"

"It's true," I admitted through clenched teeth.

"Then can you please come get him and take him home for the night? Just one night, I promise."

"Wait a minute, I have to come and *get* him, too? Are you serious?"

"Well, yes. I can't just put him in a cab. He doesn't have any money. And you're not that far. Please, big brother. Pleeeease? For me?"

I groaned in agony, because I knew the exact face she was making right now. It never failed to pierce my armor.

She laughed. "Thank you. You're the best."

"I didn't say yes." But I sat up and tossed the covers off.

"I know you. You can't say no to me."

"*Fine*. I'll come get him, and he can stay here tonight. But he better not stain anything."

"He's very clean, I promise. But you might have to lend him some pajamas or something."

I got out of bed and headed for my closet. "Christ, Ellen. Do you want me to tuck him in, too? Sing him a lullaby?"

"What? No! You know you're a terrible singer. I'd never subject anyone to that."

Switching on the closet light, I grabbed the jeans and shirt I'd had on earlier. "Remind me how mean you are next time I'm trying to say no to you."

"No way. But I love you. See you in a few."

I ended the call, set my phone aside and got dressed. From my dresser drawer I grabbed a clean pair of socks, and sat on the bed to tug them on. Then I turned off the light and went downstairs, where I stepped into one of several pairs of sneakers lined up in the hall near the back door and grabbed my keys. For a second, I paused and imagined other shoes lined up there too. A little girl's sandals. A little boy's cleats. Or maybe two little pairs of Adidas like their dad's.

Which was so stupid. Even if I hadn't fucked it up with my ex and we'd gotten married, we'd probably only have one kid by now, and it wouldn't even be out of diapers yet.

But still. I'd be a husband. A father. I'd have a family to raise. People who needed me and depended on me and loved me unconditionally, the way I loved them. Was there anything less complicated than the love between parent and child?

Stop it. You're being ridiculous, and the longer you stand here feeling sorry for yourself, the longer it will be before you're back in bed.

After checking to make sure I had my phone on me and

my wallet in my pocket, I went out the back door and pulled it shut behind me.

On the drive to the bar, I realized I hadn't double-checked the spare room to make sure it was properly made up, but I wasn't really worried. I always kept it guest-ready just in case, and the hallway bathroom had been cleaned two days ago. My friends laughed at me for having a cleaning lady come every week, especially the friends who were married with kids, because how could there possibly be any dirt in the house when there was only one person living there, and that person was the most fastidious man on earth? Their houses were always a mess—stuff *everywhere*, as if someone had turned them upside down and shaken them like snow globes. Actually, Ellen's house was like that too, and her car—oh my God, the amount of shit in her car was enough to spike my blood pressure every time I rode in it. Sometimes I wondered how we were related. Her entire life was like a bunch of loose ends scattered every which way, and mine was like a nice, neat line.

At a stoplight, I glanced into the back seat of my car, pleased to see absolutely nothing there. Nothing in the passenger seat either, and no old coffee cups or water bottles in the cup holders. No crumbs or napkins or stray French fries. It even smelled good. People who rode in my car said that all the time.

Wasn't that a good thing? Weren't you supposed to take good care of your house and your car and other things you'd paid a lot of money for? Ellen had dipped into her trust fund a million times, but I hadn't touched mine after paying for school. I'd worked hard for everything I owned, and I wanted them to last. Besides that, appearances mattered. People judged you by them.

And what else did I have?

I parked in a downtown structure and made my way to The Blind Pig. A few people were coming out as I was coming in, and I held the door open for them before moving through it.

Ellen spotted me right away. "Hey!" She came around the bar, rushing up to kiss my cheek before grabbing me in a bear hug. "Thanks so much for this. You smell good, by the way."

"Trying to flatter me?"

"Yes. But it's also true." Laughing, she let me go and glanced over her shoulder. "He's sitting over there at the bar. I feel so bad for him."

"And what's your Russian orphan's name?"

"Maxim Matveev," she said with a thick accent.

"Wait, does he speak English?" For a moment, I panicked that I was stuck with someone who wouldn't understand anything I said. My Russian vocabulary was sparse, to say the least. *Da. Nyet. Vodka.* I also knew *perestroika* thanks to a college history class, but I thought that might be a little difficult to work into a conversation.

"Yes. Don't worry, you can tell him to wipe his feet and close the lid and hang up his towel in English, and he'll totally understand."

I rolled my eyes.

"Be nice. I think he feels weird about accepting the offer. He keeps trying to tell me this is ridiculous."

"It is."

She gave me The Face, and I sighed.

"Come on. Introduce me."

She took me by the hand and pulled me through the crowd toward the bar.

I saw him first from behind. At least, I thought it was

him—he was the only person sitting alone. Light short hair. Slender, muscular build. He sat up tall, his back straight.

Ellen touched his shoulder. "Maxim, this is my brother, Derek."

He turned to face us, and even in the bar's dim light, his eyes were a startling shade of blue. He looked younger than I'd expected, and somehow less Russian. I don't know what I was expecting—Boris Yeltsin, maybe?—but not the tall, trim blond guy who stood up and offered his hand. Not the cobalt eyes. Not the sharp-angled jawline.

I wasn't expecting him at all.

I wasn't expecting any of it.

FOUR

MAXIM

I WAS A LITTLE IN SHOCK.

This man was Ellen's brother?

She'd told me he was thirty-six, not married, and not to worry if he came off a little gruff at first.

She'd failed to mention he was fucking gorgeous.

"Hey," he said. "Nice to meet you."

He offered his hand, and I met it with mine. His grip was perfect—warm and strong and just long enough.

"So I hear you've had some back luck." His voice was deep and a little gravelly. It did something to me. Something that made it difficult to look him in the eye.

I forgot my entire English.

Ellen came to my rescue. "He can tell you the whole story later—poor thing has to be exhausted by now. But tomorrow we're going to fix everything. All he needs tonight is a place to stay."

"No problem," Derek said. I liked the way he stood,

with his feet wide apart and his arms crossed over his chest. He looked strong and confident. The kind of guy who made no apologies for himself. Who took initiative and got things done. I liked it so much I forgot to argue that he didn't have to take me in for the night.

Ellen punched him on the shoulder. "You're the best, brother. Biggest sweetheart ever."

"Biggest pushover ever," he grumbled.

"That too. Now be nice to him," she said, shaking one finger at her brother. She turned to me. "Maxim, I'll see you tomorrow, okay? Don't worry about a thing. Get some rest." She gave me a quick hug, and when she let me go, I finally found my voice.

"Thank you so much, both of you. I'm sorry to be a bother."

"No bother," he said, and he seemed to mean it. "Ready to go?"

I nodded, grabbing my notebook with the picture of Liliya in it off the bar, then I followed him through the crowd and out the door. I didn't know if it was the jet lag or the theft or the alcohol on an empty stomach or the surprise gut punch of being attracted to Ellen's older brother, but something had me feeling a little off balance.

Come on, Maxim. Pull yourself together.

At the end of the block, we stopped at an intersection, waiting for a green light so we could cross the street. I took a few deep breaths, hoping the cool night air might clear my head a little.

"So." Derek glanced at me. "You're a long way from home."

"Yes," I answered. It seemed like he was waiting for me to go on, but my tongue felt tied in knots. The right words weren't coming to me.

The light changed and we crossed the street, walking side by side now. "I'm parked in the structure. Third floor."

I followed him up two flights of stairs and over to a shiny black Range Rover. *Even his car is beautiful.* He unlocked the doors and I climbed into the passenger seat. The inside was as spotless as the outside. I wanted to compliment him on it, but all I could do was stare at his hands as he buckled his seatbelt.

Then my stomach growled—one long, loud, ferocious groan.

Our eyes met, and Derek's expression was amused. "Are you hungry?"

"Uh. Yes." I laughed uneasily.

"When was the last time you ate?"

I had to think about it. "On the plane. The first one."

He nodded and started the car. "No wonder. Let's get you some food."

"You don't have to worry about it." He was already putting me up for the night. I didn't want him to have to feed me, too. "I'm fine."

"That sounded like a fucking German Shepherd in your stomach, Maxim. You need food. Don't argue."

I liked the way he said my name—it put me at ease. And besides, my mother had taught me it was rude and offensive to turn down offers of food and drinks. "Okay. Thanks."

We circled down to street level and exited the garage. As we drove through downtown, I momentarily forgot my hunger and stared out the window like a mesmerized child. We passed one old movie theater after another, and I craned my neck to keep looking at the signs. "This street is incredible. What is this?"

"It's the old Broadway Theater District," said Derek. "It does have some really cool architecture from the twenties, although not all of these buildings are theaters anymore."

"It looks exactly like what I pictured when I imagined California as a kid."

"Oh yeah?"

"Yes. My mother is obsessed with Hollywood musicals, so my sister and I grew up watching them."

"You have a sister too, huh?"

"Yes, Liliya. She's eight." Since we were stopped at a light, I pulled the photo of her from my book and held it so Derek could see.

"She's much cuter than *my* sister," he said. "And probably much less annoying."

I laughed. "I don't know. I think your sister is pretty nice."

He shook his head, accelerating again. "She's nice, I'll give her that. She's just a little crazy."

About twenty minutes later, he turned into a driveway next to a two-story brick house with a porch light on over a white front door. It was very nice, but it wasn't the kind of house I'd pictured him in. Somehow I'd imagined something more modern and masculine for Derek—a condo with lots of glass and metal and sharp edges or something, rather than something traditional.

That's ridiculous. You don't know him at all.

He parked in the garage at the back of the yard, and I followed him to the back door. He opened it and stepped aside, as if to let me go first. I hesitated. It didn't seem right to step inside someone's house before him, especially since I was an unexpected guest. I looked at Derek, and there was an awkward moment where neither of us knew what to do.

"Okay, then." He walked in first and turned on the light, and I entered behind him.

The first thing I noticed when I entered Derek's house was how good it smelled—fresh and clean, a little woodsy. I inhaled deeply as he moved around me to shut the door. "What's that smell?" I asked. "It's amazing."

He looked confused for a moment and then he sniffed. "I don't smell anything." After setting his keys on a shelf, he removed his shoes and lined them up neatly against the wall next to a few other pairs. I left mine along the wall too and followed him into the kitchen.

He turned on the lights and gestured toward a round wooden table, which was surrounded by four chairs. "Take a seat. Let me just get some lights on and then I'll get you something to eat."

"You really don't have to."

He pinned me with a stare. "I know."

My insides tightened. Is this what Ellen had meant by gruff? I kind of liked it—the intimidating look in his eye, the no-bullshit tone, the way he said how things were going to be and wouldn't listen to arguments. It was sexy as hell.

Derek disappeared through an archway, and a light came on in the next room. I looked around, taking it all in. From the polished wood floor to the dark-stained cupboards, to the light stone counters to the glass backsplash tiles in different shades of green, the room looked like something from a magazine. And it was so clean! Everything shined—the stainless appliances, the marble counters, even the green apples in a bowl on the table. Were they even real? I was leaning over inspecting them when Derek returned to the kitchen.

"You're probably hungry enough to eat plastic, but don't eat that fruit."

I laughed as I straightened up. "I wasn't sure if it was

real or not. This kitchen could be a movie set, it's so perfect."

"Thanks." He went over to the big white sink and washed his hands. "It was quite a project, but I'm happy with the way it came out."

"Did you do it yourself?" I asked, impressed.

"Most of it." He rinsed the soap from his hands and dried them with a towel that had been folded on the counter. "Which was probably why it took so long, but I never trust anyone to do a good enough job. I'm a little bit of a control freak."

I nodded. Ellen had said that exact same thing while we were waiting for him to arrive at the bar, but I didn't think I should mention it. "Could I use the bathroom, please?"

"Sure. It's right over there." He pointed toward a door off the back hall.

"Thanks. Be right back."

I went into the bathroom, pulled the door shut, and looked at myself in the mirror a moment, trying to imagine what someone like Derek saw when he looked at me. It wasn't terribly encouraging. My hair was messy. My eyes were bloodshot. My face had the pale, sallow look of someone who hasn't slept or eaten well in a couple days.

And my heart was beating faster than normal.

Good thing he couldn't see that.

FIVE

DEREK

HE SEEMED SO *YOUNG*.

Maybe it was just because he'd needed rescuing tonight. But even beyond that, there was something youthful and endearing about him. The way he'd stared out the car window at those crumbling old theaters. The excitement in his voice when he talked about coming to California. The way he wasn't being a dick about his bag being stolen at the bar. It made me feel bad that I'd grumbled so much about helping him out. Poor guy—what shitty luck he'd had, getting robbed when he'd barely gotten off the plane. He had to be exhausted as well as hot.

Hungry. I meant hungry.

Not that he wasn't attractive. A person would have to be blind not to appreciate the perfect symmetry of his features. The vivid hue of his eyes. The chiseled jaw. It was an objective fact: as human beings go, he was nice to look at. No harm in admitting that. Nothing sinful about it. And as someone who was fitness conscious, I could see that he kept himself in good shape and appreciate the work it took. I didn't have to feel bad about it.

Frowning, I concentrated on seasoning the strip steak I'd taken out of the fridge for him. I heated some oil in a pan, and when it was ready, I threw the steak on. It sizzled noisily.

I wondered how old he actually was. What he did for a living back in Russia. Whether he was single. How long he'd be here. What it was about life there that made him want to escape. The weather? The economy? The politics? I hadn't been this curious about someone in a long time.

From around the corner, I heard the toilet flush and the sink turn on.

It felt a little strange to be alone in my house with another man. I liked to entertain and had friends over for movie nights or dinner parties pretty often, but I couldn't think of one time it had just been me and another guy here hanging out. Most of my good friends were married now, and had been since I'd bought the house. I'd never even had a woman sleep over. Gabrielle and I had split before I got the keys.

I'd actually been on the verge of proposing when she'd seemed to snap, suddenly convinced I didn't really love her. Of course, *she* didn't see it as sudden—she claimed there had been distance between us for months, and she couldn't ignore it any longer.

Fragments of our final argument pummeled my brain like a hailstorm—her demands and accusations, my questions and pleas, and then finally, the sad dissolution.

Be honest for once.

Why are you doing this?

You don't want me.

Don't throw this away.
There's nothing real here.
What do you want?
I want more.
I've got nothing more to give you.

I tried to fix it, tried to make myself into the man she wanted, tried to feel the things I was supposed to feel. In the end, I was numb. Exhausted. Empty.

Next time, I'd do better.

Frowning, I recalled the earlier disaster with Carolyn. She hadn't seemed too bothered by it, but I was. There had to be something I could do to create some chemistry, but what? I went to the fridge and started pulling out ingredients for a salad—lettuce, tomato, cucumber, carrots, radishes. While I was slicing the tomato, Maxim came back into the kitchen, inhaling deeply.

"That smells so good. My mouth is watering."

"Hope steak is okay." I placed some greens on a dinner plate, added the tomato slices, and started slicing a radish. "I had one thawed out I was going to make for dinner tonight but I ended up going out."

"I'd probably eat the plate you put it on, I'm so hungry, but yes. I love steak. This is so nice of you."

I met his eyes only briefly and looked down at the cutting board again. *Fuck. That blue.* "I don't mind. I like to cook."

"I'm starting to feel glad my ride didn't show up at the airport to get me. I would not be eating so well if he had."

I finished the salad and turned the steak over. "So he just didn't show?"

He exhaled, running a hand through his hair. "Yeah. But I'm hoping it was only a miscommunication. Hey, could I charge my phone?"

"Yeah. I have a charger right there on the counter." I pointed to where I meant, and he took his phone from his pocket and plugged it in.

"Thanks. I can't believe I forgot mine."

"It happens." I noticed he was looking over my shoulder into the dining room, a curious look on his face. "Go on. You can look around if you want."

"Are you sure? I don't want to be too forward. But your house is so nice."

"I'm sure. And thank you." I grabbed a bottle of wine from the small fridge under the counter. "I decided to have a glass of wine. Would you like one?"

"No, thanks. I'm not much of a wine drinker."

"Something else?" I asked, pulling the corkscrew from a drawer. "Vodka?"

"I'm not really a vodka drinker either."

"I thought everyone drank vodka in Russia." I took a glass down from the cupboard and winced. "Sorry. That's probably a stereotype."

But he smiled. "Plenty of Russians drink vodka. It might be a generational thing."

"How old are you?" I couldn't resist asking as I yanked the cork from the bottle.

"Twenty-four."

Twenty-four. God. I poured a lot of wine into my glass. A lot.

"I take it you're a wine drinker?" he asked.

"Sometimes. I like whiskey too." I set the bottle down and took the steak off the heat. "Go on and look around. This will be ready in a few minutes."

He disappeared into the dining room, and I took a good, long drink.

SIX

MAXIM

IT WAS obvious Derek had good taste and took a lot of pride in his home. It wasn't huge or overly luxurious, but it was beautiful and clean, and every single room had small touches that made it feel warm and welcoming. Like the kitchen, each room I saw could have been a Hollywood set.

The dining room walls were painted a soft blue-gray, and a shiny silver bowl full of white blooms rested on the long rectangular table. Beyond that was the living room, where thick white rugs covered the floor, and wide chairs and couches in neutral colors were arranged around a big ottoman. Lots of framed photographs stood on the white mantle over the room's brick fireplace, and I walked over to look closer.

A picture of Derek and Ellen from their childhood made me smile. He looked about ten years old; she, maybe half his age. Another boy, a little shorter than Derek, stood between them, and I wondered if there was a third sibling.

All three of them wore bathing suits and were smiling broadly, squinting into the sun. They were all missing at least one tooth.

There were more family pictures, taken at graduations and Christmases, and someone's wedding—the other brother's, perhaps? It looked like Derek might have been the best man. I wondered if Derek had ever been married, or if he had a girlfriend. He must. What guy at his age, who looked that good and was obviously kind, smart, and successful, would still be single?

"Food's ready."

At the sound of his voice, I turned. "I was just looking at your pictures. Can I ask you about them?"

"Of course." He came into the room and stood next to me, tucking his hands into his pockets.

"You have a brother as well as a sister?"

"Yeah. David. He's two years younger." He pointed to the photo of them in formal dark suits. David was tall like Derek, but not quite as ruggedly handsome. "That was his wedding three years ago. He and his wife live in San Diego, and they have a six-month old son now, Gavin."

"Is this him?" I gestured toward a photo of Derek cradling a baby in his arms.

"Yeah. That was at his baptism. I'm his godfather." A note of pride crept into his voice, making me smile. "Anyway. Ready to eat?"

"Definitely."

We went back to the kitchen, where Derek had set a place for me at the table, complete with placemat and a linen napkin, a steak knife on the right and a fork on the left. A glass of ice water was on the table for me, too. "This is like a five star restaurant," I said as I sat down, placing the napkin on my lap. "I feel underdressed or something."

"Nah. I just have a thing about paper napkins. I hate them." He set a plate in front of me, and I could have wept, it looked so good—a perfectly seasoned seared steak and a fresh garden salad. Simple but perfect.

I dug in immediately.

Derek cleaned up the kitchen, then brought his wine to the table, taking the chair across from me. "Wow. You *were* hungry."

I grinned sheepishly and cut a bite off the last remaining portion of steak. "My grandparents grew up in hard times, and they taught me to never leave the table until I finish everything on my plate, because you never know if you're going to have a good meal tomorrow. But also—this is delicious."

"Was the steak cooked okay?"

"Perfect."

"Good. I guess I should have asked you how you like your meat."

I froze with my fork halfway to my mouth for a second before recovering. *Don't be a pervert. He meant the steak.* "I like it the way you did it," I assured him. But I couldn't look up from my plate, and I felt self-conscious as I chewed. Then I swallowed too soon and had to take a big drink of water to wash it down.

"This your first trip to the U.S.?" he asked me, crossing his arms over his chest.

"My second. I visited New York three years ago."

"How long will you stay?"

I decided to be honest. In Russia, people believe it's bad luck to talk about an undertaking before it's complete, sort of like putting a hex on it, but something about Derek made me want to confide in him. "I hope forever."

"Really? You're hoping to immigrate?"

"Yes."

"Can you? I mean, is it legal?"

"Yes and no. It's complicated." I finished the steak and took another drink of water. "I can stay for six months with no problem because of my visa. After that, I'll have to figure something out."

"You don't sound too worried about it. Are you?"

"Not really." I shrugged. "I'll do whatever it takes."

"Might be tough."

"It will definitely be tough. And probably risky, but I don't mind. I like taking risks. In Russia we say '*Kto ne riskuyet tot ne pyet shampanskoye,*' which I think roughly translates to 'He who takes no risk doesn't drink champagne.'"

He nodded thoughtfully. "Here we say, 'No guts, no glory.' Same idea, though."

"Yes, exactly."

"Do you have a lot of family in Russia? Won't you miss them?" He sounded genuinely curious.

I thought of my mother, newly divorced for the second time and struggling to support herself and Liliya, and felt a pang of guilt. "I will miss my family, yes. I hate feeling like I've abandoned my mother and sister. But my mother understood why I wanted to come here."

"And why was that?" He reached for his wine.

"I want to be a Hollywood screenwriter."

He laughed a little. "Then I guess you're in the right place. Have you written any screenplays?"

"I've started about fifty of them, but I've never completed one," I admitted. "I want to take some classes here. I've taken some online, but I think being in a classroom with a teacher and other students will be much better, especially for my English."

"Your English is already pretty fucking good. What kind of work did you do in Russia?"

"Thank you. I was a technical writer for a petrochemical company. It was okay work, but never my passion. What about you? What do you do?"

He took another drink and set the wine glass down. "Commercial property development for my dad's company."

"Do you like it?"

"I guess so."

"But it's not your passion?"

He shrugged. "I don't know that I have a passion, not like you do." Then he smiled wryly, his eyebrows lifting. "You know, I'll be honest, I was surprised when I first met you. I expected someone completely different."

"Really? Like who?"

He cringed, but then he started laughing. "Like Boris Yeltsin. In one of those furry Russian hats."

I laughed too. "What a disappointment I must be."

He sat back, the smallest smile tipping his lips. "Nah."

My heart pumped a little harder in my chest. This felt good, sitting here across the table from him, being the sole object of his attention, making him smile. I liked the grit in his voice, the easy way he leaned back in his chair, the way his eyes crinkled at the corners when he laughed. I liked the broadness of his chest, the fullness of his mouth, and the way he was looking at me right now, almost like we shared a secret. I wanted to write it all down in my notebook so I'd remember the details about tonight forever.

"I should let you get some rest." Rising to his feet, Derek picked up my plate and took it to the sink. I brought my glass over, and he rinsed everything and loaded the dishwasher.

"Where should I put the napkin?" I asked, holding it up.

"Oh, here." He took it from me, and our fingers touched. "I'll throw it in the laundry."

He disappeared down the back hall. A few seconds later, he returned to the kitchen and reached behind me to turn off the lights. For a moment, we stood there in the dark, neither of us moving. He was close enough that I could see the rise and fall of his chest, hear his breath, close enough that I found myself thinking two very dangerous words —*what if?*

Then he brushed past me. "You have to be exhausted. Come on upstairs. I'll show you your room, and then I'll come back down and turn the rest of the lights off."

Saying nothing, I followed him through the dining room and living room and up the stairs. I *was* exhausted—so exhausted my mind was playing tricks on me. Making me think crazy things.

Because for a second there, I'd almost thought Derek was about to kiss me.

Go to bed, Maxim. You're delirious.

At the top of the steps, Derek turned left. "Guest bathroom is right here," he said, opening a door off the hall and turning on the light. "Towels are right here on the sink, and —" He opened a drawer and took out a toothbrush and toothpaste, still in their boxes. "You can use these."

I stood outside the bathroom, peering in. "This is incredible. In Russia, we normally have a single bathroom for the entire apartment that all the family members share."

"Sounds crowded." He opened the shower door as if to check something. "Shampoo and conditioner are in there."

"Thank you."

He came out of the bathroom and I stepped aside to let

him by, but his shoulder brushed my chest. My stomach tightened—I hadn't been this attracted to someone in a long time.

"And you can sleep in this room," he said, opening the next door down. He moved inside and switched on the light.

The room held a big double bed neatly made up with striped bedding, a dark wood dresser beneath a huge framed mirror, and matching nightstands topped with identical lamps. Just like all the rooms downstairs, there were small, personal touches that made the guest bedroom even more welcoming—art on the walls. Candles. Plants by the windows. A bottle of water on the nightstand. Half a dozen pillows on the bed, one of which said Sweet Dreams.

"This is beautiful," I said.

"I'm sure you'd prefer a hotel, but I hope you'll be comfortable."

"Not at all." I shook my head in disbelief. "This is much better than a hotel."

He shrugged like it was no big deal and tucked his hands into his pockets. "Need anything else? I can get you something to sleep in if you'd like. Or some clothes for tomorrow?"

Normally I would have said no, but the prospect of wearing something of Derek's was too tempting. "If it's not too much trouble. I feel like I've had this stuff on for days."

"No trouble. Just give me a minute." He left the room, and I stood there feeling guilty. A couple hours ago, I hadn't even wanted to accept the offer to stay in his house. Now I was asking for his clothes? *You don't need his fucking clothes. Stop it.*

But when he came back in the room and set a stack of clothing on the bed, my pulse quickened. "Thank you."

"Let me know if you need anything else. My bedroom is across the hall."

Oh, fuck. "Okay."

He put his hands in his pockets again. "Tomorrow you'll probably want to sleep in. I'm going to the gym early in the morning, but I'll try not to wake you. I'll be back around nine."

I nodded, but I'd barely heard what he was saying. I was too busy trying not to think about his room being right across the hall.

"If you do wake up and want breakfast, help yourself to anything in the kitchen." His broad shoulders lifted. "Guess that's it."

Don't leave yet. "Derek, thank you again for all of this."

"No problem." He headed for the door. "Night."

"Night."

He shut the door behind him, and I went over to the bed, sat next to the clothing he'd brought me, and placed one hand on the top of the pile.

I told myself he was this kind to everyone.

I told myself I wasn't special—I was just a favor to his sister.

I told myself I'd only imagined the tension between us downstairs in the dark.

But I wished I hadn't.

SEVEN

DEREK

I CLOSED the guest room door behind me and stood still for a moment, my hand still on the knob. Had I thought of everything? Was there anything else he would need? I'd told him about the towels, right? Maybe he'd like an extra blanket? Some deodorant? A razor?

What the hell are you doing? Leave him alone already.

I yanked my hand off the knob as if it had burned me and went downstairs. After locking the back door and setting the alarm, I walked through the shadowy kitchen and noticed his notebook on the counter, right next to his phone. I picked it up, fighting the urge to look inside it. What was it, a journal or something? Or a screenplay? Curiosity about him battled with my conscience.

Put it down, asshole. Whatever it is, it's private.

I set it on the counter again, but I couldn't stop looking at it. Maybe he'd want it upstairs. And what about his phone? He'd need that up there, wouldn't he?

Stop it. He's probably asleep already.

I could knock softly.

You could let it go until morning.

But he might want to call his friend again tonight.

That's an excuse and you know it.

It was. And I did.

Frowning, I stood there for a few minutes with one hand on his phone. The truth was, I was drawn to him, and it wasn't only his looks. It was his warmth and optimism. His manners. His gratitude. He struck me as someone who didn't take things for granted like a lot of Americans do. And I liked the way he'd come here determined to change his life, leaving everything and everyone he knew behind. Not because he felt entitled to something better, but because he had a dream and he was willing to work for it. He was almost like someone from another era—part of a generation of immigrants that had come here and built this country into what it was today. They might not have had a lot of resources, but they had backbone. Fortitude. Grit.

And okay, fine—I liked that he'd taken his shoes off without my having to ask.

But I was worried for him too. How was he going to get by? Did he at least have some money saved? Where would he live? How was he going to eat? I felt protective of him somehow, almost like since I'd come to his rescue, now I was responsible for making sure he'd be okay here.

Don't be fucking ridiculous. He's twenty-four, not twelve. He doesn't need you. Plus, he has a friend here already.

But look how he'd let Maxim down today. How responsible could he be? And Maxim didn't know anyone else here, so maybe he'd need someone like me to help him out. At least until he met new friends.

Not that it would take long. He'd probably have a girl-friend soon, too. Of course he would. A gorgeous young blonde with huge blue eyes like his. Curves for days. Legs a mile long. They'd fall in love fast and get married right away, which would solve his immigration problem, but no one would ever think he'd married her just so he could stay —it would be obvious how crazy they were about each other. They'd be fucking perfect together. His dream life would be a reality. Cue the fucking sunset.

I was irrationally angry about it all.

But that meant it really didn't matter if I wanted a couple more minutes talking to him tonight, did it? After all, once he left tomorrow, I'd probably never see him again. This would be it.

I unplugged the charger from the outlet.

A minute later, I was standing in the upstairs hallway outside the closed bathroom door, listening to the shower running. What I should have done was leave his things in the guest room where he'd find them and go the fuck to bed. But I didn't. Instead I stood there like a fucking creeper, imagining him naked underneath the spray.

Stop it right there. Not okay.

The water went off, but I still didn't leave. I pictured him drying off with one of my towels, hanging it up (yes, in my fantasies, everyone hangs up their towels), and pulling on my clothes. I'd had some underwear still in the package as well as a couple new pairs of socks, so I'd given those to him, as well as a pair of athletic pants, a clean T-shirt, and a hoodie. I'd never loaned another guy my clothes before.

Jesus, what the fuck does it matter? Get out of the hallway before he opens the door and catches you standing here, you fucking lunatic!

I hurried into his room and placed his notebook and

phone on the nightstand, but I wasn't quick enough. He entered the room as I was turning for the door.

"Hey," he said, his expression surprised. He ran a hand through his wet hair. His chest was bare, and the sweatpants hung low on his hips, so low I could see the top half of the V on his lower abdominals. Although he wasn't bulky, every muscle on his upper body was sharply defined. My eyes traveled over his skin, lingering low. Deep inside me, something dangerous stirred.

Fuck. This was a mistake.

I forced myself to look up. "Hey. Sorry to bother you. I was just—" I blanked, unsure how to finish my sentence. "I thought you might want your phone and your notebook. I put them on the nightstand."

He smiled. "That's so nice of you. I was thinking I should probably call my mother."

I nodded quickly and moved around him toward the door, giving myself a wide berth. "Night."

"Night," he echoed.

But I was already halfway down the hall.

TEN MINUTES LATER, I was lying in bed, staring at the ceiling with my hands behind my head.

I was angry with myself. I should know better than to allow that depraved part of me to surface, however briefly. Everything I wanted to achieve in life depended on keeping those dark, confusing urges buried. And hadn't I mastered the disguise already? Hadn't I spent years learning to control my sexual appetite? Hadn't I succeeded in suppressing every forbidden desire I had to the point where I barely felt any desire at all? Why was I letting a couple hours in the company of one handsome stranger undo me?

Because it feels good, desire.

Exhaling, I closed my eyes. It did feel good, that dark and dangerous thing he had awoken in me. It made me feel virile. Carnal. Alive. It gave me hunger, thirst, want. Even now, it threatened to overcome my defenses as my right hand slid down the front of my pants.

Because it feels good, desire.

My cock grew harder inside my fist as I pictured Maxim's bare chest, tight abs, the sharp V. I threw off the covers, hating myself.

Because it feels good, desire.

His skin would be warm and damp from his shower. His mouth firm and generous. His hands strong. I wanted them on me instead of my own. I wanted mine on him. I wanted to be rough with him, punish him for making me feel this. Be punished in turn for feeling it, for giving in to it.

Because it feels good, desire.

My hand worked harder, faster, tighter. My hips flexed. My stomach muscles contracted. I imagined us together— two hard, strong, muscular bodies moving against each other —unmasked, unabashed, unapologetic. I heard my name on his lips. I tasted his skin on my tongue. I felt his entire body stiffen—or maybe it was mine—all the tension inside me pulling viciously tight, as if it was still trying to suppress the urge, keep the secret, tame the animal, but it's doomed to fail, there is nothing stronger than lust at that moment, no power so great, and all that I am burst from me in a sudden pulsing rush.

Afterward, my heart still thundering in my chest, my stomach sticky, I lay there hoping I hadn't made any noise, or that if I had, a hallway between two closed doors would be enough to smother it.

A minute later, I went into my bathroom to clean up, mad at myself for indulging in fantasy but determined to put it behind me. What I'd done was wrong, but ultimately it was meaningless. No need to agonize over it or torture myself. I wasn't confused; I'd had a moment of weakness, that's all.

But the moment was over now, and I had total control—of my body, of my mind, of my behavior.

I wouldn't lose it again.

EIGHT

MAXIM

I WOKE up thinking about him. I'd fallen asleep thinking about him too.

But that was only natural, right? I was wearing the guy's clothes, sleeping under his roof, completely in awe of his generosity. It was gratitude, that was all. I was just really, really grateful. It had nothing to do with the fact that he was so fucking hot, and it didn't matter anyway, because he was straight.

Except I couldn't stop wondering about the way he'd looked at me after my shower last night. I'd come back into the bedroom with pants on, but the way he'd stared at my body made me feel like maybe I'd forgotten them. I'd had to look down and double-check. In that moment, the attraction between us had seemed unmistakable. But he'd rushed out of the room so quickly afterward, I wasn't sure.

Perestan' vydumyvat', Maxim. Stop imagining things.

Even if Derek was gay, which he isn't, why would he be interested in you?

He wouldn't. Because he could have anyone he wanted. Someone as smart and sexy and successful as he was. Someone professional. Someone mature. Someone with a university education, a beautiful house, and a Ferrari in his garage—maybe two. That's the guy he would want, and the guy he would deserve. Not some scrappy Russian immigrant who wasn't even sure where his next meal was going to come from.

And anyway, I had enough to do today without getting distracted by Derek. I grabbed my phone to see if Jake had texted or called and saw that I had voicemail from him.

I played it, putting the phone to my ear. "Hey dude, it's Jake. I'm trying to get ahold of you but your phone keeps sending me to voicemail. You're probably on your way here already. Anyway, my car broke down in the mountains and I'm stuck here for another day or two until I get it repaired. Sorry I won't be able to pick you up at the airport, but you can get a cab and go straight to the apartment. It's in Hollywood, and I'll text you the address. My friend Mike lives there and he's expecting you. He's also the guy to ask about jobs for cash. I'll send his contact info. Sorry again about not picking you up, hope you arrive okay. Bye."

I checked my messages and saw that Jake had texted an address and shared contact info for someone named Mike Jones. I quickly texted Mike that I was Jake's friend who had rented the apartment and wanted to move in today. I also inquired about any immediate jobs for cash. I'd spoken to my mother last night, and after she'd freaked out over what had happened to me (and demanded to know if Derek was a movie star), she'd promised to wire my savings to me as soon as the bank opened on Monday. Hopefully, Mike would have some work that would get me through the next couple days.

I set my phone down and opened the nightstand drawer, hoping to find a pen. Of course, there was a pen. And a notepad, and a book light, and a book of matches. *Derek should run a hotel or something*, I thought. *He's so good at this. But he's probably good at his real job too. He's probably good at everything.*

Sitting up against the headboard, I opened the notebook to a blank page and wrote down everything about him I remembered from last night as well as how I'd felt sitting across from him. After filling up an entire page, I closed the notebook and put it back on the nightstand.

Rolling out of bed, I pulled on my jeans from yesterday, and the clean shirt and socks he'd given me. I'd never worn another man's clothes. It was strangely intimate, which was exactly what I'd wanted, of course. I felt guilty again. *Stop thinking about him that way.*

I made the bed and left the pants I'd slept in neatly folded at the foot. In the bathroom, I used the toothbrush and toothpaste he'd left for me once more and wet my hair a little.

As soon as I started down the stairs, I smelled breakfast cooking and coffee brewing. My stomach rumbled hungrily. When I got to the kitchen, I saw Derek at the stove. He looked over his shoulder at me as I entered the room.

"Morning," he said. He was freshly showered, his dark hair still a little bit damp. He wore jeans and a fitted black T-shirt that showed off his muscular arms and back.

"Morning." I tried not to stare.

He turned back to the stove. "Sleep okay?"

"Yes. More than okay."

"I see the clothes fit."

"Yes. I'll get them back to you right away."

"No rush. Are you hungry? Want some breakfast?"

"Yes," I admitted. "It smells delicious. Although you've already fed me once, and I don't want to be greedy."

"You're not. It's just eggs. And like I said, I enjoy cooking for people." He began filling two plates with food. "Help yourself to coffee. There's a cup there for you."

Grateful for something to do, I tucked my phone into my pocket and poured coffee from the pot into the empty cup next to it. I noticed his cup was only half full. "Can I pour some more for you?"

"Sure. Thanks."

Our elbows bumped as I filled it up, but he didn't move away. I replaced the pot and brought the coffee to the table, setting the cups down at what I thought of as "our places" from last night. "Would you like me to set the table?"

"Sure. Mats are in this drawer." He nodded toward a drawer near his hip. "Silverware is in that one on the far right."

"Got it," I said, opening the drawer with the placemats in it. Every time I got close to him, my stomach jumped.

I set the placemats and silverware on the table, and Derek brought the plates over a minute later. I almost laughed out loud when I saw them. What he had called "just eggs" was actually an omelet full of vegetables, crispy strips of bacon, and two slices of fresh melon. "This looks so good. You must have been a chef in a past life."

He rolled his eyes as we sat down. "You sound like Ellen. Don't tell me you believe in that stuff."

I smiled. "Okay, I won't."

He groaned loudly, and something about the sound turned me on.

"You don't believe in anything she does?" I asked as we began to eat.

"No. I need to see something to believe it. Did you get ahold of your friend?"

"Yes. He's stuck in the mountains because his car broke down, but he apologized and sent me the address for the apartment I rented."

"Where is it?"

"In Hollywood. Perfect for me, right?"

He picked up his coffee and took a drink without answering. After setting it back down, he said, "After breakfast, I'll take you."

"I thought Ellen—"

"I talked to her earlier. She forgot about something she had to do today, of course, so I offered to take you."

"Oh." I felt guilty for being glad Ellen was busy, but I liked the prospect of more time with Derek, even if it was just a car ride. "Thank you. You've done so much for me already. I hope this doesn't interfere with your day."

He didn't look up from his breakfast. "No big deal. I'm having some friends over for dinner, but that's not until later. I'll have plenty of time to prepare."

"Are you sure?" I asked. "With guests coming, it feels like too much to ask of you."

He finally met my eyes. "It's not. I want to take you."

Our eyes met, and gooseflesh blanketed my arms. Nothing else was said, yet it felt as if something more was exchanged.

But then he looked down again, and the feeling was gone.

NINE

DEREK

WHILE I'D BEEN at the gym punishing myself with an especially grueling workout this morning, Ellen had called and left a voicemail begging me for another favor—could I please help Maxim locate his friend today and drive him where he needed to go?

On the way home, I'd called her back and given her a ton of shit about it, although secretly I didn't mind. I genuinely liked Maxim and wanted to make sure he was okay, plus my head felt much clearer this morning.

It was the dark that had gotten to me last night.

The late hour.

The wine.

The loneliness.

And Maxim was very charismatic. It was exactly the right combination of factors to mess with me, make me think I wanted something I didn't. Today would be different. I could never confess my sin out loud, but I could at least atone for it by doing him kindness. And if I felt any inkling of what I'd felt last night, I wouldn't let it overwhelm me— I'd fight back.

Then I saw him in my clothes, and the first thing I thought was, *Take them off. Not because I don't want you to have them, but because I want to put them on right now, feel them on my body like I want to feel you there.*

Not exactly fighting words.

But I rallied, keeping my thoughts clean even as he moved around my kitchen like he lived there. It felt so good I had to talk myself down. *It's not him. It's because you're lonely. You want someone to share your life with. You want this kind of closeness with someone. You like taking care of people, and he seems to need it. Don't confuse that for anything else.*

During breakfast, I'd been okay as long as we didn't make eye contact. Because every time we did, I felt like I unwittingly gave away a little piece of my secret. It was unnerving, the effect he had on me. I'd never experienced anything like it.

Sunglasses. That would help.

I reached for a pair on the back hall shelf and slipped them on. "Ready to go?"

"Yes," he said, showing me the screen of his phone. "Here's the address."

I cringed a little at the thought of an apartment in that area, but to Maxim Hollywood probably sounded like the most glamorous address in California. I didn't want to hurt his feelings. "Got it."

On the way there, I asked him what his plan was.

"My plan for what?"

I glanced his way. He looked completely unconcerned, even though he had nothing but a phone, a bag of dirty clothes, and a notebook to his name. "For living here. You must have made a plan before you came, right? What you'll do, how you'll live."

"Oh." He was quiet for a moment. "In Russia, we say, *'Yesli khochesh' rassmeshit' Boga, rasskazhi yemu o svoikh planakh.'* It means 'If you want to make God laugh, tell Him about your plans.'"

I rolled my eyes. "God's not asking you. I am. And I'm pretty sure God's a planner, anyway."

"Well, I have the apartment. I paid my first month already."

"And it's nice enough?"

"I don't know. I've never seen it."

I frowned. "What do you mean you've never seen it? You said you paid rent already."

"I had to, in order to make sure I would get it. Jake—that's the guy who was supposed to pick me up—says there aren't a lot of places for what I can pay in rent when I'm starting out."

"You paid for a place you've never even *seen?*" I was shocked, but Maxim didn't seem too bothered.

"Yeah," he said with a shrug. "But other than that, I really don't have a plan. Because even though I've wanted to move here for a few years, the decision to actually do it was sort of... I can't think of the word. You know like when you do something without really thinking first what will happen afterward?" He looked at me for help.

"Impulsive?"

"Yes—impulsive. My decision to come here was impulsive. I didn't really think or talk about it too much."

"That's a pretty big decision to make impulsively."

"It was. But I think if you plan everything in your life, you might be so focused on the plan, you don't notice all the other possibilities. You might ignore gut instincts. And I like to go with my gut. I think if you do that, you always make the right decision."

I wasn't too sure about that. I was a man who liked a plan and didn't always trust my gut to act in my best interest. Gut instincts could be useful, but they were still instincts—based on innate compulsion, not on reason or fact. And I had some pretty frightening innate compulsions.

But I didn't want to get into that with Maxim. This was about his life, not mine. "Okay, but let's think practically for a moment. How will you eat?" I looked over my shoulder before changing lanes. "Do you have money saved up or will you try to work?"

"Eventually, I will have to work, but for now, my mother is wiring my savings to me. It shouldn't take too long."

"Like how long?"

"Just a couple days."

"A couple days?" I looked at him. "You can't go a couple days without eating, Maxim."

"I won't. The guy who's renting me the apartment has some jobs for cash for me."

That sounded sketchy to me. "Doing what?"

"I don't know. But don't worry about me, really. You've done enough." He reached over like he might touch my arm or something, but then pulled back. "My mother asked if you were a movie star."

That made me laugh. "Really?"

"Yes. In her mind, Hollywood is crawling with movie stars. They're on every corner. She also thinks all Americans love guns and eat McDonald's every day."

"Uh, no and no. Not this American, anyway." I thought for a moment. "But I can't really blame her. All I know about Russians are stereotypes, not that you fit any of them."

"You mean that we're all cold and unfriendly and never smile? We sit around drinking vodka and frowning about life?"

"Actually, yes."

"Russians smile, we just don't do it as often as Americans, or as randomly, and we definitely don't smile at strangers. We're not as open and friendly right away with people we don't know."

"*You* are."

He shrugged. "I'm learning to adapt."

"So what are Russians *really* like?"

"Hmmm. Warm after we know you. Generous. Resilient and resourceful, because we've had to be. Oh, and we are totally superstitious."

I liked the way he said "totally." He pronounced the second *t* the same as the first one, whereas an American would turn it into a *d*. "Yeah? About what?"

"Pretty much everything. For instance, I realized I forgot my phone charger on the way to the airport in Kiev, but going back for it would have been bad luck. Russians believe you should never return home for forgotten items."

"Seriously?"

"Yes, and if you do go back for something, you have to look in a mirror before you go out again."

I shook my head, but I was laughing. "That is fucking absurd."

"Here's another one," he said. "You should never use hand gestures on yourself or anyone else when describing something negative. Like if you were talking about a terrible scar on someone's face, never gesture toward your own face as the example. And if you do it by accident, you need to wipe the bad energy off your face and throw it away."

"Ridiculous. My God, no wonder you and Ellen clicked. You're *both* crazy." But they both made me laugh, too. And they were both fearless and spontaneous and completely confident that no matter what life threw at them, they could handle it. Deep down, I envied that. I had strength and tenacity, but sometimes I wondered if I'd have made different choices if I'd had some of Ellen's free spiritedness. Or cared less what other people thought of me.

"Your sister was telling me last night about twelve-year life cycles," Maxim went on, "and how every cycle should start in a new place so it's good thing I came here right after turning twenty-four."

"Be careful. Next thing you know, she'll have you at one of her crazy dream analysis sessions or take you to get a psychic reading. Total bullshit."

He studied me. "You really don't believe in anything you can't see?"

I thought about it. "It's not that so much. I mean, I believe in God. I guess I just believe in free will over fate. I don't think anything is inevitable—you always have choices, and your beliefs guide those choices. If you don't want something to happen, you don't let it happen. And if you want something badly enough, you go after it."

"I definitely agree with that," Maxim said. "That's why I came here. But I also like believing that some things are meant to be. That some things are bound to happen because a force beyond our control is at work. Even feelings are sometimes beyond our control."

Fuck yes, they are. "But our actions aren't," I argued. "Feeling something doesn't mean you should act on it. If everybody went around doing what they felt, we'd live in complete chaos."

"And chaos is messy."

"Yes."

"And you don't like things that are messy."

I glanced at him sideways and then stared straight ahead. For someone I'd met less than twenty-four hours ago, that was pretty damn intuitive. It kind of annoyed me. "No. I don't."

"I understand." He was quiet for a moment, then spoke again. "I admire your discipline and self-control. I could probably use some of it. And I didn't like paying for the apartment without seeing it, but what choice did I have? I wanted to come here more than anything. I was willing to risk it."

I softened a little. Maxim was young—I had to remember that. Some of that fearlessness I envied was simply not knowing better. Someone his age needed to make mistakes in order to learn—I certainly had. And I couldn't fault him for going after something he wanted. "I get that. You just have to think things through a little more. Be practical. Plan ahead. Consider all the possible consequences before you take a risk."

"I'll try," he said. "I really want to make my life here work."

And before I knew what I was saying, the words were out of my mouth. "I'll help you. I can help you."

As soon as I said it, I was sorry, not because I didn't like him or want him to succeed, but because I wasn't comfortable with the way he made me feel. I'd thought showing him kindness today would make me feel less distressed about last night, but it wasn't. Even being in the car with him had me on edge—the interior of the Range Rover had felt perfectly spacious yesterday, but with Maxim in the passenger seat it felt snug. I was constantly aware of how close he was. My skin hummed with it.

All I wanted was to get him to his apartment, wish him well, and put him out of my head.

THE ADDRESS MAXIM had given me was an old two-story building a couple blocks from the Hollywood freeway. I frowned as we pulled up. No self-respecting Angeleno would want to live in this area. It was nothing but traffic, tourists, and homeless people. The building itself looked like a World War II bunker, complete with crumbling facade and scorched lawn in front. "You're sure this is it?" I asked him.

"Yes. It looks nice, doesn't it?"

Are you fucking kidding me? I thought. But I didn't say anything as he jumped out of the car. Who knew what his living conditions had been like back in Russia? Maybe this place looked like a palace to him.

Still.

"How long are you planning to stay here?" I got out of the car and shut the door, making sure I locked it. "This isn't the greatest area."

"For a little while, at least." He glanced around the parking lot. "I hope it's close to public transportation. I'll need that."

"Public transportation? You won't get too far on public transit around here."

"No? I guess I'll get around by walking then."

I stared at him. "Maxim, this is L.A. Nobody walks in L.A. Haven't you heard that song?"

His face was blank. "No."

I took a deep breath, feeling my blood pressure rise. How was it possible someone could make a transatlantic move with so little preparation? Was he one of those people that things just worked out for somehow? Who succeeded solely on instincts, determination, and charm? Maybe Maxim was truly poised on the edge of achieving the American Dream, but I had a bad feeling about this place. While I was trying to figure out how to help him without getting too invested, he held out his hand.

"Hey, thank you for driving me. And for—everything. I won't forget this."

I shook his hand, ignoring the heat that ricocheted up my arm at the clasp of our palms. "You sure you're all right here? Maybe I should wait. Make sure this is the right place."

"No." His voice was firm. "You've done enough for me. And I'll return the clothes as fast as possible."

"Keep them." I liked the thought of him in my clothes. I could allow myself that one small thing, maybe even file it under being charitable, since he had so little.

We looked at each other for a moment, and I was glad I had the sunglasses on. To keep myself from saying or doing something I'd regret, I shoved my hands into my pockets. "Well. Good luck."

"Thanks. See you around, I guess." With one last smile, he turned and walked toward the entrance.

He got about ten feet.

"Maxim!" I jogged to catch up with him, even though every instinct in my body was telling me to get the fuck in the car and go home. "Let me stay and make sure you get in okay." That was reasonable, right? That's what Ellen would have done. There were all kinds of weirdos around here. And what if the address was wrong?

"You can if you want to, but it's not necessary."

"I'll feel better if I do. Ellen will never forgive me if anything else goes wrong for you," I joked. By the time we reached the door, I had myself mostly convinced I was doing it for Ellen.

The door opened into a stairwell, which immediately struck me as a safety hazard. So anyone could simply walk in?

"It's apartment 202," Maxim said, glancing at his phone as he climbed the stairs. "Second level."

On the second floor, we entered a dark, humid hallway that smelled like old fried food. My stomach turned.

Apartment 202 was right across from the stairs. The door was open slightly, and Maxim knocked before pushing it all the way open.

The air was hazy inside and the lighting dim, so it took my eyes a moment to adjust. The first person I saw was a stocky, dark-haired guy in a white tank top smoking in the kitchen, which was over to the right side of one big room. On the opposite side there were a few people slouched on a dingy couch staring at their screens. One of the two girls said hi and the other one waved, but the guy didn't even pick up his head. He was all into his laptop, which was covered with stickers. The TV sat on the floor, tuned to CNN, though no one appeared to be watching. The place reeked of stale cigarette smoke.

"He didn't tell me there were two of you," said the guy in the tank top.

"There aren't. My friend is just dropping me off," Maxim said. "Are you Mike?"

The guy nodded.

"Nice to meet you. Is this the apartment?" Maxim asked.

I wondered if he was praying the guy would say no, like I was.

"Yeah. See that hallway there, your room is on the left." Mike poked his cigarette in the other direction. "Bathroom right over there, but someone's in it right now."

"How many people live here?" I asked.

"Right now, six."

"Six?" My jaw fell open as I glanced around again. There was no way this place was big enough for six people. "Where does everyone sleep?"

Mike shrugged. "Anywhere they can. Come on, I'll show you the room."

We followed Mike out of the kitchen and down the hall. As I walked, I felt something like sand crunching beneath my feet. Mike pushed open a door that looked like it had been kicked a lot, and entered the room. I stood behind Maxim in the doorway, peering over his shoulder.

It was tiny and cramped. It had one window facing a parking lot outside, a bare twin mattress on the floor, a beat-up dresser with sagging drawers. Every available surface was covered with dust and grime, and the mint green paint on the walls was peeling. My left eyelid started to twitch. Why the hell had I insisted on seeing this place?

"What's that?" Maxim asked, pointing to a door opposite us.

"That goes to my room," Mike said. "But don't worry, I'll try not to wake you up when I come and go."

"Wait a minute." I held up one hand. "You have to go through this room to get to your room?"

"Yeah," Mike said, like it was no big deal. "It used to be the closet." Then he pointed to the mattress, which was stained and lumpy. "That's yours if you want it. The girl that lived in here before left it." A roach scuttled across the floor and Mike stomped on it with his boot. "Fuck. I'll get that cleaned up." He shouldered by us, and lumbered down the hall.

Maxim moved into the room to look around while I struggled with my conscience. On one hand, Maxim wasn't a puppy I needed to save—he was a grown man who was perfectly capable of taking care of himself. And bringing him home with me again was a bad idea for a good fucking reason. But could I really leave him in this bug-infested hell-hole with its dirty floors and grungy couch and polluted air, a complete stranger marching through his bedroom multiple times a day, nothing but a stained mattress to sleep on? He didn't even have any sheets! I shuddered at the thought of it.

"Maxim. You can't stay here."

"There's no other option." He eyed the peeling paint, the bare mattress.

"There's always another option. You can stay with me until your savings get here." Two days. I could handle that, right? "Will you be able to get a better place then?"

"I don't think so. My savings aren't huge, and I need to buy a laptop. I'd also like to save some money for screen-writing classes." He shook his head and spoke with certainty. "You've done enough for me, Derek. I appreciate the offer, but this is what I can afford, so it's where I'm going to live for now. I'll be fine."

Mike entered the room again, a wad of paper towels in his hand, which he used to wipe up the cockroach mess.

I exhaled, my eyes closing briefly. *Just get out of here. He's not your responsibility. He made the choice to move here impulsively, now let him deal with the consequences of his actions.*

But I couldn't make myself leave.

"So, what's the deal? You staying or not?" Mike asked.

"Yes," said Maxim.

"No." I met his eyes, squaring my shoulders defiantly.

He squared his too. "*Yes*. Thank you for everything, Derek, but I don't need your help."

"I know you don't. But you're going to take it. Now let's go." I turned and strode as quickly as I could out of the apartment, through the lobby, and out the front door, gulping the fresh air.

Motherfucker.

What had I done?

TEN

MAXIM

I COULD HAVE RESISTED. I almost did.

I'd come here knowing it would be a struggle. I wasn't afraid of it. And I didn't want Derek to think I couldn't handle myself. Didn't want him to feel like my problems were his problems. Didn't want him to see me as someone who needed to be rescued, because I didn't.

But hell if I didn't follow him out of that apartment anyway. I justified it by telling myself only a fool would let his pride keep him trapped in that filthy place, but deep down, I knew better.

The truth was, I liked Derek. I liked the way he took control of a situation. I liked the sharp edges of his gravelly voice. I liked the look in his eye when he wanted something done his way, the one that said *don't fuck with me*. And when I looked at his life, I saw someone who had done things right. He'd decided what he wanted, and he'd gone after it. I knew I could learn from him.

He was just outside the stairwell door when I caught up with him. "Hey," I said. "You don't have to do this."

"I know I don't." He slipped his sunglasses on again. "What did you pay for that piece of shit mattress?"

"Four hundred dollars."

"Get it back. For half that, I'll rent you my guest room for two weeks." He started walking toward the parking lot, and I followed.

"I'll pay the full four hundred." Accepting his generosity was one thing, but I wanted to do my part. My pride demanded it.

"You can't afford it right now, Max. Trust me. I know what decent apartments cost here."

"Then I'll pay it back eventually," I argued, only slightly distracted that he'd shortened my name. It suggested familiarity, closeness even. I liked it.

We reached the car and got in. "How much is in your savings?" he asked.

"About two thousand dollars."

He looked at me. Blinked. "We need to find you a job."

"Of course. I was planning on it."

"You didn't say that when I asked about a plan before." His brow furrowed.

"Because if I did," I admitted, "I might cause it not to happen."

His expression grew even more puzzled, and then suspicious. "Is this a Russian thing?"

I almost smiled. "Yes."

Exhaling, he turned on the engine. "At the risk of causing you bad juju or whatever, I'll see if I can help you find something. Ellen might even have some work for you at the bar."

"I'd love to work for Ellen. And I have some experience working at a bar."

"Great," he said, pulling into traffic. "Although you know how Ellen is. She claims to hire people based on their *auras*, not their resumes. How's your aura?"

I laughed. "Pretty good, I think? Although I'm not really sure what an aura is, exactly."

"Me neither." He shook his head. "But somehow it's worked out for her so far. The bar does well."

"That's wonderful."

"It is. I'm happy for her. For a while, I was worried she'd never figure her life out. Name a profession and she's probably wanted to be that at one point—astronaut, circus performer, veterinarian, ballerina, flight attendant. She's always been all over the place. Totally opposite of me."

"But you get along so well."

"We do," he mused. "It's funny because our brother, David, is sort of the opposite of both of us. He never wanted to work for the family business because he wants nothing to do with corporate culture. Says he doesn't have the stomach for negotiation. But he was always really focused on studying marine biology and becoming a professor."

"A professor. That's awesome."

Derek shrugged. "He seems happy, especially now that he's married and has a baby. I wish they lived closer, although he's probably glad for the distance from my parents. He doesn't get along with my dad very well."

I didn't know what to say. Curiosity burned in me, but I'd never ask. Luckily, he went on.

"It's nothing big, they're just really different. And my dad was hard on us growing up. Very religious, very demanding. But also very proud of us when we met his expectations. I was better at handling the pressure than David was."

I nodded, taking it all in. "Your family is religious?"

"My parents are. I'm not, not really. But I went to Catholic schools. I was an altar boy and all that. I don't necessarily agree with everything the Church says and does, but when you've had the doctrine drilled into you for that long, at home and at school, some of it sticks with you, whether you want it to or not."

"Ah."

"I like *some* of its basic ideas," Derek continued, "the value of human life, the importance of family and community, the obligation to help others."

"I can tell both you and your sister like to help others."

He seemed a little embarrassed by the compliment, his cheeks coloring. "What about your family? Are you close?"

"To my mother, yes. I barely know my dad."

"Really?"

"Yeah. He and my mother were really young when they had me, and he took off soon after."

"What about your sister?"

"Different father. But that guy took off too."

"Fuck. Guess your mom really has a type."

"Yeah. I feel bad for her. I think she always wanted that perfect family."

He didn't say anything after that, and I wondered if he was thinking that she should have controlled her feelings more. Not acted on them when it was clear she wouldn't end up happy. But I didn't really get that—how could you help acting on your feelings? What else was there to act on?

A few minutes later, we arrived at his house. "Dammit," he said, slowing down as he pulled into the drive.

"What's the matter?"

"I just noticed the landscapers didn't show again. They were supposed to come this morning. I don't know why I give these assholes a second chance."

"What do you need done?"

He made a noise. "Everything. And I can do some of it, but I inherited these fucking rose bushes with the house that are more high-maintenance than a beautiful woman. And if I didn't like the way they looked so much, I'd tear them the hell out."

"I can take care of it."

He looked at me like I was nuts. "You have landscaping experience too?"

I shrugged. "I've had a lot of different jobs. And growing up, I spent every summer at my grandparents' country house, and I helped take care of the gardens there. And yes, we had roses. My grandmother treated them like babies."

"You have *roses* in Russia?"

"Yes, Derek." I laughed, enjoying the feel of his name in my mouth. "It's not snow and ice all the time there. We do have sun and warmth in summer."

"Sorry." He grimaced as he pulled into the garage. "I promise to get over my preconceived ideas about where you come from."

"And I promise to help you out around here and then get out of your way in two weeks."

Derek turned off the car. "You're not in my way."

We sat there in the darkened car for a moment, and I thought he was going to say something else, but he didn't.

There were more flowerbeds and gardens in the back-yard. Derek stood in the driveway frowning at all of them before checking his watch. "Fuck, it's two o'clock already, and I haven't even gone to the store yet. I might not be able to use the patio tonight. It's all weedy and overgrown back here."

It wasn't, the yard actually looked very nice, and the patio was beautiful. But I knew that for Derek, there was no such thing as "good enough." It had to be perfect. "I can do it all. Honestly. Just show me where everything is, and I'll get it done in a few hours."

He looked at me sideways. "You sure?"

"Positive. I like this work, and I'm good with my hands."

The sunglasses covered his eyes, but the slight drop of his chin made me think he looked at my hands after I said that. He cleared his throat a second later. "Okay, then. The job's yours. I'll deduct from your rent."

"No. This is a favor, Derek," I said as we walked toward the house. "I'll still pay the full rent."

He unlocked the back door and pushed it open. "Whatever. But you're going to need some money for clothes too."

Oh, yeah. I'd sort of forgotten about that. While I was trying to think of a solution, he went on.

"Let's not worry about rent for now, okay?" He set his keys and sunglasses on the shelf and took off his shoes. "When your savings get here, we can talk. I'll help you make a budget. And we'll get you that job so you can start saving for classes."

I removed my shoes too, and followed him into the kitchen. "That sounds perfect. I don't know how to thank you." (A total lie. I could think of plenty of ways to thank him.)

He leaned back against the counter and took out his phone. "Pay it forward someday."

"I will." Turning away from him, I removed the hoodie he'd loaned me and hung it on the back of a chair. It was warm enough outside that I wouldn't need it. When I was done working, I'd ask him if I could wash some things, and then stay out of sight during his dinner party. "I'm going to get started out there."

"Tools are in the garage." He didn't look up from his phone. "I'll be out in a minute. I'm just going over my grocery list."

"Okay." I put my shoes on again and went out the back door into the sunshine, unable to keep the smile off my face.

This already felt like a new life.

ELEVEN

DEREK

I KEPT my eyes on my phone until I knew he was out of my view.

Then I exhaled.

This wouldn't be easy, having him around for two weeks. And yet...it would be completely easy. Enjoyable, even. It was the craziest thing—I felt comfortable with Maxim in a lot of ways. He was easy to talk to, he made me laugh, he was interesting and fun and different. I liked hearing about his life in Russia, too. It gave me some insight into why he was the way he was.

Where it got uncomfortable was when my body reacted to him. A hitch in my breath. A tightening in my chest. Heat in my blood. Provocation of that thing in me that existed only to want and didn't care about the consequences.

It was maddening that I couldn't feel those things for someone like Carolyn, who was perfect for me in every other way. Why should it be Maxim who ignited that fire in me, rather than her? What was it about him that wouldn't let me out of its grasp? Why was I being punished this way?

As if being pulled by magnetic force, I walked over to the chair where he'd hung the sweatshirt I'd loaned him. Glancing out the sliding glass door to the patio, I saw him standing by the rosebushes at the side of the yard, the sun glinting off the gold in his hair. I picked up the sweatshirt and brought it to my face.

It was still warm from his body.

I inhaled slowly. Soap. Fabric softener. But there was something else there, too. At the deep end of my breath was the heady, masculine scent of his skin, and I held it captive in my lungs, closed my eyes.

You inside me.

My mind feasted on the scent. I felt my lips on his skin, my hands on his back, my chest against his. He was warm and strong and hard and—

Two quick knocks on the glass door made me jump, my eyes flying open to find Maxim standing there on the patio, his head turned, so he was looking away from me. I immediately dropped the sweatshirt onto the chair and slid the door open.

"Hey."

He looked at me, his face impassive. "Hey. Do you have some gloves?"

"Uh, yeah." My face was probably fifty fucking shades of red. But he hadn't seen anything, right? "Be right out."

I put my shoes on again and went out to the garage, where I rummaged around on my workbench shelves. Where the hell were those gloves? I knew where everything was in this garage, so why the fuck couldn't I find them? My mind was cloudy with confusion and shame. Had he seen what I was doing? He couldn't have. He wasn't even looking at me when he knocked. And even if he had, he knew how I was about neatness. He probably thought I was going to hang the sweatshirt up somewhere, or put it in the guest room.

My heart rate slowed, and I remembered where the gloves were. I pulled them off the shelf and slipped them on for a second, flexing and fisting my hands.

"Find some?" Maxim called from outside.

"Yeah." Quickly I tugged them off and headed into the sunshine, squinting at the light. I'd forgotten to put my sunglasses back on. "Here you go."

I handed them to him and watched him put them on, sliding his fingers into the spaces mine had occupied a moment before.

It was almost like touching him.

"HEY." I switched my phone to my left hand and reached for a couple lemons with my right.

"Hey, big brother. How'd it go today with our Russian orphan? Thanks again for doing that."

"No problem. It was, uh, interesting." I grabbed a few limes too, in case anyone wanted them for cocktails.

"Did you drop him off?"

"Yes and no."

"Yes and no?"

I frowned at the bunches of herbs, scanning the selection for thyme. "I took him to the apartment he was supposed to live in, but I couldn't leave him there."

"Why not?"

"It was disgusting."

Ellen laughed. "Like what, the toilet seat was up? There were damp towels on the floor? Cookie crumbs on the counter?"

"No, like roach-infested, filthy dirty, stained-mattress, you-couldn't-pay-me-a-million-dollars-to-stay-one-night-there disgusting." A woman perusing vegetables to my right gave me a horrified look and moved away.

My sister gasped. "Seriously? So he wouldn't stay?"

"No, *he* was fine with it. I mean, he wasn't, of course he wasn't, but he said he'd be okay and it was what he could afford and it was only temporary."

"Wait, I thought he was staying with a friend, the one that didn't show up last night."

"No. That guy was just going to give him a ride to the apartment. But his car broke down in the mountains or something."

She laughed. "Thanks for nothing."

"Exactly. Anyway, I couldn't leave him. It was that bad."

"Wow. So what did you do with him?"

"What could I do with him? His mom is wiring his savings, but it won't be here until Monday. So I brought him home with me."

"Of course you did." She giggled. "You big softie."

I grimaced, scouring the tiers of root vegetables. Where the fuck was the fennel? "I'm not a softie. It's only temporary, and I'm telling you, nobody could have left a friend in that place."

"You guys are friends now? That's so cute."

"We're not friends exactly, I just—I don't know what we are." Spying a bag of fennel, I grabbed it and tossed it into my cart. "But I said I'd help him."

"Help him with what?"

"With everything, Ellen. He's the nicest guy in the world, but he moved here, like, on a whim and really didn't plan for it."

"He moved here? I thought he was just visiting."

"He wants to stay." I switched my phone to my right ear and pushed my cart toward crates of potatoes and onions in the middle of the produce section. "He wants to be a screenwriter."

"Doesn't everybody?"

"Right. So he's got about two thousand dollars saved up, with which he needs to buy food, shelter, a laptop, and screenwriting classes for the foreseeable future."

"Yeah, that's not gonna happen."

"That's what I told him." I tossed a few onions and a big bag of Russet potatoes into my cart. "I said he could stay for two weeks, during which I'm going to help him make a budget and find somewhere to move that he can afford once he gets a job."

"A job?"

"That's where you come in. Can you hire him?"

"I'd be glad to. Is it legal?"

I frowned. "Not really. You'd have to pay him in cash. Keep it all under the table."

"Okay." Ellen didn't sound bothered in the least. "I'm not working tonight, but I can bring him in tomorrow."

"Great." Some of the tension eased from my upper back. "He says he's got some experience."

"Sounds good. Where is he now?"

"He's back at the house doing some yard work for me."

"You put him to work already?" She snorted. "That's so you."

"Ha ha. He offered, thank you very much. He said he

had experience with gardening too, although he could be back there butchering my rose bushes for all I know."

"He's a real jack-of-all-trades, huh?"

"Apparently."

"Too bad he's so unattractive."

His handsome face popped into my mind, and I forced it out. "Unattractive?"

"It was a joke, Derek! I was kidding. For God's sake, the guy looks like a Calvin Klein underwear billboard come to life."

"I guess." *Don't think about him in his underwear. Don't think about him in his underwear. Don't think about him in his underwear.*

"You guess? I'm sorry, but you'd have to be dead not to find him attractive. And not even recently dead. Like a hundred years dead." She sighed. "Too bad he's gay."

I froze, my entire body on edge. "What?"

"He's gay. One of my servers overheard him telling some girl at the bar that last night." She laughed. "From the sound of it, she was pretty disappointed. Poor girl."

"Oh my God." The store was spinning.

"What difference does it make? Are you going to be all Dad about this?"

"No! It makes no difference at all. I just didn't realize." My voice sounded strange to me.

"Good. You scared me for a second. I can only take one narrow-minded relative. Anyway, I better go. I still have a shit ton of inventory to do."

"Okay."

"Hey, what are you guys doing tonight? I'm off. Want to see a movie or something?"

"Uh, no. I mean, I can't. Maybe Maxim would like to." His name felt different on my lips.

"Why can't you?"

"I'm having friends over for dinner."

"Whatcha making?"

"Roasted chicken and vegetables." Which I was supposed to be shopping for, so I could get the fuck home and make it, but I was still anchored to my spot by the potatoes.

"Yum! Got room for one more?"

"Sure," I said absentmindedly.

"Great! What time should I come over?"

"Uh, seven is good."

"Perfect. Gives me time to go home and clean up. Who else is coming?"

I forced myself to start walking again, focus on the task at hand. *Chicken. I need a chicken.* "Um, Gage and Lanie. Carolyn."

"Ooh, is that the girlfriend?"

"She's not my girlfriend. She's just—someone I'm seeing."

"Well, whatever. You've mentioned her, and I've been hoping to meet her. I'll see you tonight!"

"Okay. Bye." I ended the call and brought up my grocery list so I could finish shopping, but I found myself having to look at it again and again, my mind was so preoccupied with what Ellen had told me.

Maxim was gay?

If I'd made any peace at all with his presence in my house for the next two weeks, it was all undone by that news.

Was it true? Did it even matter?

Hell yes it did. My attraction to him suddenly felt a thousand times more dangerous, now that I knew it was possible it could be reciprocated.

And was it? Was Maxim attracted to me? I replayed last night and today in my head, looking for a telltale sign—a word, a touch, a look—something that would give him away, but I came up with nothing. Maybe it was because he felt nothing. Maybe it was because he was Russian and had that detached face mastered. Or maybe it was because I'd been so obsessed with my own feelings, constantly focused inward on what he did to *me*, that I could find no evidence I'd captured his attention like he'd captured mine.

For a split second, I was disappointed.

What the hell, asshole? That's a good thing. The last thing you need is for him to be interested in you. You don't want it. You can't want it. It's wrong. Nothing is going to happen.

I took a few deep breaths and repeated the words in my head.

Nothing is going to happen.

TWELVE

MAXIM

I SAW HIM.

Through the glass, I saw him.

I'd been looking at the roses, seeing what needed to be done, and I realized I'd need gloves to even get started. As I walked toward the house, I saw Derek through the large glass door off the patio and decided to knock on it. Then I got closer and saw him holding the sweatshirt I'd worn. His face was buried in it.

At first I thought it was a trick of the light on the glass, my mind bending a reflection into a fantasy. But I blinked several times, and he was still there.

My pulse quickened. Why would a man smell another man's shirt that way, unless he was trying to smell the man? My stomach flipped over.

But rather than stand there and risk being caught, I decided to look away as I knocked. Make him think I hadn't seen anything. The alternative would've been way too awkward for both of us.

Luckily, I was a good actor. I asked him about the gloves without a tremor in my voice and kept my face expressionless. In contrast, his cheeks were deep red, and he refused to make eye contact. It was the most flustered I'd ever seen him. He came outside and hurried into the garage without even glancing my way.

But by the time he found the gloves and handed them over, he'd appeared composed again, his usual self. He told me what he wanted done in the yard overall, what the priorities were today, and where all the tools were. I listened and asked questions and assured him I could handle everything he wanted done, but in my head all I could see was his face buried in that shirt.

I obsessed over it all afternoon, adding up all the significant details—the lack of a girlfriend or wife. The odd moment in the kitchen, where I'd had the crazy thought he might kiss me. The way he'd looked at me last night in my bedroom.

Maybe I wasn't crazy.

Was it possible I *had* felt some chemistry between us? Was it possible the attraction was mutual? Was it possible he'd smelled that shirt for the same reason I'd asked to borrow his clothes in the first place—to experience the illusion of intimacy without actual physical touch?

This morning, I'd have said it wasn't.

Now I was starting to wonder.

WHEN DEREK RETURNED from the store, he took bags of groceries straight into the house with barely a glance in my direction. He spent the entire afternoon cooking and preparing for dinner without saying anything to me, although at one point he came out and set a plate with a sandwich and some chips on it on the patio table—a long wooden table with two benches on either side. Next to it, he set a tall glass of ice water. "Lunch," he called to me before going right back inside.

Grateful, I took a short break to eat and cool off, and when I was done, I left the plate and glass on the table, figuring I'd bring it inside when I was done. But a little later, I looked over and discovered he'd taken them in already.

At that point, I was ready to conclude I'd been totally off about him before. He wasn't acting like someone who was into me at all. In fact, if I didn't know better, I might have thought he was irritated with me for some reason.

Eventually, he did come outside to talk to me. I was in the middle of mowing the lawn, and he wandered over, hands in his pockets. It had been a warm afternoon, so I'd taken off my T-shirt earlier, and even though he wore sunglasses I could see the way he stared at my upper body. The sun was hot on my back, but his eyes on my chest were hotter.

"You need sunscreen," he told me.

I turned off the mower. "Maybe. But the sun feels so good on my skin."

His gaze stayed on me another few seconds before scanning the yard. "You did a lot of work out here today. And actually, I think you did a better job than my landscapers."

"Thanks. I haven't gotten to the rosebushes yet."

"Don't worry about it. It can wait until tomorrow."

"I'll get it done by tonight."

"Well, dinner is at about seven-thirty tonight, and it's about six right now. I wasn't sure how much time you needed to clean up, or if you wanted to wash some clothes, or borrow something."

"Thanks, but I don't need to come to your dinner party. I can stay upstairs once your guests arrive."

"Actually, you'll be doing me a favor if you come."

"A favor?"

"Yeah." His expression was a little embarrassed, and his eyes dropped to his shoes. "Originally it was just going to be my friend and his wife and this woman I've been seeing, Carolyn."

He's seeing a woman. Disappointment punched me in the gut.

"But while I was talking to my sister earlier, she asked if she could come and I said yes without thinking. That would make five people," he said, as if that explained the problem.

I was a little confused. "Five people?"

"I have a thing about an odd number of people at the dinner table." He rolled his eyes and shrugged. "I know it sounds weird, but I can't stand it. I like an even number. That doesn't mean I'm superstitious," he said defensively, probably because I'd started to grin. "It just means that visually, I like all the seats filled. It's a personal preference."

"Of course."

"I have plenty of food, and I know Ellen would love to see you, so it would be great if you'd join us." He finally looked me in the eye, and said the words I wanted to hear. "I'd *like* you to join us."

I felt it again—that pull between us.

"Then I will." Truthfully, I'd have said yes even if he hadn't told me he wanted me there, because I liked the idea of doing him a favor. "You said seven thirty?"

"Yeah."

"I'll finish quickly." I looked down at my muddy jeans

and chest, which was smudged with dirt and shiny with sweat. "Then I'll clean up and maybe do some laundry."

Derek didn't seem to know where to look—he went from my torso to my eyes to the house in the space of five seconds. "I'll put a few more things on your bed that I think might fit, and we can throw your stuff in the wash."

I nodded. "Thank you."

He went back inside, and I finished up the lawn, cleaned up, and put the tools I'd used back exactly where I'd found them. I knew how Derek was about staying organized.

When I was done, I scooped up my sweaty T-shirt from the driveway and went up to the guest bedroom. Derek had placed a pair of jeans and two shirts on my bed, along with more new socks and underwear. I shook my head in disbelief. How much new stuff could one man possibly have on hand, the tags still attached?

I undressed, shoving all the dirty things in the bag I'd used earlier. I took a quick shower, scrubbing off the sweat and dirt of the day, and tried very hard not to imagine hands other than mine running over my skin. *He's dating a woman, remember? Not into guys, not into you, not into anything you're thinking. So get him out of your head.*

Derek had left a new towel folded on the sink, and it was slightly warm, like maybe it had just come out of the dryer. He'd also left a little travel kit packed with basics like a razor, deodorant, a comb, and a couple different hair products. *He's being so good to me.* But was it only his belief in helping people out? Did he feel obligated to be this kind, or was there something more to it?

After messing with my hair a little, I hung up my towel and went into the bedroom, where I dressed in Derek's clothes again. I was glad they belonged to him and weren't new—it meant he'd worn them before. In fact, before I slipped my arms into the sleeves of the shirt, I found myself smelling the neck of it, looking for any trace of the man, feeling cheated when I didn't find it. When I was dressed, I checked my reflection in the full-length mirror on the closet door.

It pleased me that his clothing fit almost perfectly. No, it was more than that—it turned me on. I felt like we were sharing something (which we weren't). I felt a physical closeness between us (which didn't exist). I felt my body respond when I imagined him taking them off me, replacing them with the heat of his skin (which would never happen).

Enough.

I closed my eyes, willing the blood to stop rushing, the desire to stop building, the hum beneath my skin to go away. The insane thing was, my attraction had seemed to grow stronger since hearing that he was dating a woman. What was that about?

It's about wanting what you can't have, asshole. Now quit being stupid about him. He's just a really nice guy. He's not interested in you and never will be. Get over it.

Nothing is going to happen.

THIRTEEN

DEREK

I'D INVITED Maxim to dinner for a reason.

Beyond the fact that I couldn't stand empty chairs at the table when I had guests, I'd hoped to prove some things to myself: That whatever confusion Maxim stirred up in me was simply displaced desire to be with someone like Carolyn, who was so perfect my subconscious probably felt she was too good for me. That seeing them together would make it abundantly clear that my attraction to Maxim wasn't real, it was just a desperate attempt to make a connection with someone because I'd been feeling a little lonely. That God wasn't punishing me for my sins—He was testing me.

It was my job to prove I was stronger than temptation, no matter how powerful it was. I could rise above it. I could win.

It was not going well.

"So, Maxim, did I hear earlier you'd like to be a screen-writer?" Carolyn asked.

She was seated to my right, looking beautiful in a silky red blouse that bared her shoulders and second-skin jeans with high heels. When she'd arrived, I'd greeted her with a big kiss on the lips. It had felt weird and forced, and I'd only done it because Maxim had been standing nearby. He'd looked away, and I'd been angry.

Look at me. This is who I am.

But it wasn't. I couldn't have cared less about her ass in her tight jeans, but I couldn't get enough of Maxim's in mine. I was angry about that, too.

"That's the goal," Maxim said, "but I need to do some studying first." I'd seated him at the far end of the table because it was the farthest chair away from me, but of course that put us directly opposite each other, and all I'd done was stare at him all night. Even dimming the lights hadn't helped, because that asshole looked even better by candlelight.

"Oooh, you could write Russian spy movies." Ellen poured more wine in her glass and giggled. "Whenever I think of Russia, I think of spies. Is that terrible of me? Wait, you're not a spy, are you?"

"No, I'm not." He flashed her a mischievous grin I wish he'd given to me. "Not that I would tell you if I was."

Ellen gasped playfully, then she snapped her fingers. "Damn. I thought maybe I could brag about sitting next to the KGB at dinner."

"Does the KGB still exist?" asked Gage. He'd been my best friend since seventh grade, and I'd been the best man at his wedding to Lanie eight years ago. Now they had three kids under age six and rarely got out much socially, but he and I tried to have a beer a few times a month to keep up. "I'm kind of embarrassed I don't know."

"It's sort of sad that all we know about Russians, or all they know about us, are stereotypes from movies," said Lanie. "Why is that?"

"Because it's fucking *far*?" said Gage, reaching for his drink.

"It is far," said Maxim with a smile, "but I think our cultural differences can make it hard to understand each other, even when people are in the same place. I was telling Derek earlier that Russians have a reputation for being cold, but we're not. Not really. We just express ourselves in a more modest way. And even when we're curious about someone or something, we don't ask personal questions because we don't want to be rude."

"And in America, that would seem like indifference," said Ellen. "Maybe even rudeness, like you didn't care enough to ask or smile at someone."

"Yes." Maxim nodded. "I think it's just a part of an eastern culture where people are more submerged in their own world than tuned in to what happens around them. If you take a subway somewhere in Moscow, for example, you won't see too many smiling people. Everybody is thinking their own thoughts, and their faces don't react to you. But if you get to meet them, you'll find they're actually very nice. In fact, if you go to a Russian house for dinner or something, you'd be surprised to find how welcoming and generous the hosts are."

"I have to admit, I always picture Russia as being cold but exotic. Women in fur coats, dripping with diamonds and eating caviar." Carolyn giggled. "But that's probably from the movies too."

"There are wealthy people in Russia, but it's also very

common for those who had a poor childhood to really like nice things, luxury things." Maxim shrugged. "Lots of people never had new clothes or toys. Sometimes food was scarce. When you grow up this way, you don't want to feel like that again. It's my story, too."

"I get that," Lanie said.

He had a poor childhood, I thought, hungry for any personal details about him. I wondered how poor. Did he grow up impoverished? Hungry? Lacking for anything?

"We also like to impress," he went on, a glint in his eye. "This is why some Russians drive luxurious cars while living in a tiny apartment, or wear designer brands or go to expensive restaurants—because they didn't have a taste of it before and they want to show it's different now."

"Speaking of taste, my old roommate dated a Russian girl," said Gage. "She used to bring us all these amazing left-overs from her family functions. And she'd come over and make these potato pancakes..." He closed his eyes and moaned. "So good."

"They are good." Maxim nodded. "I make those sometimes."

"You can cook?" Ellen asked.

"A little. My mom worked a lot, so I had to help out with meals growing up. She taught me to make some things." He caught my eye and grinned. "But nothing like Derek. I told him he must have been a chef in a past life."

"Yes!" Ellen exclaimed. "He definitely got all the cooking skills in the family. I can barely boil water."

"Dinner is excellent, Derek." Carolyn touched my arm. "Thank you for inviting me."

I put my hand over hers. "You're welcome. I'm glad you're here." For all the wrong reasons, of course, but I was still glad.

"Maxim, your English is so good," Lanie praised. "I teach high school, and I've got students who've lived here their entire lives and don't speak it as well as you."

"Thank you." Maxim lowered his chin as if he were embarrassed by the compliment, and even from all the way across the table I could see how long his eyelashes were.

What the fuck? His *eyelashes?*

Get a grip on yourself.

But I couldn't, so instead, I gripped Carolyn's hand and held it in my lap. She sent me a surprised smile, and I returned it, but my pulse didn't quicken the way it should have with her hand so close to my crotch.

"I still can't believe your bag was stolen at my bar," said Ellen. She'd told the story of Maxim's first night in America with great dramatic flair during drinks on the patio, including plenty of nonsensical rhapsodizing about fate, as if it hadn't been a random cab driver's suggestion that had brought him into the bar. "I feel so bad about it."

"Don't," Maxim said. "Everything turned out fine. Better than fine. I made new friends."

"Good thing you were home when Ellen called you, Derek." Carolyn squeezed my hand. "Now I'm glad I didn't keep you out too late."

"I figured he'd be home, since he goes to the gym so early Saturday mornings." Ellen's eyes glittered with mischief. "And we all know Derek does not miss a Saturday morning at the gym."

"Heaven forbid he get off schedule." Lanie clutched her heart.

"Or leave the garage door open," added Gage.

"Or dishes in the sink." Ellen loved this game.

"Or eat in his car."

"Or wear shoes in the house."

"Or let dust bunnies form under the beds."

"Enough," I muttered, feeling my neck get hot under my collar.

"You really lucked out, Maxim. Hotel Derek is nicer, cleaner, and has better food than any place in L.A," Lanie said.

"All true. But it wasn't luck," Ellen insisted, her expression smug.

"I believe it was more than luck, too." Maxim met my eyes, and I saw it—the wanting. *I saw it.* Something in me splintered. "I believe some things are meant to be."

Fuck.

I kept drinking. With every swallow, I tried to numb the feelings that not only refused to stay buried but insisted on growing as the night wore on. It was as if seeing the desire in his eyes had unlocked the prison where I'd kept mine. I stole furtive looks at him, noticing small details I'd missed before —the length of his fingers, the fullness of his mouth, the veins on the backs of his hands. They reminded me of the veins I'd seen on his abdomen last night, the ones that snaked beneath the waistband of his pants.

I wanted to trace them with my tongue.

Somehow I got through coffee—mine was spiked—and dessert, although I didn't touch the chocolate cake Carolyn had brought. I had no appetite for anything but him.

Gage and Lanie left first, saying they had to get their sitter home by eleven. I hugged Lanie and shook Gage's hand, promising to see him later this week for a beer. Ellen helped Maxim bring all the dishes into the kitchen before she left, hugging all three of us and telling Maxim she'd call tomorrow about working at the bar.

"That would be amazing," he said. "I'll do whatever you need. Can I walk you to your car?"

"Sure. Bye, you guys!" She blew me a kiss and swept out of the room with Maxim on her heels.

I finished loading the dishwasher while Carolyn blew out all the candles and collected the linens. "Can I help you do the rest by hand?" she asked, pushing up her sleeves.

"No. You've done enough. I'm too tired to do them tonight, anyway. I'll do them tomorrow." It was a lie, I'd never go to sleep with the sink full of dirty dishes, but I couldn't take any more pretending tonight. I was half drunk, totally frustrated, seriously angry, and I wanted to be alone so I could hate myself in peace. (And probably jerk off while I did it.)

"Are you sure?" She bit her lip, clearly disappointed. "I really don't mind staying." Slipping her hands around my waist, she rose up on tiptoe to whisper in my ear. "I don't have to be home by eleven. Or anytime tonight at all."

I laughed uncomfortably and disengaged her arms. "I'm sorry. I'm just *really* tired."

"Oh." Her face fell, and I felt horrible.

You're such a fuck-up. This is the second night in a row you have to make excuses for yourself. She's not going to wait around forever, asshole. She deserves better.

"Can I walk you to your car?" I asked.

She nodded. "Okay. Let me grab my purse."

Maxim came in the front door as we were going out. "I'm walking Carolyn to her car," I said, avoiding eye contact with him.

He nodded and held out his hand. "It was so nice to meet you, Carolyn."

"Same." She shook his hand and smiled brightly. "I hope to see you again."

"You can go up to bed, Maxim. I'll clean up tomorrow." Without giving him a chance to argue, I guided Carolyn out the front door and yanked it shut behind us. Guilt had me taking her hand as I led her down the porch steps and front walk.

"I had a great time tonight," she said. "I loved meeting your sister and your friends."

"I'm glad."

"And Maxim is so interesting. It's so nice what you're doing for him."

"It's nothing."

When we reached her Audi, she let go of my hand and took out her keys. I gave her a quick kiss on the cheek and stuck my hands in my pockets.

"Derek," she said, and I could hear the puzzle in her voice, "is everything going okay for you? With us, I mean?"

"Of course it is." I lied, but I lied for her sake. Okay, for both our sakes. But I didn't want to hurt her feelings with words that wouldn't make sense to her, and I didn't want to give up on myself yet. I could still beat whatever this was inside me. I knew I could. But not tonight. "I'm just tired."

"Okay." She didn't sound sure of it. "I just want to make sure. Sometimes tonight it seemed like it was, but other times, it felt off. And I'm not rushing you or anything. I just don't want to waste your time—or mine. If this isn't going anywhere, I want to know."

"I understand," I said quietly. Closing my eyes, I exhaled and offered her something closer to the truth. "I'm going through something right now, and I feel a little off. I get like this sometimes. Where I don't feel like myself."

"Is it...depression?" she asked tentatively.

"No. I don't think so. It's more like...anxiety or something. I get anxious about things and have to work them out before I can move on."

"Oh." She smiled hopefully. "Can I help you in any way?"

"You're sweet, but no. It's something I have to do on my own."

"What do you do?" she asked, then she shook her head. "I'm sorry. You don't have to answer that. It's none of my business."

"It's okay. There's no magic bullet or anything. I just try to step back and give it time. Make sure my priorities are straight. Re-evaluate my goals in life. Remind myself what's important."

"I think everybody should step back and do that some-time. Myself included."

"I can give you some space if you need it."

"No. That's okay. I've thought about you a lot, Derek. And I've thought about what I want in a relationship a lot. I really like you, but I'm looking for a commitment. Not a ring or anything, but a commitment. Because that's what would make me happy, and I deserve to be happy." She smiled. "It took me three years of therapy to say that. How'd I do?"

I smiled, although I felt horrible inside. "Great. And it's true. You deserve to be happy."

She grinned. "Thank you. It made me happy when you held my hand tonight at the table."

"Good." Jesus fuck, I was a dick. "Night."

"Night." She got into her car, and I watched her drive away before turning around and trudging up the sidewalk toward home. I felt like shit. I felt like a failure. I felt like everything I had planned for my life was slipping through my grasp, and it was my own fucking fault. I couldn't even blame Maxim. I was struggling with myself long before I'd ever laid eyes on him. Being around him just made it worse.

You'd better be upstairs already, Maxim. You'd better be out of sight, asleep, behind a closed door. I can't fight myself anymore tonight.

I let myself into the house and locked the door behind me. Right away I heard the clank of dishes and the kitchen sink running. *Fuck, he's still down here.* Taking a deep breath, I squared my shoulders and tried to put the mask back on before walking back to the kitchen.

As soon as I saw him, it started to slip.

He was at the sink, washing the remaining dishes. I went straight for the whiskey bottle and threw back a shot. "Didn't I tell you to go to bed?"

"You did, but I knew you weren't really going to go to bed without cleaning up."

"Oh yeah? How'd you know that?" I tossed back a couple more fingers, taking solace in the fiery warmth pouring down my throat, spreading through my chest.

"Because I know *you.*"

"After only one day?"

"In your case, some things were obvious right from the start."

"You're just like the rest of them," I grumbled. "Did you hear how they make fun of me?"

"Yes, but I don't understand why. When you have a house as beautiful as this one, why wouldn't you take care of it?"

"Thank you!" I shouted, throwing my hands in the air. I nearly knocked the whiskey bottle over too. "Finally, somebody fucking gets it."

Figuring I'd had enough booze to blunt his effect on me, I rolled up the sleeves of my black button-down shirt and moved next to him. "I'll help you."

"Okay."

I caught him trying to not to look at my wrists and fore-arms, and it made me smile. *How does it feel to want someone and have to hide it?* "You wash, I'll dry?"

"Sounds good."

We worked in silence, shoulder to shoulder, and I found myself increasingly—and disturbingly—pleased at the thought of him being attracted to me and being forced to conceal it. It was fucking horrible of me to take pleasure in his discomfort, but I liked being secretly wanted. Being illic-itly desired. Being the object of his covert glances and maybe even his darkest, dirtiest thoughts. I let our arms touch more than necessary, as thrilled by the physical contact as I was by the thought of what it might be doing to him.

For there is no man who does not sin.

My dick started to get hard, clearly unbothered by the whiskey that was breaking down my inhibitions, pushing past all my defenses, and letting my imagination run wild.

What's in that gorgeous head of yours, Maxim? What's behind those cobalt eyes? What would you do to me, if I let you? What would you let me do to you?

"Carolyn is so nice," he said, handing me the last serving dish left to be dried.

What? He was thinking about *Carolyn* right now? He wasn't supposed to be thinking about Carolyn—*I* was, goddammit!

But I wasn't. "Yeah."

He turned off the water. Rested his wet hands on the edge of the sink. "I didn't realize you had a girlfriend."

And I heard it in his voice—the slightest edge of jeal-ousy, so faint I might never have noticed it had I not been so hyperaware of everything about him right now. I fucking loved it.

"She's not my girlfriend."

"Oh." Now there was confusion. "I guess I misunderstood."

"She *wants* to be my girlfriend."

Silence.

Of course there was silence. Maxim would never ask what the problem was. But I wanted to tell him. I wanted him to know. I wanted to share the impossible longing I felt with one person who might understand it.

"The problem is me."

He was completely still. Before I could stop myself, I covered his right hand with my left. "Sometimes I don't know what I want."

He yanked his hand from beneath mine and we faced each other.

For the first time tonight, I looked him right in the eye. Nothing around us existed for me anymore. I heard only his breath. Smelled only his skin. Saw only his guarded expression.

I had to have him.

Now or never.

I grabbed him by the arms and crushed my mouth to his. *Oh my fucking God.*

For the first time in my life I was touching another man's lips with my own. They were so different than a woman's—bigger, firmer, fuller. I devoured them with the ferocious hunger of a starving lion.

He opened his mouth, sliding his tongue between my lips. His hands gripped my hips, pulling my lower body against his. *Fuck.* I felt the bulge in my jeans grow bigger and harder, and *I felt his on the other side.* As we kissed, he backed me up to the counter and moved against me, his cock rubbing up and down alongside mine. I was out of my mind at the thought of it, the feel of it.

This can't be happening.

Everything about this—his mouth, his hands, his body, this kiss, this friction, this madness I felt, this caged thing inside me desperate to get out—was unreal.

Maxim slid a hand between us, gripping me through my jeans. Even through denim I felt the heat of his palm. "Can I?" he asked, his breath warm against my mouth.

"Yes."

His lips still on mine, he unfastened my belt and unbuttoned my jeans. A moment later I felt his hand—*another man's hand*—wrapping around my cock. It was warm and solid and strong, and I groaned in agonizing pleasure as he worked it up and down my shaft. He moved his mouth across my jaw and down my neck. "You smell so fucking good," he said, and his voice—low and intense—made my dick throb in his fist.

Next thing I knew, he'd dropped to his knees and a warm, wet mouth was closing over the tip of my cock. In some kind of spiraling motion that nearly drove me insane, he slowly took it deeper and deeper into his mouth until it was buried. Then he moved faster, rubbing his tongue over my crown, sucking me hard and deep, taking me to the back of his throat.

Holy fuck, he knows what he's doing.

And when I looked down and saw him on his knees for me, saw his lips moving up and down my cock, felt his deep, driving hunger in the way he sucked and squeezed and stroked me, I was lost.

Lost to him, lost to myself, lost to this aching, pulsing need inside me to let go. To stop pretending I didn't want this. To surrender to it because I wanted it and it felt so fucking *good*.

But I didn't even try to make it last.

I grabbed the back of his neck with one hand and fucked his gorgeous mouth like the selfish, savage animal I was, my lower body contracting rhythmically as I poured myself inside of him.

I felt like a god. I felt like a monster.

I felt like nothing in my life would ever be the same.

FOURTEEN

MAXIM

I SAT BACK on my heels, momentarily stunned. I don't know who was breathing harder, Derek or me.

Oh my God. I can't believe that just happened.

I looked up at him, and he was staring at me like he'd never seen me before.

"Jesus," he whispered.

Then he was gone. I don't even think he zipped up his pants, he just took off. A moment later I heard footsteps on the stairs, followed by a slamming door.

Fuck. Was he angry? About what? I hadn't forced him. *He'd* kissed *me.* Maybe I'd pushed it too far? But I'd asked before touching him, hadn't I? And he never told me to stop, never pushed me away, never once indicated he wasn't enjoying it. In fact, he'd seemed to enjoy it a hell of a lot.

Almost as much as I did.

I got to my feet and adjusted the crotch of my jeans. Apparently my dick hadn't gotten the message that we were done here. It was still hard, and thinking about what had just happened was only making it harder. I could still hear Derek's rasping growl, still smell him in the air, still feel his cock sliding between my lips.

I can still taste him.

Taking deep breaths, I braced myself against the counter and closed my eyes, trying to calm my body down. But God, the way he'd lost control was so fucking hot. I hadn't expected it—I hadn't expected anything, of course. There hadn't been any time to think. But he'd gone from standing still and letting me have my way with him to grabbing my neck and pounding his cock to the back of my throat in an instant, almost like he'd snapped. It had surprised me somehow. The quickness of it. The violence of it. The intensity of it. I'd loved every fucking minute.

Not that it had taken very many of them. The whole thing had happened so fast, my head was spinning.

I turned around and leaned back against the counter, staring at the sink where we'd washed the dishes. It had been killing me how close he was standing, so close that I'd started to wonder if he was doing it on purpose. When he'd put his hand over mine, I'd been even more confused—straight guys didn't touch each other that way, did they?

Then his words. *Sometimes I don't know what I want.* I don't have the best gaydar in the world, and English isn't my first language or anything, but at that point I was pretty sure he was telling me he was attracted to me. It had both thrilled and terrified me—I wanted him like crazy, but what if I was wrong? What if I made a move and he was offended? What if he was just being American and opening up about his personal problems and it had nothing to do with me? Being Russian, I was used to people being indirect, but this was more than casual conversation. The stakes were high.

So I'd pulled my hand away. If he wanted me, he'd have to show it.

And he had. I'd almost had a heart attack when he grabbed me by the arms. But the way he'd kissed me, as if he were suffocating and I was fresh air, left no room for doubt —he felt it too, that thing between us. Whether he was gay or straight or something in between, it was there, and *oh my God* it was hot.

So what was Derek's problem? What could he be upset about? Was it guilt? He'd said Carolyn wasn't his girlfriend, although even so, he might feel bad for fooling around with me behind her back or something. Derek was such a good guy, that could totally be it. I hadn't noticed any hot chemistry between them tonight, but that might have been because I hadn't wanted to.

It was also possible Derek felt bad because I was a guest in his home, and he was doing so much for me. Maybe he was worried I'd felt pressured to repay him with sex or something. It was ridiculous, and hopefully it had been obvious to him how much I'd been into it, but I could see him feeling that way.

Or maybe he was horrified by what we'd done. Maybe it disgusted him. Maybe he was upstairs right now scrubbing away the evidence and begging God to forgive him.

I hoped not, but no matter what, it was clear that he was not okay with what had happened.

Upset by the thought, I turned off all the lights and went upstairs, glancing at Derek's closed bedroom door but going straight into the guest room, making as little noise as possible. When I was undressed and lying on my back beneath the blankets, hands behind my head, I wondered how tomorrow would go. What he'd say. How he'd act.

In my gut I felt it would be best to let him take the lead, and then follow it. If he wanted to pretend it had never happened, fine. We didn't need to talk about it. Nothing had to change, either, and I hoped he wouldn't want me out of the house just because things had gotten heated between us. It wasn't that big of a deal. We could go back to the way things had been before he grabbed me. Brush it off. Remain friends. It's not like I wasn't used to keeping my sexuality to myself, and I hadn't expected anything to happen with Derek in the first place.

That said, I'd do it all again in a heartbeat.

I'd do more than that.

FIFTEEN

DEREK

GUILT. Shame. Anger.

I lay on my back, staring at my bedroom ceiling and drowning in anguish.

What the fuck had I done?

You shot twenty years' worth of repressed desire and sexual frustration down another guy's throat, that's what. And then you left him kneeling on the kitchen floor without saying a word.

It was all my fault. I was a terrible person.

I shouldn't have grabbed him. I shouldn't have kissed him. I shouldn't have let him touch me that way. I shouldn't have liked his mouth on me. I shouldn't have lost control. I shouldn't have had the best orgasm of my entire life with another guy.

But I had. I'd never felt anything like it.

Why was that? It's not like I hadn't had good blowjobs from women before—at least, I'd thought they were good.

But Maxim took it to an entirely new level. It had almost been like an out-of-body experience. Was he really that good? Or was it the *thought* that made it so mind-blowing? The idea that I'd finally given in to a forbidden desire *just this once*, and I'd never have it again?

Either way, I couldn't deny how powerful it had been. How intense. The fucking walls had trembled.

Weak. I was so weak.

How had I let this happen?

It's not like I was gay. I was attracted to women, too. And I wanted a traditional family—a wife and kids. I didn't want a fucking boyfriend. That was ridiculous. Was I supposed to bring a *guy* home to my parents? To client dinners? Company picnics? Corporate fundraisers? Was my father going to turn over his business to someone he saw as less than a man? Less than himself? Less than perfect?

Fuck no. And I'd worked too hard to give it all up.

If only sex with women was more satisfying. Maybe that was my problem. It's not that I didn't enjoy it, but somehow, no matter how beautiful or eager or passionate the woman was, no matter how willing she was to please, no matter how rough she let me get, I was always left feeling vaguely unsatisfied. Like there was supposed to be more, and somehow I was missing it.

Like the walls were supposed to tremble.

I closed my eyes, inhaling and exhaling. Never again. It didn't matter what the walls had done, because there were more important things at stake than sexual satisfaction. My career. My reputation. My self-image. My relationship with my family. My plans for the future. Allowing myself to be with Maxim that way jeopardized all of that.

I'd told Maxim last night that I didn't have a dream, but that wasn't true. My dream was to be normal. To live the kind of life people around me approved of and admired. To be seen as someone who had it all, even if he knew deep down it wasn't true.

What good had truth ever done me, anyway?

―――――

I HADN'T FALLEN asleep until nearly three o'clock in the morning, so I let myself sleep in, which was rare. Usually I'm up and about pretty early on weekend mornings, getting things done. But today it was almost eleven when I finally got out of bed, and I didn't even feel all that rested. My head was aching and my mouth was dry. I'd definitely overdone it with the whiskey last night.

I stepped into the shower, trying to plan out exactly how to handle Maxim. Poor guy—he had to be so confused, maybe even angry. I'd been so totally out of line to take advantage of him like that. To use him as a weapon in this fight against myself. He was totally innocent.

Well, not totally.

My blood heated and my dick started to rise as I remembered looking down at him last night. Oh my God, he'd looked so hot with his mouth on me.

No. This is what gets you into trouble. Stop thinking about him that way. Frowning, I went completely still, closed my eyes, and thought about the least sexy thing I could conjure up—my second grade teacher back in Ohio, Sister Mary Ruth, and how she used to call us all liars and snap our hands with rubber bands when she thought she'd caught us fibbing. *God sees you lying,* she'd say. *God sees everything you do.*

Thirty seconds later, my body was my own again, and I continued soaping up and wondering what to do. Should I apologize? Should I pretend it hadn't happened? Should I say I was drunk and don't remember a thing after dinner? Part of me wanted it to be that easy: What? A blowjob in the kitchen? I have no idea what you're talking about.

You fucking coward. You can't do that. At least be man enough to own what you did. Tell him you're sorry. Tell him you don't know what came over you. Tell him you've never done anything like that before and never will again.

Grimacing, I rinsed off and stood there under the spray for a few more minutes, delaying the inevitable. This would be the most uncomfortable conversation I'd ever had. Fucking brutal. But at the very least, maybe it would deter me from ever giving in to those feelings again.

I got out of the shower, dressed in jeans and a T-shirt, and brushed my teeth. In the mirror, I noticed my eyes were bloodshot, and the circles beneath them were dark. I put some drops in them, but told myself I deserved to look like shit after what I'd done. Then I took a few deep breaths, pushed my shoulders back, and opened my bedroom door.

The guest room door was open too, but I didn't hear anything downstairs. Slowly, I made my way down the steps and into the kitchen, bracing myself to find him there.

But he wasn't. And I saw no evidence that he'd been there at all—no coffee made, no dishes in the sink, no smell of breakfast lingering. Confused, I checked the back hall and noticed his shoes weren't there. What the fuck? Had he just left? How? He didn't have a car or any means to get a cab. Had Ellen picked him up? From the corner of my eye, I caught movement in the yard. I pushed open the back door and went outside in my bare feet.

He had lined up my potted plants on the driveway and was standing over them with the hose.

"Morning," I said, walking over to him.

"Morning." He glanced at me but returned his focus to the plants a second later. His expression was unreadable.

I shoved my hands in my pockets. "Sleep okay?"

"Great. You?"

Shrugging, I made some noncommittal answer, something between a grunt and a murmur.

"I think I finally beat the jet lag. I woke up around eight and had all this energy, so I came out here to finish up what I didn't get to yesterday."

I surveyed the yard and realized how much he'd done—the beds had been weeded and watered, the roses had been deadheaded and cut back, the patio had been swept. "Wow. Thanks."

"I enjoyed it."

I studied him again, my insides tightening. He wore my jeans again, and one of my shirts. He hadn't shaved since he'd been here, and his stubble was growing in slightly darker than the hair on his head. No gray in sight, of course. And under that shirt I knew his skin was perfectly smooth. Abs perfectly taut. He was so young—and I was old enough to know better. Here I'd lectured him about actions and consequences, and it had been *me* who'd gotten carried away by my feelings. Who hadn't thought before he acted. Who sincerely regretted what he'd done, even if it had led to the best orgasm of my life.

Don't think about that. Do what you came out here to do and move on.

"Maxim, I owe you an apology."

"No, you don't." He didn't look at me.

"Yeah, I do. I don't know what the fuck I was thinking."

No reaction.

"I've never done anything like that before in my life." It

wasn't even a lie. But the next part was. "It must have been the whiskey."

Finally, he met my eyes. Studied my face. "Okay."

"Because I'm straight. I'm not into guys at all. I just— lost control for a minute there." I concentrated on not blinking, not looking away, not surrendering anything. The defensive walls were up and they were going to stay up.

He nodded slowly.

"But it didn't mean anything. And it won't happen again." I said it firmly and meant it.

He focused on the plants again, his face impassive.

Jesus, Maxim. Could you please be a little less Russian right now and let me know what you're thinking? Are you mad? Insulted? Fine with this? Do you even give a fuck?

"So let's forget it happened. That work for you?" I asked, crossing my arms over my chest.

He moved to the next plant. "Of course."

"Good."

An awkward pause.

"So...you about done out here? Have you eaten yet? Thought maybe I could make us some lunch and then we can look online for some options for apartments." The more normal I could make this, the better. I'd thought about asking him to leave, or even paying for him to stay at a hotel, but decided that would be worse. That would be acknowledging outwardly that he had affected me, and I couldn't do that. The only way to pass the test I'd failed last night was to try again.

"That would be great, thanks."

"Okay. I'll get something going and give you a shout when it's ready."

"Sounds good."

I walked back into the house, feeling his eyes on me the

entire time. Once I was inside, the door closed behind me, I exhaled and tried to feel relieved. That had gone well, hadn't it? So why did I still feel so uneasy? It wasn't like his reaction had been upsetting. On the contrary, he'd barely seemed to care. Why was that?

I found myself getting unreasonably grumpy about it as I made sandwiches for lunch. Had our interlude in the kitchen not affected him at all? How could he be so cool about it? Had he not enjoyed it as much as I had?

Why didn't he appear to want me anymore? He'd certainly been all over me last night.

Christ Almighty, have you gone insane? Are you even listening to yourself? He reacted exactly how you wanted him to! How you needed him to! You can't have him living here for two more weeks, coming on to you all the time. You'll lose your mind! This is the best possible outcome from your stupid mistake.

Don't fuck with it.

SIXTEEN

MAXIM

IT WASN'T the damn whiskey.

He was lying. About some of it, at least. I could hear it in the tone of his voice, defensive and insistent, and see it in his face—a carefully controlled mask.

But why?

As I finished watering the flowers, I went over his remarks again in my head. *I owe you an apology. I don't know what the fuck I was thinking. I've never done anything like that before. It must have been the whiskey. I'm not into guys at all. It didn't mean anything. Forget it happened.*

Even though I'd been prepared for it, I didn't like it.

I didn't want his apology—I wanted his body, his attention, his permission to feel this way. I wanted to be invited in. Just...more of him. I wanted more of him.

And it was fucking terrible and greedy and selfish of me to want more than he was willing to give. He was being so generous, and I certainly didn't feel like I deserved any of it, but I couldn't help feeling that way. I didn't even really understand it. I'd never been the guy who wanted *more*. Give me no-strings sex without the complications of *more* any day of the week.

But this felt different. He was special to me. I wanted to be special to him.

The more I thought about his words, the more bothered I became. Maybe it was true that he'd never done anything like that before, but he hadn't done it because he was drunk. If he hadn't said yes when I asked permission, if he hadn't been so hard in my hand, if he hadn't come so hard and so fast and so long in my mouth it nearly choked me, then maybe I'd believe it was the whiskey.

But no. He'd done it because he'd wanted to. *That's what you were thinking, Derek. I want this. Plain and simple.* And he'd wanted it badly—enough to risk rejection. Enough to go after it hard. Enough to say *fuck the consequences and put your mouth on me.* I was one hundred percent certain about that.

And maybe that was it. Maybe that's what had me a little riled up. If he'd come out here and simply said *I'm sorry about the way I acted, it was a mistake, let's forget it and move on*, that would be different. At least then he wouldn't be denying the truth.

I was hurt and angry for about thirty seconds before realizing how childish I sounded.

Jesus, Maxim. Get over yourself. What good would it do for him to admit the truth? What difference would it make? If he doesn't want more of you, there's nothing you can do about it. He's done so much for you, the least you can do is respect his feelings on this.

A few minutes later, I turned off the hose and wound it up on the reel mounted to the side of the garage, vowing to honor his wishes. Whatever his reasons were, they were good enough for me, and as much fun as last night had been, however good it had felt to be so close to him, I'd try to forget it had happened.

But when I went into the house and saw him at the kitchen table, my thoughts ran away from me. *I want to kiss you again. I want my hands on you. I want your skin on mine.*

I couldn't think of one person who'd ever had such a powerful pull on me. It was as if gravity was somehow stronger between us, as if it wasn't a feeling at all, but an inescapable force. It left me feeling disoriented and off-center and almost powerless.

I liked it. And I didn't like it.

But one thing was certain—I had to keep it hidden.

AFTER LUNCH, during which neither of us spoke much, Derek brought his laptop to the kitchen table, along with pen and paper. "Let's see what's out there for apartments right now. Want to sit over here so you can see?"

"Okay." I moved to his side of the table, but I was careful to keep some distance between our chairs. Getting too close to him was not a good idea.

"That's for you to take notes." He slid the paper and pen in front of me. "And after we ballpark what your rent will cost, we can make a monthly budget."

"Ballpark?" I wondered.

"Oh—it means to make a reasonable guess at something. To get close to a number, even if you're not exact."

"Got it."

Derek started the search, and as the minutes ticked by,

it was increasingly clear that I'd have to double my savings in order to move in anywhere decent. Even a small room and bath in a shared apartment would cost at least a thousand dollars a month. First and last months' rent would eat up what I already had saved, and I had to think about utilities, groceries, transportation, and clothing, too. Derek helped me estimate what those things might cost per month, and we added up the numbers. The total was slightly alarming.

"Wow," I said, running a hand through my hair. "California is expensive."

"It is," Derek agreed.

"And I still need a laptop."

"I thought about that," he said. "I know it's high on your priority list, but realistically, getting a new one will have to wait until you're on your feet. In the meantime, I have one you can use."

"You do?"

"Yes. It's older, so it's not very powerful or fast, but it's something. I just have to wipe it clean, and it's yours as long as you need it."

"Thank you." I met his eyes and realized we hadn't left enough space between us at all. "I don't know what to say."

"It's nothing." He licked his lips. Stared at mine. "Just an old laptop."

"It's everything." *What are you thinking right now?* "And it means so much to me."

We both went silent, the tension between us so heavy I felt smothered by it. The hum of the refrigerator receded as my heart thundered louder in my chest. He leaned toward me slightly, and it took all my willpower to stay still. *Kiss me again. I want you to. I want it all.*

His breath came faster, his chest expanding and

contracting. I knew what I'd feel if I put my hand on it—the riotous banging that clamored inside my ribcage too.

"You should hate me for last night," he said, his voice deep and quiet.

"I don't."

"I hate myself for it."

My heart squeezed. "Why?"

"Because it's wrong."

So that's it. "Didn't it feel good?"

He closed his eyes and exhaled. "It felt fucking incredible." Then he looked at me again. "But Maxim, it's not who I am. Do you understand? I don't want that. I can't."

"Okay." As much as I wanted to argue, I knew it wasn't the right thing to do. His problem wasn't with me—it was with himself and his beliefs, and he'd only dig his heels in deeper if I pointed out the truth. But having me here had to make it worse for him. "Derek, I should find somewhere else to stay."

"No, that's not what I meant. I don't want you to go, I just—we just have to forget it happened," he insisted, as if I'd said otherwise. "That's the only way."

"Okay. That's what we'll do." I'd agreed with him, but you'd have thought I hadn't from the tortured look on his face. *Don't look at me like that. This isn't what I want, but you're not giving me any choice.*

A second later, his phone vibrated on the counter behind us. He jumped up and grabbed it. "Hello."

Grateful for the breathing room, I sucked in lungfuls of air free of his scent, willing my heart rate to return to normal.

"Yes. You want to talk to him?"

I turned in my chair and Derek handed me his phone. "It's Ellen."

"Thanks." I brought the phone to my ear and watched him leave the kitchen and go into the back hall. "Hello?"

"Hi, Maxim!" Ellen chirped. "Are you busy?"

I heard the bathroom door shut. "No."

"Want to head over to the bar? Derek said he'd bring you."

"Oh. Sure. Do I have time to clean up? I was working in the yard this morning."

"Don't worry about it. You'll want to shower when you get home from the bar anyway. I always do."

"Okay. I guess I'm ready, then." If I could get my pulse to stop hammering.

"Super! I had a barback quit this week and I'm short-handed. See you in a few."

"Sounds good. Bye." I ended the call and set the phone on the table as Derek came back into the kitchen, looking much more like himself. Calm, cool, in control.

"Ready?" he asked.

"Almost. I'm going to change clothes really quick. My laundry still in the dryer from last night?"

"Yep." As if our previous conversation hadn't happened, he picked up his phone and leaned back against the counter, focused on the screen. God, he could go from hot to cold quickly—and from cold to hot just as fast, like he'd shown me last night. It was dizzying. I grabbed my clean clothes from the dryer and headed upstairs to change, grateful for a reason to leave the house.

SEVENTEEN

DEREK

WHY DOESN'T HE CARE?

It was making me crazy. Everything about him was making me crazy. The way I wanted him, the memory of last night, the fact that he seemed completely unbothered by the fact that I was demanding we forget anything happened. In fact, it had been *me* to bring it up again at the table! How fucked up was that?

But nothing I said had provoked him, and his ability to remain cool and detached while I was coming out of my skin made me want to scream. He'd been totally into me last night! The blowjob had been *his* idea! *Why. Didn't. He. Care.*

Worse than that, why did I care so much?

After a silent car ride to the bar, I'd dropped him off and drove in fucking circles for an hour, trying to get my head on straight. When that didn't work, I parked at the mall and went into a few stores, telling myself to pick out a birthday present for Ellen but grabbing a bunch of things for Maxim instead. Maybe it was seeing him in my clothes that was the problem. Maybe if I took away that strange and possessive sense of closeness, I wouldn't be so confused. On my way home, I called Gage and asked if I could stop by. I needed distraction, and his house was always in complete chaos.

"Sure, man. Come on over. We're in the yard."

Thirty minutes later, I was sitting on their patio, a cold beer in my hand, watching their kids splash around in a little plastic pool. Lanie was in the house prepping kebabs for the grill, and Gage was sitting next to me, blowing up a giant alligator float that was way too big for the pool. When he was done, he handed it to Pennie, his oldest, and told her to share it.

"No," she said, running away with it. "Uncle Derek, watch me!"

He tipped back his beer. "Whose idea was it to have kids?"

"Come on, you have great kids." I applauded and whistled when Pennie took a flying leap into the pool on her raft.

"I know, but they ruined my life. Hey, Will!" he yelled to his five-year-old. "Don't push your brother like that! He'll fall in, and I'll have to get out of this chair to save him, and I don't really want to get out of this chair!"

"I heard that!" Lanie hollered through the screen.

"You hear everything," muttered Gage. He set his beer on the table and stretched out his legs, crossing them at the ankle. His arms were crossed over his stomach, which showed the first traces of a belly. "God, I'm tired. Remember when I could stay up past ten o'clock and not be exhausted the next day?"

"Vaguely."

"Those were good times."

I took a slow, long sip of my beer. "Maybe, but I wouldn't trade what you have to go back."

"You wouldn't?" He raised his voice. "Pennie, if you try to ride that on the ground, it will get a hole in it!"

"No way. You've got it all, man. I envy you."

He glanced at me. "Envy me? Of what, my soul-crushing mortgage? My Dad bod? My messy house? My ability to change a dirty diaper with one hand?"

I winced. "Maybe not the diaper thing. Or the Dad bod. But everything else—your easy relationship with Lanie, your house full of kids, your Saturday soccer games and Sunday barbecues. I wish I had all that."

"No marriage is easy," he assured me. "Half the time Lanie and I want to strangle each other. The other half of the time, we want to strangle the kids. But you're right. I wouldn't trade it."

I lifted the bottle to my lips again. "Told you."

"So have a family," he said, as easily as he would say *have a kebab*. "What are you waiting for?"

"The right person, obviously." I laughed gruffly, but it was fake. "I can't seem to find her."

"Carolyn seems cool."

"She is, but...I don't know. She's perfect on paper, but there's not much chemistry. I'm afraid of getting serious with her and never feeling anything more than I do now."

"Which is what?"

"I *like* her a lot, but..."

"You don't want to bang her."

"No," I admitted.

He ran a hand through his unruly brown hair. "Dude, do not marry a woman you don't want to bang, because that is the only person you have permission to bang until death do you part. Did you hear that? *Death*."

I frowned. "Right."

"Maybe you're being too picky," he suggested. "I know you hate hearing that, but maybe you don't have to have the A-plus-on-paper woman. Maybe you should look for the woman you want to bang who's like, a B-minus on paper."

"Maybe."

"I mean, you could have anyone," Gage went on. "Girls have always lined up to be with you. How hard can it be to find a cute little twenty-nine-year-old neat freak who loves vacuuming and hates sand as much as you do?"

"I don't hate sand," I said, rolling my eyes. "I just don't like the way it gets everywhere."

"I'm fucking with you." He hit me on the arm. "Look, give it some time. If it's not happening with Carolyn, then move on. It's bound to happen with someone."

I nodded, tipping back the beer again before glancing over my shoulder to make sure Lanie was still in the house. Then I spoke quietly. "Do you ever get the urge to cheat on Lanie? Like, are you ever attracted to other people?"

"I wouldn't say I have the urge to cheat." Gage spoke softly too. "But yeah, I'm attracted to other women some-times. I'm human. But I don't act on it. Not worth it."

"What do you do about it? To make it go away?"

"It sort of goes away on its own once I think about what I have with Lanie. I've never been so attracted to anyone I'd risk losing her or hurting my family."

Of course not. But that didn't help me.

Gage crossed his arms over his chest and went on. "Probably the most tempted I've ever been to sleep with someone I wasn't supposed to was when I fell for Lanie. We'd been friends for so long, and I'd dated one of her roommates, and she was kind of seeing this douchebag named Brodie. There were all these reasons why we shouldn't hook up. But I couldn't stop thinking about her. Then one night, she broke it off with the douchebag, and I was like fuck it—I need to see what this is. We might ruin our friendship, but I need to know."

I nodded in understanding, because I got that—the desperate urge to understand what you felt. I wished it were as simple as that between Maxim and me.

But in our case, I'm not sure I wanted to know. What good would it do me?

I stayed at Gage and Lanie's for hours, eating and drinking and letting their kids climb all over me as the sun set behind the hills. They were noisy and sticky and their popsicles melted all over my shirt, but I didn't mind. This was what I wanted—family and friends in the backyard on a warm summer night.

Around nine-thirty I got a text from Ellen telling me she'd bring Maxim home later, so I didn't have to wait up to come get him. By then, the kids were getting to that sunburned-and-tired meltdown stage, so I said goodnight and headed home.

My house felt emptier than usual.

EIGHTEEN

MAXIM

"YOU SURVIVED." Ellen grinned and handed me an envelope with cash stuffed inside. "Here you go. It's a little more than a hundred bucks. Sorry it's not more, but it was kind of slow tonight. Eventually I'll pay you weekly, but for now I'll pay you at the end of your shifts."

I couldn't believe it. A *hundred bucks*, right now? That was a quarter of my rent to Derek! Even better, it was the first money I'd made in the U.S. I thumbed through it in disbelief, wishing I didn't need this money and could frame it as my first big achievement here. Ellen might not think a hundred bucks was a big deal, but I felt rich. And so, so grateful. In fact, I had to turn away from her, scared I might actually tear up. "Ellen, thank you so much. You have no idea how glad I am to have this job."

"Of course. What are friends for? I hope it wasn't too terrible."

"Not at all." I'd been so busy the first few hours, the

time had flown. I spent most of the time assisting Ellen behind the bar, washing glasses, refilling ice, running down to the basement to get more beer and wine, and occasionally taking food orders to tables if the wait staff was slammed. The last couple hours I'd spent helping Ellen clean up and restocking the bar, with only a quick break for dinner.

"We can take off now. My other manager is going to close up."

"Okay. What do I owe you for the shirts?" When we'd arrived, she'd given me two black T-shirts with the bar's logo on them. One I'd put on right away, and the other was folded under my arm, along with the shirt I'd worn here.

"Nothing." She laughed. "That's your uniform."

She called goodnight to the staff that was left and we went out the back door to where her car was parked.

"Jump in," she said, opening the driver's side door of a beat-up Jeep.

"You don't lock your doors?" I went around to the passenger side and attempted to get in, but first Ellen had to throw a bunch of things that had been on the seat into the back—water bottles, coffee cups, clothing, shoes, plastic bags.

"Nah. What for?" She started the car as I buckled up. "Nothing worth stealing in here, and if someone wants this piece of shit badly enough, they can have it."

I laughed. "You are *so* different from Derek."

"Oh Jesus, his car is ridiculous. You could eat off the floor." She backed out of her parking spot. "Not that he lets anyone eat in it. And he practically has heart palpitations any time he has to ride in mine."

I couldn't resist asking more about him. "Was he always so neat and organized? Even as a kid?"

"Yep. Always kept his bedroom perfectly clean, never

left his toys out, used to love washing his bike more than riding it. His friends would be like, 'Derek, it's called a dirt bike! It's supposed to have dirt on it!'"

I laughed, picturing that gap-toothed, dark-haired boy I'd seen in the picture over the fireplace scrubbing away at his spokes. "I can see that."

"He's such a good guy, but he takes himself so seriously sometimes. Always has."

"But he's so successful. He's got that beautiful house, and a good job, a great car. He takes such good care of everything. He's so generous to everyone. He seems perfect to me." For a second, I thought I'd said too much, but Ellen didn't seem fazed.

"He's pretty close to perfect, I suppose. If you're judging by appearances. But I don't know how happy he is."

I had to know more. "You don't think he's happy?"

She thought for a moment. "I think he's lonely. But he doesn't really talk about his feelings."

"I can understand that."

"But I know he wants a family and thought he'd have one by now, and I think that affects him. I don't know if he's told you, but he had a really serious girlfriend for a while. In fact, he bought the house intending to move into it with her. They were going to get married."

My stomach felt like I'd swallowed rocks. "Oh."

"He had this perfect life all mapped out—the house, the wife, the kids. Then she broke it off, and I think he's been sort of lost ever since. Felt like he'd failed, and if there's anything Derek hates more than dirt, it's failure."

I smiled, but I felt for Derek. My biggest fear was failure, too. Questions I didn't allow myself to ask were constantly threatening like storm clouds in the back of my mind. What if I couldn't make it here? What if I had to go back to Russia? What if I wasn't good enough, smart enough, driven enough to achieve what I wanted?

"Part of that comes from our parents," Ellen went on. "Or at least our dad. He was really hard on the boys growing up—strict rules, high standards, lots of pressure to be the best at everything, whether it was sports or school. I probably had it the easiest, or maybe I just cared the least what my parents wanted." She laughed. "I was the black sheep. I spent a lot of time being grounded."

"But you turned out pretty successful, too."

"Thanks." She flashed me a smile. "That was fun last night, wasn't it?"

You have no idea. "Yes."

"And I'm so glad I got to meet Carolyn."

"Have they been together long?" I felt guilty even asking, like it was disrespectful to Derek. But I couldn't help myself.

"Not too long. And I don't think it's too serious between them, but since the breakup three years ago, he's hardly dated anyone. I don't know if he's just ridiculously picky or if there really isn't anyone out there good enough for him, but it's such a shame, you know? Here's a guy who's dying to have a family, and he'd be the best husband and dad ever because he's got a great career and great house and he loves taking care of people, but he just can't meet the right girl. Maybe Carolyn will break the spell."

I didn't think so, but I wouldn't say that to Ellen. In my mind I heard Derek's voice. *The problem is me. Sometimes I don't know what I want.*

Unbelievably, Ellen said this next: "I've even wondered if Derek was gay."

My pulse pounded in my ears. "Really?"

"Yeah, I mean there are some signs. I'd never ask him flat out, but I have wondered."

I had no idea what to say. Thankfully, Ellen was a talker.

"It's hard because we were raised to believe it's wrong. I love my dad, but he can be a real asshole about some things, and that's one of them. He grew up in a religious household in a very conservative part of the country, and that was all he knew. When we moved out here from Ohio and first started to see gay couples, he made a lot of negative comments about it being unnatural and immoral and all that. It's bullshit, but he believes it."

"Does Derek believe it?"

"No, I don't think so. But Derek has always wanted my father's approval, more than any of us. I don't see him doing anything that would lower himself in our father's eyes, even now." She waved a hand in the air. "And anyway, I could be way off. He's always dated women, and I know he planned to marry his ex. He's probably not gay. He's just a perfectionist. Please don't tell him I said anything."

"I won't," I promised. And I wouldn't.

But my heart ached for Derek. The more I learned about him, the more I realized that the problem wasn't that he didn't know what he wanted, the problem was that he *did* know—he just didn't like it. He didn't *want* to want it. It wasn't right in his eyes, it wasn't natural, it wasn't perfect. But he couldn't make it stop.

It explained why he'd done what he did last night in the kitchen, and why he ran away afterward. It explained his excuses this morning. It explained why he said he hated himself.

I wished I could help him, but I had no idea how.

When we pulled into Derek's driveway, I said good-night to Ellen and thanked her again.

"Thank *you*," she said. "Same time tomorrow?"

"Sure." I'd have to figure out how to take public transportation, so Derek and Ellen didn't have to drive me everywhere. Maybe I could do that tomorrow. "See you then."

I let myself into the house with the key Derek had given me this afternoon. All the lights were off downstairs, and the house was silent. After locking the front door behind me, I went upstairs, stepping softly to avoid making noise. Derek probably had to get up early for work, and it was nearly midnight. His bedroom door was closed.

What had he done tonight? Had he eaten dinner alone? Watched television? Worked? I thought about what Ellen had said, that maybe he was lonely, and wondered if it was true. Could someone as handsome and kind and sexy as Derek really be lonely? It didn't seem possible.

After a quick shower, I brushed my teeth and got in bed, but I couldn't sleep. My brain was buzzing with everything I'd learned. I reached for the lamp and turned it on, then picked up my notebook and pen, scribbling for ten minutes about what Ellen had told me and how I felt about it. Mostly what I felt was sorry and helpless. Derek was doing so much for me, and my staying here at his house could not be easy for him. Not only was I a constant reminder of something he wanted to forget, but if he wanted me half as badly as I wanted him, it was torture knowing we were only separated by one hallway and two closed doors.

When I was done, I put the notebook and pen back in the drawer and turned off the lamp.

Two minutes later, there was a knock on the door.

NINETEEN

DEREK

MADNESS. It was madness inside me.

The way I wanted him. The way I needed him. The way I'd lain awake for hours thinking of him and promising myself I'd stay away.

It was madness that had me clutching at the sheets, as if they'd anchor me to the bed. It was madness that had me growing hard as I listened to him take a shower. It was madness that had me getting out of bed, opening my bedroom door, moving through the darkness like a ghost. It was madness telling me to knock, to seek out the truth, to know for sure.

What else could it be? When I'd left Gage's earlier, I'd been resolute—nothing good could come of being with Maxim again. Nothing.

And yet here I was at his bedroom door, my heart pounding, my adrenaline rushing, my cock aching with need.

He opened it.

Rushing forward, I grabbed his head and brought my face close to his. "I can't forget it," I growled. "And I don't fucking want to."

Then I savagely claimed his mouth with mine, plunging my tongue between his full, firm lips, desperate to get inside him any way I could. He kissed me back just as hard, his hands stealing to my waist, sliding around to my lower back. It drove me crazy to think of his hands on my skin—strong, solid, masculine hands that would grab and pull and punish.

"Goddamn you," I whispered, walking him deeper into the room. "Goddamn you for doing this to me." Grabbing one of his hands, I put it over my cock, painfully hard and thick inside my pants. "Goddamn you for making me want more."

"Let me give it to you." He tried to reach inside my pants, but I pushed his hand away.

"No. Not this time." There were things I wanted, and if I let Maxim get his hands and mouth on me, this would be over before it began. I wanted *him* to feel exposed this time. "I want to see you naked."

He shoved down the boxer briefs he wore and stepped out of them. Immediately I put my hand on his cock, groaning at the hot, heavy length of it. He got even harder as I stroked him, and feeling him swell and surge inside my fist had blood pounding through me. He moved closer to me, his mouth traveling down my neck, his tongue warm and wet on my throat. I gripped him tighter, pulled at him faster. When he moaned, I felt the sound move through my body, and all of me vibrated with wanting him, as if my veins were live wires.

"What else?" He slipped his fingertips inside the waist of my pants. "What else do you want?"

"I want to touch you. Everywhere." I let my hands roam over hard muscle and hot skin, barely suppressing the animal urge inside me to throw him on the bed and satisfy this fucking insatiable hunger gnawing at my insides. I dragged my lips and teeth and tongue over him, kissing his collarbone, biting his shoulder, licking his neck. I couldn't get enough of the way he smelled—no flowery perfumes, no fruity lotions, nothing false or fake or feminine. Just the clean, masculine scent of soap and skin.

He untied the drawstring of my pants, and they pooled at my feet. His mouth sought mine as his hands slid down over my ass. As his tongue stroked between my lips, he squeezed my flesh and pulled me against him, trapping our erections between us. My breath caught, a growl rumbling deep in my chest as he rocked his hips, rubbing his bare cock against mine. I slid my hands up his chest, over his shoulders, into his hair. The friction between us had my thigh muscles clenching, a firestorm building deep in the center of my body.

My God, was this really happening? I had to see it. Breaking the kiss, I looked down at the juncture where our bodies touched. It fascinated me—two male torsos, tight and firm and lined with muscle and veins; two thick, hard cocks standing at attention, darker than the skin on our abdomens —and I reached between us. A strangled sound escaped Maxim as I wrapped us both in one fist and moved my hand up and down, exactly like I'd jerk myself off, but a thousand times hotter because it was both of us. Our breathing was ragged and rough, and his fingers were digging into my sides. I imagined him leaving bruises, and it thrilled me. *Yes. Leave your mark.*

It only took a moment before I felt us grow slick beneath my fingers, and I found myself close to orgasm.

Maxim was close too—I could hear it in his throat and see it in his muscles and feel it in the hot, swollen cock inside my hand. It got to me, that I could bring him to this panting, heated, untamed place, that it was my body, my grasp, my movement driving him to it. I loved watching him—so different than watching a woman, and yet familiar too. His body was like mine, and I saw all my pleasure reflected in it, as if he were a mirror.

I loved the hitch of his chest, the wideness of his shoulders tapering to the tautness of his waist, the angle of his back as he leaned slightly away and pushed his hips forward. I loved the rippling muscles on his stomach, the faint trail of hair beneath his belly button, the silver sheen to his skin in the dark. And I loved the agony on his face, the open mouth, the half-shut eyes, the struggle in his expression. Was he fighting it?

The thought pleased me, that there was torture inside him, that he was suffering for me somehow, and that I could relieve it.

"I want you to come," I rasped through clenched teeth. "I want to watch you. I want to feel it in my hand. I want you dripping down my stomach."

He spoke unintelligible words of anguish, maybe not even in English, his head turning to the side, as if he were still intent on lasting longer. His profile was so beautiful it made me angry.

"Now," I demanded, stroking harder and faster, feeling my legs go weak as climax threatened. *Fuck*—I didn't want to lose control before he did, but everything I did to him, I did to myself too. "Goddamn you, don't deny me. *Now*. Now!"

He did what I asked, clutching me hard and rolling his hips as he came in silky, hot spurts, moaning something that was probably *there, you fucking asshole* in Russian. The thought of it—that I was dominating my own wayward desire by dominating its object—was arousing enough, but the sight of it—another man's cum—hitting my stomach and chest, gliding over my fist, getting all over my cock, pushed me over the edge. Everything tightened and twisted and tensed before suddenly releasing in a roaring rush of bliss as I exploded all over both of us.

Madness. That's what it was.

And I could no longer contain it.

TWENTY

MAXIM

WE STOOD THERE, breathing hard and dripping with each other, his hand still wrapped around us both. I blinked a few times, not entirely sure he wasn't a ghost. Or maybe a dream.

But he stayed where he was, his hips solid and firm and real beneath my hands, his breath warm on my face. I didn't want to move or speak for fear I'd break the spell. Was that the rapid fire of his heart I was hearing? Or was it mine?

"Uh. Sorry." Careful not to get anything on the carpet, he let go of us both.

"Don't apologize." Disappointed, I took my hands off him, even though what I wanted to do was pull him closer. "That felt great."

"Yeah." He exhaled, his eyes closing briefly. "Give me a minute."

He scooped up his pants and left the room, and I quickly used the hallway bath. Back in the guest room, I switched on the bedside lamp and tugged on underwear and the athletic pants he'd loaned me. The whole time, all I could think was, *What the hell? Why did he keep apologizing? Was he going to brush me off again?*

"Hey."

At the sound of his voice, I looked up. He stood in the doorway, jeans on, no shirt. In contrast to the way he'd stormed in before, all fire and muscle, now he looked almost afraid to enter.

"Hey." I smiled at him. "You can come in."

He walked into the room a few feet, stopping well short of where I stood. Fidgeted. Shoved his hands into his pockets. "Look, I know you don't want another apology or excuse, but I feel like I at least owe you an explanation."

"Okay."

"You must think I'm such an asshole," he went on, "barging in here like that, saying those things to you."

"I don't think you're an asshole at all."

"You must think *some*thing," he went on, running a hand through his hair, messing it up. Frustration edged his tone. "You barely reacted at all today when we talked about what happened last night. It was driving me crazy."

"How was I supposed to react?" I stared at him in disbelief. "You said it meant nothing. You said you were drunk. You said to forget it. That's what I was trying to do." I hesitated, debating how forthright I should be and deciding to go for it. Maybe he wanted to hear this. Maybe it would make a difference. "But it's useless, Derek. I'll never forget what happened between us—last night or tonight. And I don't think you will either. But if you really didn't like it and want to pretend like nothing happened—*again*—no problem."

His stubborn jaw twitched, but he didn't say anything for a moment. "I never said I didn't like it."

"So you did like it?"

He cocked a brow. "I think that was pretty obvious, don't you?"

I had to smile.

"But Maxim, I didn't *want* to like it. It only causes problems for me." Sighing heavily, he leaned back against the dresser, his shoulders slumped. "I meant what I said this morning. I've never been with a guy before you. But I've... thought about it. I've wanted to know what it would be like."

"And now that you know?"

"My head is even more fucked up. If I hadn't come in here, the not-knowing would still be driving me insane. But now that I know, it's almost worse." He shook his head. "What the fuck is wrong with me?"

If I'd thought it would help, I'd have gone to him. Touched him. Reassured him what we'd done was okay, that *he* was okay. But somehow I felt like it would be the wrong move. Instead, I chose my words carefully. "There is nothing wrong with you, Derek. Don't be so hard on yourself. You were curious, and so was I. Things happened. If you want to forget it, we can, but if you feel like you might want to see where this goes...I'd be up for that, too."

"I don't know what I want. I mean, I know what I want *physically*, at least with you, but it doesn't gel at all with the vision I have for my life."

"Which is what?"

"A wife and kids. I want a family."

I nodded slowly. I wasn't sure exactly where Derek and I could go from here, but I *was* sure it wouldn't lead to a wife and kids. While I was trying to come up with some-thing to say, he went on.

"I told you before, I was raised in a religious household. My parents..." He shook his head. "They would never understand. They would never be okay with this. *I've* never been okay with this."

"How long have you struggled with it?"

"A long time. Maybe since I was twelve or thirteen. But I always understood it as something wrong with me. A defect or faulty wiring. Because I liked girls too."

"Lots of people do."

That actually caused him to crack a smile, but it disap-peared fast. "Anyway, I've never done anything about those feelings except hate them and hide them. Pray for them to go away. But then..."

"But then?"

He looked at me with hungry eyes. "There's just some-thing about you."

"I feel bad for liking that. Sort of."

"No. Don't feel bad." His brow furrowed with anger. "I'm sorry. None of this is your fault, and I'm treating you as if it is."

"You're not," I said, shaking my head. "Derek, you've been so good to me. You've treated me better than anyone ever has. I don't know what I did to deserve your kindness and help, but I'm so thankful for it. I'll never forget it."

A tiny, sad smile appeared on his lips. "It makes me feel good to hear that."

"It's the truth. And I like making you feel good," I added.

His smile widened, but it was still mournful somehow. "Do you? I feel like shit even saying all this to you. I hope you don't think I'm judging you. My problem is only with myself."

"I understand."

"You do?"

"Yes. I've never struggled with this like you are, probably because it was always very clear to me I wasn't attracted to girls, but also because of where I grew up. Being openly gay in Russia is not accepted. Not like it is here."

"I know. And I wish I was different. I wish I could be someone else, the kind of guy who doesn't care what anyone thinks, because being with you feels so good. I just don't know if I can. Something in me refuses to give."

Seeing him so conflicted, wishing he could be someone else for me, was heartbreaking. "Derek, if you want me to leave, if that will make it easier for you, say the word, and I'm gone. I'll have my savings tomorrow, and I can find a place to stay."

He closed his eyes, exhaling slowly. "Let me think about it."

"Of course." I thought he would say goodnight and leave then, but he kept standing there, leaning against the dresser.

"Maxim. Come here."

Surprised, I stayed put. "What?"

He met my eyes and spoke more firmly. "Come here."

I made my way toward him, but it wasn't until I stood right in front of him that he reached for me. Wrapped his arms around my waist. Pulled me close and tipped his forehead onto my chest.

I put my arms around him. His body was warm, but chills swept over my back. Pure happiness flooded me, soaking me right down to the bone. I wanted to say things. *Stay with me. Let me hold you all night. I'll make you feel good.* Maybe he wanted to say things too—*don't let me go, I want this with you, show me how.*

But a moment later, he ended the embrace and left the room, neither of us saying anything except goodnight.

I got back in bed, but lay awake for what seemed like hours, my mind refusing to shut off. Was Derek still awake? What was he thinking? Would he ask me to go? I thought about everything he'd told me tonight and felt so good that he'd trusted me with his feelings. Even if it hadn't been exactly what I wanted to hear, at least he'd given me honesty. He'd revealed something to me that he'd never spoken about to anyone. It made me feel like I had something of his, something more precious than clothing or shelter or even time. I had a piece of him no one else had. I had a truth about him no one else knew. I had one of his secrets.

I wanted them all.

For the first time, I wanted to know every dark corner of someone's mind. I wanted to taste every hidden place on his body. I wanted to stay with him.

I wanted not just more, but *all.*

Frankly, it was a little terrifying.

TWENTY-ONE

DEREK

I WAS SHATTERED.

Last night had ruined me.

Turning my desk chair to face the window, I looked out at downtown L.A. skyscrapers packed with offices and apartments. Streets congested with traffic. Block after block of businesses, stores, restaurants. Sidewalks full of people. How was it possible, in a city of millions, to feel so achingly alone?

But I did. I had for so long. Having Maxim around for the weekend made me realize it. I'd forgotten how good it felt to have breakfast with someone. Run errands for someone. Kiss someone in the dark.

Having him there made my house less empty. It gave me purpose. It made me feel needed and useful and trusted. I couldn't stop thinking about that—Maxim *trusted* me. Had I taken advantage of that last night? Had I used him in an attempt to answer some question about myself? And now that I had my answer—now that I *knew*—could I walk away from it? Walk away from the one person in the entire world with whom I'd been my deepest, darkest, truest self? The one person I'd entrusted with my secret?

I was scared that I couldn't, and that fear gripped me as hard as the madness of wanting him. God, how I wanted him.

My stomach hollowed as I thought about last night. It had felt so good. So honest. So intense. I wanted nothing more than to do it again, and again, and again. To feel that closeness with him. To deepen it. Reveal more of myself and discover more of him. But at what price?

Was I really prepared to let go of my fantasy of the perfect life? A perfect family? Had I honestly done everything I could to make it happen? Was I ready to face the censure of my parents and colleagues and strangers and God and myself? Would that really make me happy? Then again, was I going to be happy married to someone I didn't feel passionate about? Living a life that required me to hide part of who I really was? Forever stifling whatever it was that had made me feel so fucking *alive* last night? Maybe that would be my punishment. My cross to bear.

At least I'd have a family.

But what about Maxim?

Maxim. So young, so full of life, so ready to take on the world. He had so much to offer and so much to learn. Mistakes to make and successes to celebrate. Personal goals to achieve. He was still in that stage of life where all you thought about was sex, food, and getting ahead. I remembered it well, but it was long behind me.

He'd probably get tired of me sooner rather than later. He'd want to go to clubs and meet industry people and experience being a gorgeous twenty-something in L.A., with their selfies and their Snapchats and their hashtags. I was closer to forty than twenty, I hadn't been to a club in years, and hashtags could #fuckrightoff. Other than Maxim, I wouldn't even know how to talk to a twenty-something. What the hell did he see in me anyway? Me, with my gray hair and cracking bones and early Saturday nights. He could have anybody.

And he certainly wouldn't be thinking about a family in the next few years. But I didn't want to be fifty and pushing a stroller around the neighborhood. How much longer was I going to wait? Maxim had said he was willing to "see where this goes," but it didn't seem right to fuck with his feelings when I knew it couldn't go anywhere.

You can't have everything. It's either short term gratification or big picture goals. Make your choice.

Grimacing, I spun to face my desk again, picked up my phone and made a call.

"Hello?"

"Hey Carolyn, it's Derek. How are you?"

"Good. How are you?"

"Good. Listen, can I take you to dinner tonight?"

"I'd love that. What time were you thinking?"

"How's seven?"

"Perfect. That gives me time to get a run in after my class."

"Great. You know, we should run together sometime."

"That sounds like fun." She paused. "Wow, you sound so much better than you did Saturday night."

Could she tell what an effort it was? "I'll pick you up at seven."

"Sounds good. See you then."

This was it. One last-ditch effort to be someone else.

My phone was still in my hand when it buzzed with a text from my sister.

Hey!! Just wanted to let you know it went really well with Maxim last night. He's such a hard worker! LOL you should have seen his face when I handed him his cash at the end of the night—it was like I gave him a million dollars!

At the sight of his name, I felt guilty. I'd have to tell Maxim what I was doing with Carolyn. Not because I'd made any promises or anything, but because we'd left some things up in the air last night, and I didn't want to string him along. He deserved to find someone braver than me. **Is he working tonight?**

Three little dots faded in and out as she replied. **Yes. I'm picking him up at 3:30. He tried to tell me he'd take a bus.** This was followed by laughing emojis with tears.

I'd have smiled, but I couldn't. **Are you able to bring him home?**

She replied with a thumbs up.

For a few minutes, I sat there staring at my phone, trying to think of what I was going to say to Maxim, how I was going to explain it. For all I knew, he wouldn't even care.

But as I made the call, my gut told me he would.

"Hello?"

"Hi. It's me."

"Hi." He sounded so happy to hear from me, I cringed.

"What are you up to?" I asked lamely.

"I'm walking to Western Union right now. I found a location only two kilometers from your house. My mother called at three A.M. this morning to let me know she had wired my savings."

I love the way he says kilometers. "Good. That's good."

"Yes, and I made a list of things I need to do after that. Aren't you proud of me?"

Oh fuck, that's cute. "Yes. What's on the list?"

"Open a bank account, apply for a credit card, buy some clothes."

With all the turmoil last night, I'd forgotten to give him the things I'd purchased. Now I wasn't even sure I should. "Good thinking."

"How is your day?"

Terrible. "Good." I frowned. "Maxim, I just wanted to let you know, I'm taking Carolyn out tonight."

Silence. "Oh."

"I wanted to be honest, because you were so compassionate during our conversation last night. I decided I'm not really into letting things go any further with us. I just can't."

"Okay."

"I feel like I owe it to myself, and to her, to give it one more chance." I was rambling, but I couldn't stop.

"I get it."

"But that doesn't mean I want you to leave. I don't." *I want to have it both ways.*

"Thank you. Have a great time tonight."

"Thanks."

I hung up and lowered my forehead to my desk, picturing him standing in front of Western Union, staring at his phone, thinking *what a fucking coward.* That's what I felt like, anyway.

A moment later, I picked up my head and shook it off. I'd made the right decision. I hadn't been rash, I'd been realistic. I'd considered the options, weighed the pros and cons, and made my choice based on my long-held, long-term goals. That's what I always did. It's who I was. Or at least, it's who I was pretending to be. Sooner or later, my feelings would catch up.

They had to.

"I'M SO glad you called me." Beaming, Carolyn reached over and tapped my thigh as I drove downtown. "I was worried about you."

"Me?" I feigned surprise.

"Yes. You really seemed bothered the other night."

"Nah. Nothing to worry about."

"Good. So where should we go?"

"I thought maybe I'd take you to my sister's bar. You mentioned you've never been to The Blind Pig." I ignored the voice in my head telling me that wasn't the real reason I wanted to go there. The one that knew I was a fraud. The one that recognized my inability to stay away from him.

"I haven't!" Carolyn was delighted. "I'd love to go there! Your sister is so nice. I really like her."

"She likes you, too."

"Did she say that? Oh, God." She waved a hand in the air. "That sounded so middle school of me. Forget that."

"As a matter of fact, not only Ellen said that, but Maxim and Gage and Lanie all made a point to tell me how wonderful you are." It was a little bit of an exaggeration, but I liked the blush it put on her cheeks, and it was a relief to know I could still be charming when I wanted to be.

I continued to pour it on, opening the car door for her, helping her out, taking her arm as we walked from the parking garage to the bar. She looked radiantly happy, more beautiful than I'd ever seen her, really, and I'm sure we looked like the perfect couple on the outside.

But as soon as we walked into the bar, I looked around for Maxim, and when I saw him hurry by carrying an armful of liquor bottles, my insides twisted. What the fuck was I doing? This was so unfair, bringing Carolyn here, parading her right under his nose. And now that I saw him, I wanted him even more. The difference in my body's reaction to him compared to its reaction to Carolyn was staggering.

Just keep it off your face, I told myself, putting an arm around Carolyn's back. *If you can't bury it altogether, at least keep it off your face.*

It wasn't easy—every time I saw him out of the corner of my eye, I lost track of what Carolyn was saying—but I thought I did a fairly good job. Maxim did even better. Granted, he was at work and I was out socially, but he barely even glanced at us the entire time we were there. He'd nodded hello when we'd come in, but that was it. Was he mad? The thought angered me. He said he'd be fine either way! Did he think this was easy, sitting across the table from one person and craving to be with another? Having to hide it? Feeling horrible and ashamed and guilty for it? *It's so easy for you, isn't it, Maxim? You know exactly who you are and what you want, and you don't care what anyone thinks. Well, that's not how it is for me, so don't tell me you understand and then judge me.*

Even worse than his ignoring me was the way I saw him flirting with customers. Flirting! With women! Giving them his sly Russian smiles and big blue eyes and probably charming them with his accent. And they laughed and batted their lashes and touched him on the arm or chest. They probably thought he'd go home with them. It took everything I had not to run over there and yell *Fuck you, he doesn't even like your parts!*

I tried harder with Carolyn. I was attentive and polite. I laughed at her jokes. I told her she looked beautiful. I asked about her family, her job, and her favorite music. I made a big deal about how much patience she must have to be a teacher, how much better at math she probably was than me, and how I admired her for running marathons. I took her hand when we walked back to the car. I kissed her on her porch, a chaste press of my lips against hers I hoped would fire me up.

It didn't.

End this fucking charade. It's painful.

While I was trying to think of a way to break it off without seeming like a total asshole, Carolyn spoke up.

"Derek," she said, tucking her hair behind her ears. "I hope you won't take this the wrong way, but—" She gave me an embarrassed smile. "I don't think we have enough chemistry for some reason. Or the right kind of chemistry. I really like you, and I think you like me, but..." She shook her head. "Something's missing. I was really hoping it would develop or we'd find it somewhere along the way, but it hasn't happened." She took on a tortured expression. "And it's *really* a shame, because you're hot, and you're a great guy, and you're single, and I am too, and I haven't had sex in a really, really, really ridiculously long time, but my gut is telling me we're better off as friends."

Relief rushed through me. "Carolyn, I'm sorry."

"Don't be. I've had fun with you. And I don't want you to be a stranger, either."

"I've had fun with you, too. And I wish things were different."

"Me too. Who knows, maybe in another life, we'd have

been more than friends," she said airily, tucking her hands into her back pockets. "But this life is what we have, and I'd like to spend the rest of mine with someone crazy about me." She smiled ruefully. "Just have to find him first."

"You will. You're fantastic, Carolyn. And some lucky guy is going to cross your path and fall hard for you. I know it."

"Maybe." She shrugged, but she looked happy at the thought. "What about you?"

I wasn't sure what she meant. "What about me?"

"You okay with this?"

"Of course. To be honest, I felt the same, but I didn't want to say anything without giving us a fair chance."

"We had a fair chance. It just wasn't meant to be." She hesitated, like she wanted to say more and wasn't sure she should.

"What?" I prompted.

She tilted her head. "Can I say something? It's kind of crazy, and I could be wrong, but it's been in the back of my mind for two days, and I don't want to offend you, but maybe it—"

"Carolyn."

"Okay." She took a deep breath. "I might be way off here, but I sensed something between you and Maxim Saturday night. Maybe it was all in my imagination, but—"

"It was," I said quickly. "You're way off."

She flashed her palms at me. "Like I said, I could be wrong."

"You are." I needed to get out of here. The back of my neck was burning hot, and I was afraid my face was giving me away. I was not prepared for this. "I should go."

Her face fell. "Okay. I'm really sorry, Derek. I didn't mean to offend you. I just know how hard it is to find someone you have chemistry with, and you mentioned you were struggling with something, and I thought—"

"You thought wrong." I took a step back. "But it's okay. I'm not offended."

"Good. Well...goodnight."

"Night."

I stepped off her porch and headed down the front walk, feeling her eyes on me. *She knows. It was obvious, and she knows.* But how? No one else had said anything! Then again, no one else had been focused on me romantically, or paying close attention to me like she had been. Plus Carolyn was smart and intuitive. She'd probably noticed me staring at him Saturday night, maybe even tonight. I hadn't been careful enough.

Suppressing a groan, I got into the car and started it up, more conflicted than ever.

Damn you, Maxim. Damn you for coming here and fucking with me like this. I had a plan, and you derailed it. Maybe I made the first move—and the second—but why'd you have to give in to me so easily? Why didn't you shut the door in my face? Why did you let me do that to you?

I drove home, angry and confused and less sure than ever that I wouldn't try to do it again tonight.

In fact, I was fairly certain I would.

TWENTY-TWO

MAXIM

I HAD no right to be angry. I knew that. Rationally, I knew that Derek had every right to say no to being with me and go on a date with Carolyn. Or with anyone.

But did he have to bring her *here*, where he knew I'd see them? Where I'd have to watch him pay her all the attention I wanted from him? Where I'd be forced to face the reality that he didn't want me enough to get over his fears? That *I* wasn't enough?

There had to be a thousand restaurants in this city. Why did he have to choose the one where I worked?

He'd done it on purpose, just to torture me. Why?

I spent the entire evening being mad at him, and in turn at myself for being mad in the first place. It was a ridiculous, twisted circuit of anger that had my head throbbing by the end of the night. I spent a ridiculous amount of energy flirting with girls just to spite him. I hoped he saw.

God, had I really thought he was going to choose me?

That just because he let me suck him off in the kitchen or jerk me off in the dark I would matter to him? I'd only known him for three days! He'd spent like twenty years playing totally straight because he thought his attraction to guys was wrong. Had I really thought I would be the one to change that? Maybe I'd been the one to finally tempt him enough to act on his closeted sexual impulses, but that didn't mean anything more than surface attraction. In the end, that's all I was to him—a hook-up.

And I didn't want to be his charity case. As soon as humanly possible, I was going to move out. I had my savings now, and I had a job making *way* better money than I'd ever made before. I might not have a Range Rover or a Rolex, but I had street smarts and survival skills, and I came from a long line of people who'd done what they had to do to get by. I didn't need anyone to hand me luxury on a fancy plate —I could earn it myself, and I would. First thing tomorrow, I'd find another place to live.

I was silent and sullen on the ride back to Derek's, and Ellen took note.

"Hey." She glanced at me. "You okay tonight?"

"Yes."

"You don't seem okay. I know Russians aren't chatty by nature, but you're broody even for a Russian tonight. And your aura is a little disturbed."

"Is it?"

"Yeah. It's dark. Very dark. I thought so when I picked you up today, but now I can *really* sense it."

"Sorry." I tried to think of a light color, so maybe my aura wouldn't bother her.

"Don't be sorry. Everyone is entitled to a dark aura now and again. But did something happen at work?"

"No."

After a minute or so of silence, she said, "Did you know Derek was bringing Carolyn there tonight?"

"No." I wondered what they were doing right now. Was he kissing her? Touching her? Fucking her? Jealousy spiked in me, unwelcome and unfamiliar. *It's none of your business what they do.*

"She's so nice, but..." Her voice trailed off, but my ears perked up. "I don't know if they're right for each other. Something's off. It's like they're trying too hard."

"Mmm."

Ellen laughed. "Just sounds now, huh? Not even words?" She patted my leg. "You poor thing. I'll leave you alone."

At first I was grateful, but maybe I should have let her keep talking because my brain filled the silence with the memory of Derek's voice, growling and deep. His heavy breaths. His tortured groans. Was he giving them to her right now? Was he telling her he wanted more? Was he demanding her orgasm the way he'd demanded mine? Maybe he was. Maybe that was standard procedure with him. Maybe he even had a script.

After saying a terse thank-you-good-night to Ellen, I let myself in the front door and locked it behind me. All the lights were out and the house was completely silent, so I froze when I heard what sounded like the clink of ice in a glass coming from the living room.

That's weird. Derek was home? And sitting alone in the dark? Or was Carolyn with him?

The last thing I wanted to do was interrupt, but on the off chance that it wasn't Derek in there but some kind of intruder, I stood at the threshold of the room and peered into the darkness. I thought I made out a lone figure sitting on the couch, but my eyes were still adjusting when he spoke.

"Come in."

It was him. "No, thank you."

"Come. In."

Always have to have your way, don't you? I hated myself for it, but I entered the room. He stood, went over to the bar cart near the window and poured something into his glass. The silver-gray light filtering through the blinds outlined his silhouette, and his shoulders appeared even bigger than I remembered. My dick betrayed me by trying to get hard.

"Drink?" he asked.

"No, thank you." I played cool Russian because I knew it would bother him.

Still facing away from me, he lifted the glass to his lips. "How was your night?"

"Great," I lied. "Yours?"

"Fine." He didn't elaborate, and I wasn't about to ask.

"Guess I'll head up to bed. It's late." And then I stood there for some stupid reason, as if I expected him to object.

He didn't.

I puffed up my chest a little. "Tomorrow, I'm leaving. I'll find another place to stay."

A pause while he drank. "Why?"

"Because it's the right thing to do."

"The right thing to do," he repeated, and I wondered if he was drunk. He tipped back the rest of whatever he'd poured and set down the glass. Then he walked over to me, and we stood chest to chest. "The right thing to do would be to go upstairs and lock your door. But you're not going to do that, are you?"

It was a challenge, and I took it.

Turning away from him, I tried to leave the room, but he grabbed my arm and yanked me backward. Then his mouth was on mine, hot and hard and heavy, one hand gripping the back of my neck, the other wrapped around my forearm.

After a few seconds of stunned ecstasy—*he still wants me*—I shoved him away from me. Hard.

"Yes. Fight me," he seethed, whipping his shirt over his head. "Fight back." He came at me again, all strength and rage and heat, pushing me back against the living room wall. "I *want* you to say no. I *want* you to push me away. I want you to be the one to stop this because I fucking can't." His lower body anchored mine, the solid bulge of his erection digging into the front of my hip. "I fucking can't."

I'd never felt so torn between pride and lust before. I wanted him as badly as I wanted to turn him down. Because this was all a game to Derek—he was fucking with me like I was some kind of toy.

But goddamn, he was hot like this—fueled by fury and passion and whiskey, unable to hold back. He wanted a fight? I could give him one. But I let him kiss me first, let his tongue invade my mouth, even stroked it with my own, but when his hand moved to the crotch of my jeans, I shoved him back again.

"Now you want me? What about Carolyn? Pick a side, Derek."

"I saw you tonight, flirting with people." His fists were clenched at his sides. "I didn't fucking like it."

"I saw *you* tonight—the way you must have wanted me to—on a romantic date with a woman." I walked toward him, and he backed up slightly. "So which is it?" Grabbing my T-shirt at the back of my neck, I pulled it off and tossed it aside. "What do you want? This or that?"

"Fuck you." He rushed toward me and our bodies crashed together, all groping hands and open mouths and heavy, choked-off breaths. I hooked one leg behind his and took him down to his knees, and he pushed me onto my back, his body sprawled on top of mine.

His weight on me felt so fucking good, and through our jeans, our cocks strained to get closer, bulging against the denim as Derek rocked his hips over mine—delicious, agonizing friction. My hands were everywhere.

"God help me, I have to have you," he whispered. He dragged his mouth down my neck and chest, over the tightly knotted muscles of my stomach. When he reached the waistband of my jeans, he pushed back onto his knees, straddling my legs. I propped myself up on my elbows in disbelief and watched as he unbuttoned, unzipped, and yanked them down to my thighs, my cock springing free.

I thought he might hesitate. I thought he might ask. I thought he might do any number of things that would indicate he'd never sucked a dick before and perhaps felt some ambivalence about it.

Nope.

Fisting my shaft with one hand he angled it toward his mouth and lowered his head, taking me between his lips. I groaned as his tongue swept over my crown and he began to suck, his head moving up and down my length. Oh my God, was this really happening? How was it possible to get the best blowjob I'd ever had from a complete novice? How did he take me so deep, suck me so hard, stroke me just the right way with his tongue?

Because it's Derek. He's perfect at everything.

"Jesus," I whispered, closing my eyes as I hit the back of his throat again and again and again. If I kept watching, this was going to be over quickly, and I wanted this hot, wet, mind-blowing rapture to go on forever. But even the sounds were enough to do me in—he wasn't holding anything back—and I knew I wasn't going to last.

I opened my eyes as he looked up at me. *Oh, fuck.*

"Gonna come," I choked out.

He went at me even harder, a ferocious growl escaping his throat, almost like he was ordering me to do it, threatening me if I didn't. No problem, because a second later my climax ripped me wide open, and I was groaning and gasping and cursing as my cock pulsed and streamed inside his mouth, watching the whole thing happen with wide, disbelieving eyes.

When he'd swallowed every last drop, he released me and crawled back up my body to claim my mouth. He tasted like whiskey and sex, and I couldn't get enough. "I want to fuck you," he said, the words hot against my lips.

My body, which should have been completely sapped, ignited once more. "We need—"

"Upstairs." His voice thick with urgency. "My bedroom."

Two seconds later, we were tearing up the stairs and he was pulling me into his pitch-dark bedroom. With frantic hands, we shoved off shoes and socks, tugged off jeans and underwear, and then fell onto the bed, our mouths joined. I ended up on my back and he settled between my legs, grinding his slick, hard cock against mine, which was rising fast.

"I fucking love your body." His words sent fireworks shooting through me.

"I feel the same," I said, running my hands over his wide, muscular shoulders and back.

"More," he said in that commanding tone of his. "I want more."

"Take it."

He got to his knees, and I heard the sound of a drawer open and close. A series of clicks. Hands rubbing together. In the shadowy dark, I could see the outline of him preparing to fuck me, and my heart pounded furiously in my chest. I watched as he began to stroke himself, a tremor moving through my body when I felt his warm, silky fingers slide between my legs. Deftly, unabashedly, he explored me, his touch so expert I almost couldn't believe he'd never done this before. *I love your hands.*

I bent my knees and opened wider for him, inviting a more intimate touch. He eased one finger inside me, and my stomach muscles tensed at the sweet, tight burn of it. "Yes," I whispered. One finger became two, teasing and stroking and stretching me. Whether by happy accident or on purpose, he rubbed my prostate, and my lower body started to hum. *Fuck, that feels good.* Fully hard again, I took my cock in my fist and rocked my hips, fucking his hand and mine at the same time.

He grunted. "Jesus. That's so fucking hot. Don't stop."

I kept doing it, careful not to go at it too enthusiastically so I wouldn't come yet. But his fingers were too deep, his eyes on me too hot, and you can only work against your own body for so long before it tells you to fuck off, *this is happening.* And I wanted it to happen with him. "Derek." I struggled to speak. "Now."

I'd never wanted anyone this badly, and I'd never cared so much about making it perfect for someone. It wasn't that I'd been a selfish lover, but in the past it had mostly been about the physicality of sex. The arousal, the fuck, the release. With Derek, it was different—I was conscious of his desire for me on another level. I knew it had to be powerful enough to overcome fears that resided at the very core of his being. I was aware that he had chosen me not just over another man, but over *himself*.

I wanted to be worth it.

TWENTY-THREE

DEREK

THIS WAS IT. No turning back.

Not that I wanted to. All my inhibitions were gone, annihilated by my physical need to *have* this man. To *take* him. To *know*, once and for all.

I could barely contain myself as I tore open the condom packet and eased it over my aching cock. My fingers shook. It was a different kind of excitement than I'd ever felt—a storming, swirling mass of nerves, desire, anticipation, fear, hope, dread, greed, thrill. And at the center of it all, the eye of the storm, was my awareness of him. Maxim. It wasn't only that I wanted the answer to a question. I wanted *him*.

After coming home from Carolyn's, I'd tried to numb myself with whiskey—would I never fucking learn—and forget the feelings I'd had watching him flirt with those women. But it was no use. I knew it was no use the moment I heard his key in the lock. I knew what I was going to do the moment I saw him from where I sat in the lonely dark. I just hoped he'd have the good sense to stop me.

But he hadn't. And the more we kissed and touched and struggled against what I finally saw as the inevitable conclusion of such passion, the more I wanted to surrender to it.

So I had—I shed every last doubt and let my deepest instincts take over. And now I was being rewarded for it.

His body beneath mine. His cock in my mouth. His cum down my throat. His tight, hot ass grinding against my fingers. His hand on his dick.

Easy, easy now.

My heart was pounding. I couldn't breathe. Maxim's sweet, low voice in the dark was like a secret I wanted to keep forever.

He closed his eyes, his expression tense and his breaths deep and measured as I gently pushed the tip of my cock inside him.

I couldn't talk. I didn't even have sentences in my head —just words that jumbled together as my brain tried to process what I was feeling as I slid deeper, inch by inch. Fuck. Yes. Hot. Tight. This. More. Want.

When I was buried inside him, I fell forward, bracing myself above him, my lips an inch from his. I closed my eyes. "Sweet Jesus."

He wrapped his arms and legs around me. "Does it feel good?"

I swallowed, afraid to move, because I knew I would come in two thrusts. "Yes."

He kissed me, his tongue teasing between my lips. "I want this to be everything you imagined."

But I hadn't imagined anything even close to this.

Slowly, with control that shocked me, I began to roll my hips, easing in and out of that unbelievable heat. He moaned against my lips, and I loved the sound of it so much, I moved a little faster, a little harder, just so he'd do it again. *It's so good, so fucking good.* I'd never felt anything like it.

"You're perfect," he whispered, "so fucking perfect."

It was all perfect, every single thing—his legs around me, his hands on my back, his breath on my lips. It made me feel close to him. Like what we were doing wasn't just about sex—it was about *us.* I lifted my head up slightly to see his face, and our eyes locked. *Fuck.* Right then, I understood why he'd come so quickly in the living room when I'd looked up at him. There was something so intimate, so powerful, so blistering hot about eye contact in a moment like that. It was more than contact. It was *connection,* and it was intense.

My body reacted, moving faster and harder and deeper until I was bucking wildly over him, every brutal thrust punctuated with a sound from the back of my throat and the slap of skin on skin. I grabbed the headboard, almost desperately, as if I needed to hold on. He brought a hand back to his cock and jerked himself as unrestrainedly as I was fucking him, all the muscles in his arm and abs and chest flexing, his legs tightening around me. It's everything I'd always wanted sex to be—sweaty and hard and rough and animalistic and *fuck, fuck, I'm going to come* and then it was the sight of him losing control beneath me that finally pushed me over.

But it wasn't the sight of his muscles or his hand or his cock. I wasn't even looking at it.

It was his eyes. It was the connection. It was the answer to everything, because it wasn't only a connection to him—it was a connection to *myself,* a path to understanding a part of me I'd always found incomprehensible, foreign, ugly.

With Maxim, it made sense. It was as much a part of me

as the heart beating in my chest or the blood rushing through my veins. And it was beautiful.

With him, it was beautiful.

I COLLAPSED ON HIS CHEST, my face buried in his neck. "Oh my God."

His hands slid up and down my sides. "I think you were lying to me."

"About what?"

"About never being with a guy before."

"I wasn't lying. You're the first."

"I'm really happy about that."

"I am too." For a moment, I wondered if there would even have been a first without Maxim's appearance in my life. I couldn't imagine there was any other guy in the universe who could have driven me to this. It was all him.

"So you're okay with this?"

"Yeah. I think so." I took a breath. "But I don't know where we go from here."

"Where do you want to go?"

I thought for a moment. "I don't know. I'd be lying if I said I could walk away from this."

"Good." He kissed my head. "I don't want to walk away either."

"But you and me together..." I lifted my chest off him, braced myself with my fists on the mattress. "I have no idea what that looks like. How we go about it. I'm not ready to go public."

"I get it. And I'm not really a public person in that respect, anyway."

"So we just...what? Hang out here together?"

"Sure."

"Does that mean you're not leaving tomorrow?"

He smiled. "Yeah. That's what it means."

"Good."

"But I am leaving in two weeks. You'll be tired of me by then, anyway."

I laughed, but a few minutes later, when I was alone in my bathroom washing my hands, I wondered if he was right. Would I grow tired of him? Was this going to be a brief, passionate fling? As short as it was intense? Were we going to play house here for a couple weeks and then be done with each other when he moved out? In a way, it was probably what I should hope for. That whatever this thing was between us would burn out before it affected my life on any long-term basis. Chemistry as hot as ours wasn't sustainable anyway, right? That kind of spark always fizzled, whether you were gay or straight. I heard about it all the time from married friends.

So I decided not to beat myself up over what we were doing. It wouldn't last long, I'd get it out of my system, and we'd both move on, free to pursue our larger goals. This was like a little side trip. All in fun. How long had it been since I'd done something just for fun? Something spontaneous, purely for pleasure?

Satisfied with that, I brushed my teeth, turned off the light and went back into my bedroom. Maxim wasn't there, and his clothing was gone too. I wandered into the hallway, and saw that he wasn't in the bathroom. His bedroom door was half-open, and the lamp was on.

I frowned. Should I say goodnight? We hadn't really said it before. I'd sort of just gotten up to use the bathroom and he'd done the same. I don't know why I assumed he'd come back to my bed. I wasn't even sure I wanted him to.

But this seemed like kind of an anti-climactic ending to a magnificently climactic night.

His lamp clicked off, and I went back into my room, feeling slightly disappointed, and then aggravated with myself for it. *Don't get weird. He's not your boyfriend. He's more like a...fuck buddy. Remember those? They don't stay the night.*

Right. It was better to keep some clear boundaries. Clearly even Maxim recognized that. What a relief we were on the same page. Turning back the covers, I got into bed, set my alarm, and switched off my lamp. When I lay back on my pillow, I realized I could still smell him on the sheets.

I closed my eyes and inhaled deeply.

TWENTY-FOUR

MAXIM

I FINISHED WRITING in my notebook, tucked it into the drawer, and turned off the light. I hadn't written much, just a few immediate thoughts, but I never wanted to forget how good this felt. And if I woke up tomorrow and none of this was real, at least I'd have a record of it.

I glanced at the door, which I'd left half-open as a sort of half-invitation. Because even though I'd have loved to sleep next to him—actually what I really wanted to do was stay up talking and kissing and touching each other all night, something I'd *never* done or even wanted before—going back into his bed seemed way too presumptive of me. If he wanted me there, he could come find me, but if he didn't, that was okay, too. I understood that there were lines he did not want to cross. Not yet, anyway.

After a few minutes of silence, I knew he'd gone to bed, and I settled in beneath the covers. In the darkness, I didn't even have to close my eyes to picture my favorite moments from tonight. His eyes looking up at me with my cock in his mouth. The way he moved inside me, slowly at first, and then with all the heated passion of a summer storm. His voice, deep and soft. *I'd be lying if I said I could walk away from this.*

It had easily been the hottest blowjob I'd ever had, the best sex I'd ever had, and I'd never forget the way Derek looked as he got lost inside me. He'd surrendered to it so completely, so passionately. But it was his words I loved best. Or maybe it was his honesty. His willingness to take a chance on me. He'd come a long way in a few days.

Neither of us knew where we might end up, but this was America. Anything was possible, right?

Smiling, I turned onto my stomach and stretched out. I hadn't been looking for this. But I was damn happy I'd found it.

THE NEXT MORNING, I showered, dressed, and came downstairs to a surprise—Derek was at the breakfast table, drinking coffee and looking at his laptop. His hair was a little damp, and he was dressed in jeans and a casual shirt. His feet were bare. I might have imagined it, but to me he looked much more relaxed than he had in the last three days. No furrowed brow, no tight lips, no tension in his neck.

"Good morning," I said, unable to keep a grin off my face. "I thought you'd be at work."

He set down his coffee cup. "I didn't have anything major scheduled, so I shuffled a few minor things to be able to take the day off. I haven't done that in forever."

"What will you do with your day off?"

"I have some errands to run, but I also wondered if you wanted to do some shopping. I actually picked up a few things for you on Sunday, but I'm not sure if they'll fit or if you'll even want them." He shrugged like it was no big deal. "I meant to leave them in your room for you yesterday, but it was sort of a hectic day, and I forgot."

"You bought clothing for me on Sunday?" I don't know why I was so surprised—it was exactly like Derek to do something so nice. "You didn't have to do that."

He waved a hand in the air, dismissing it. "They might not even fit. And it's only one pair of pants and two shirts. You'll need more than that."

I nodded. "Shopping today would be great. I just have to be back at three-thirty for Ellen to pick me up."

"I can drop you off at work when we're done. Coffee's still hot if you want some."

"Thank you." I took a cup from the cupboard and filled it. To make sure I was actually awake, I pinched myself. Twice. "Have you had breakfast?"

"Not yet. I can make some, or we can go out."

An idea came to me. "Actually, let me do it."

His eyebrows rose. "Do what?"

"Cook breakfast," I said excitedly. "There's something I'd love to make for you if you have the right ingredients. It's called *syrniki*, and it is the most amazing thing in the world. My mom used to make them for me."

"What is it?" He looked suspicious.

"Don't you trust me?" I teased. "I promise it will be delicious, and I'll clean up the kitchen, too. Can I look in your fridge for what I'll need?"

"Ask me. I'll tell you if I have it."

I thought for a moment. "Eggs. Cottage cheese. Lemon. Butter."

"Yes to all."

"Flour and sugar?"

"Yes."

"How about raisins?"

He tilted his head and squinted. "I think so. Maybe in the pantry."

"Sour cream and honey?"

"Yes."

"Good! That's everything."

He started to get up. "What kind of cookware do you need?"

"Just a frying pan, but you sit down," I scolded. "Enjoy your morning off. I want to do everything."

He looked amused but sat down again. "Okay. Have at it."

I gathered all my ingredients but found that I couldn't remember exact amounts for things. After searching for a recipe online that was close to my mother's and coming up empty, I decided to call her. It was ten P.M. there, but she was a bit of a night owl, and I thought she might be up.

Liliya answered the phone and squealed when she heard my voice. "Maxim!"

"Hello, *malyshka*," I said warmly. Her voice reminded me of home, and I felt a tug of longing for the people I loved there. I spoke Russian to her. "What are you doing awake?" From his chair at the table, Derek watched me, a curious look on his face. "My sister," I whispered in English. "I called my mom to ask her something about the recipe." He nodded in understanding.

"I'm terrible," Liliya said crossly. "I can't sleep."

"Why not?"

"I had the bad dream again."

"About the monster?"

"Yes."

"What did he do this time?"

"He said I would never see you again."

My heart squeezed. "That's not true. I promise."

"But why did you go so far away?"

"I wanted an adventure, remember? I wanted to see new things. Speak a different language. Meet movie stars."

"Did you meet one yet?"

"Not yet. But do you know what I'm looking at right now?" I walked over to the sliding glass door and looked out into the yard.

"What?"

"Sunshine and palm trees and tropical flowers. Everything is bright and sunny and colorful. And when I breathe in the air, it smells like oranges."

"Can I visit you?"

"Yes. As soon as I can arrange it. But it will take a while for me to get settled, okay?"

"Okay."

"Can you put Mom on, please?"

"Yes, but don't hang up. I want to talk again."

I smiled, meeting Derek's eyes. "She misses me," I told him.

"Of course she does."

My insides melted a little.

"Maxim!" My mother sounded worried. "Is everything okay?"

"Yes, fine. How are you?"

"Good." Then her voice was muffled. "Liliya, stop! I'll give you the phone in a minute. Sorry," she said clearly again. "Liliya misses you."

"I miss her too. I miss both of you. But I'm thinking of you because I want to make *syrniki*, and I forgot parts of the recipe. Can you tell me how much of each ingredient to put in?"

"I just guess at it by now, but I think I have it written down here somewhere. Hold on."

While she looked, I asked Derek where I could find a pen and paper to write it down. He came around the counter, opened a drawer, and took out a pencil and stack of yellow Post-It notes. Then he refilled his cup of coffee while my mother recited her old recipe and I wrote it down.

"Perfect, Mom. Thank you so much." I turned around and found Derek leaning back against the counter across from me, lifting his cup to his lips. I switched to English. "I don't want to screw it up because I'm making it for someone special, and he's very picky."

He rolled his eyes, but smiled too.

"Let me know how they like it," my mother said. "Liliya wants to talk again."

"Okay. And then I should go."

"Okay. Bye, honey. I love you."

"I love you too."

My sister came back on. "Maxim, sing me the song."

I cringed. 'The song' was the theme to *Spokoynoy nochi, malyshi*, a Russian children's show that had been around forever. It was silly and childish and I did *not* want to sing it in front of Derek. I don't even have a decent voice. "No, *malyshka*. I can't sing it right now."

"Please, Maxim! I can't sleep without it. It's the only thing that will help."

A stab to the heart. "Can't Mom sing it for you?"

"No. She doesn't remember it."

I groaned, and Derek looked at me quizzically.

"Please, Maxim. I miss you so much."

I exhaled, defeated. "Okay." Then I closed my eyes—as

if that would save me from mortification—and started to sing, at a much quicker tempo than usual.

Liliya caught me. "Slow down, Maxim! You're doing it too fast!"

I dutifully slowed down and sang it the right way, my voice cracking in all the usual places, making her giggle. When I got to the last line, I peeked at Derek, whose amused expression made me want to bury my face in my shirt.

"Okay now? Think you can sleep?" I asked Liliya.

"Yes," she said. "Goodnight."

"Goodnight, *malyshka. Ya tebya lublu.*"

"I love you, too. Bye."

I hung up, set my phone on the counter, and braved a look at Derek. Tried to hold my chin up. He drank his coffee, his eyes dancing with glee over the rim of the cup.

"What?" I said, feeling the heat in my face. "She couldn't sleep. That's a kid's song from an old Russian television show I sometimes sing to relax her."

"Nothing. It's adorable. I didn't know you sang lullabies."

"I don't. Only that one."

"Maybe you'll sing it to me sometime." He tried not to smile but couldn't help it.

God, I love making him smile. "Ha ha. Go ahead and make fun of me. You'll be sorry when I don't share my *syrniki* with you." I turned my back to him and opened the bag of flour.

A moment later, he stood right behind me, pressed against my back. He looped his arms around my waist and kissed my neck. "I'm only teasing. I actually find it very sexy that you'd sing your little sister a song to help her sleep."

"You do?" I looked at him over my shoulder.

"Yes." He put his lips on mine, and it was sweet and soft and easy, much different than the fiery kisses we'd shared last night. We weren't racing to undress or touch each other or get to the next hot thing. We were content with a kiss.

We were in the moment, and it just felt good.

TWENTY-FIVE

DEREK

A LULLABY.

I couldn't get over it. He sang a lullaby to his little sister when she couldn't sleep. Of all the things about Maxim that I'd learned, that one was my favorite. And he'd looked so miserable as he sang it in my kitchen. His singing voice was almost as terrible as mine.

But it was so fucking sweet. And I hadn't been lying when I said I found it sexy—I did. There wasn't much about Maxim I didn't find sexy. Even in my old jeans—or maybe especially in my old jeans—and his work shirt, he looked amazing. But he was amazing on the inside too. Smart and funny, kind and genuine.

And I *trusted* him. It was astonishing to me how much I trusted Maxim after such a short period of time. We'd only met four days ago, and yet I felt more at ease with him than I'd felt with anyone in a long time. I could be myself around him in a way I couldn't around other people. My real self, without hiding anything. There was such relief in that, and I felt incredibly grateful for it. If he never paid me a dime for the clothes or the rent or anything else I did for him, I wouldn't care. This feeling was worth everything, even if it wouldn't last forever.

"Okay, here you go." He set a plate down in front of me, and I moaned in anticipation, my mouth watering. On it was what looked like four thick pancakes, fried to a golden brown, dusted with powdered sugar, and drizzled with honey. A big spoonful of something white—sour cream, maybe?—sat off to one side, and raspberries were scattered on top of it all.

"This looks delicious. What are they again?"

"*Syrniki.* You say it now."

I made an attempt, which I thought was pretty good, but Maxim laughed anyway.

"There, your first Russian word. I want you to learn four more by the end of the day." He put his plate down and took the chair across from me. I noticed how he'd known where everything was to set the table, from the placemats to the napkins to the utensils, and got a ridiculous kick from seeing him so familiar with my kitchen.

"I'll try," I promised. Unable to wait a second longer, I picked up my fork and knife and cut a bite, making sure to get a little of everything so I'd taste all the flavors. I put it in my mouth and moaned again.

Maxim grinned. "Good, right?"

I chewed slowly, appreciating the slight crisp on the outside and the soft, doughy inside. A little sweet, a little savory, the perfect balance. "How do you say delicious in Russian?"

"In this case, *vkusnyy.*"

"Well, this is fucking *vkusnyy.*"

He laughed. "I'm so glad you like it. You'll have to let me cook dinner for you sometime too."

"You can cook for me any time you want," I mumbled, my mouth full. "This is so good."

He smiled, his cheeks flushing slightly. "Thank you."

After breakfast, I helped Maxim clean up the kitchen and we went up to my bedroom so I could give him the clothing I'd bought. He stood near the doorway while I went to my closet and retrieved the bag, pulling out the receipt and tucking it into my pocket. He'd see the price tags, so it was probably a silly gesture, but maybe I could convince him they'd been on sale. I had a feeling he was going to protest they were too expensive.

When I came back in the room, he was still standing by the door, looking around curiously. "Looks different in here in the light," he said sheepishly.

"Oh. Right." I glanced at the bed, which I'd made this morning after changing the sheets. The sight of it made my stomach muscles clench. Was it too soon to do it again? Was he sore? *Don't think about it.* "So. Here you go." I handed him the bag. "If you want to try them on in here, you can. I have a full-length mirror on the door."

"Okay."

"I'll give you some privacy," I said, moving toward the door. I didn't want him to think I was trying to get him to strip in front of me—not that I'd complain. But he caught my arm.

"You can stay." He smiled. "I don't mind."

Fuck, every time he gave me that look, the one that said *I'll show you mine if you show me yours*, I wanted to throw him down and roll around naked.

I cleared my throat and perched on the edge of the bed. "Okay."

He took off his clothes, and I openly stared at his body. Jesus. No wonder I'd lost my mind last night. In fact, I was kind of sad to see his legs and ass disappear into the new jeans, but glad they fit him. "They look great," I said, repositioning myself so my swelling erection wasn't trapped uncomfortably.

"Thanks." He shrugged into one of the shirts I'd picked out and buttoned it up. "What do you think?"

I think you're perfect. "Is it a little too big? It might be too baggy around your waist. But I'm not sure the next size down would fit you in the shoulders."

He frowned. "I don't know. It feels comfortable."

"Try the other one."

He traded the first shirt for the second. "This one feels good too. How does it look?"

Like I want to rip it off you. "Great. You like it?"

"Yes."

"It's yours. I think we should take the other one back."

He looked worried. "Take it back? But you took it home and I wore it. They will do it?"

"Yes. The tags are still on. I promise they'll do it."

He smoothed the shirt over his stomach. "I really like this. I'm glad you chose it."

"Good. Do you want to look in the mirror?"

"No, that's okay." He smiled. "If you say it looks good on me, I'll believe you."

"It does. Do you want to wear it today?"

He thought for a second. "I better wear my work shirt in case we don't have time to come back here." As he was taking off the button-down, he noticed a price tag hanging from the label. "Eighty dollars?" he asked incredulously. "For one shirt?"

"It's not that much." I rose to my feet and picked up the

one to be returned and placed it in the bag. That one had cost even more.

"To me, it is." His blue eyes were wide.

"I told you, you don't have to pay me back right away."

"I want to," he said firmly, putting the shirt in the bag. "So we need to return this one, too. Someday I will be able to afford luxury clothes, but not yet."

It kind of broke my heart that he thought an eighty-dollar shirt was a luxury item. "Maxim, please keep it. As a gift."

"No."

"Listen, it makes me happy to do things for people. So it's not for you, it's for *me*. Keep it for *me*, so I can feel good about myself."

He shook his head, but he smiled. "You're crazy."

"I'm not. I just like you."

His smile grew wider as he reached down and grabbed his work shirt and pulled it on. "I like you, too. And I'm so —" He looked down at his chest. "Oh, fuck."

"What?"

"I put my shirt on inside out." Quickly, he scrambled to get it off.

"So?"

"If you put your shirt on inside out, it means you will get beaten."

"Beaten! By who?"

"By anyone." He turned the shirt right side out and put it on again. "That's why you should punch me."

I shrank back. "Are you insane?"

"No! It's symbolic. You have to punch me so that I will get the beating from you, not from someone who really wants to do it." He said this in all seriousness, then turned to face me. "I'm ready. Go ahead."

"Maxim, I'm not going to punch you."

"You have to!" But he was laughing now. "A little punch, okay? Otherwise, I won't feel right."

"Oh my God. I can't even believe this. What's the Russian word for crazy?"

"*Sumasshedshiy.* Say it. Then punch me."

"*Sumasshedshiy.*" I completely mangled it, then I gently nudged his rock-hard abs with my fist. "That's all you get."

He narrowed his eyes. "You punch like a girl."

"What?" I dropped the shopping bag and tackled him, throwing him onto the bed, pinning him beneath me. "Take it back."

He was laughing so hard his eyes were shiny. "Even Liliya hits harder than you."

"*Take it back.*"

"No, because then you'll get off me, and I'm enjoying this."

I was too, of course. What was better than Maxim trapped beneath me? It reminded me of last night. My dick, which had never really settled down after seeing Maxim undress, was now on its way to full tilt. I pressed it into him. "You'd enjoy it even more with your pants off."

His eyes lit up. "I agree."

A minute later, we were buck naked and right back where we'd been before, with me straddling his hips. We kissed feverishly as I moved my body over his. God, I'd never get enough of the way it felt to be pressed skin to skin, muscle to muscle with him this way. For a second, two weeks seemed much too short a time limit.

Well, that's what you've got. So make the most of it.

"Derek. Will you do something for me?"

"What?"

"Turn around."

"Turn around?"

"Yes." He put his lips to my ear. "I want my mouth on you."

I hesitated, feeling strangely proprietary about my ass, given what I'd done to his last night. But it had been nighttime then. It had been dark. There had been whiskey involved. Right now it was daytime, the room was light, and I was all hopped up on caffeine and sugar.

"Please," he said, his tongue tracing my earlobe, sucking it into his mouth. "I promise, it will feel so good."

I was curious. I wanted to know what it felt like. And I was obsessively fastidious about my body, so I was shaven and clean. But...could I? Was there such a thing as being *too* gay? What transgressions were allowable and what was too much? At what intrusion would I draw the line?

He wants this. Don't overthink it. "Okay."

I flipped around so I was straddling his upper body, my hands braced on either side of him. He hooked his arms under my thighs and pulled me back so my ass was right in his face. I didn't even have time to feel self-conscious before his tongue swept slowly up the crease, sending me into near paroxysms. I could have wept for how divine it felt. How hot and wet. How intimate. I'd totally planned on blowing him since my mouth was down there and all, but I couldn't do a goddamn thing except groan and writhe and let my eyeballs roll back in my head. Maxim held nothing back. He used his tongue, his lips, his teeth, his hands. He moaned with pleasure, as if I was the best thing he'd ever tasted. His thick, hard cock twitched on his abdomen, a few drops of cum oozing from its tip. *This is turning him on.*

The thought of it sent me spiraling selfishly toward release. I rocked my hips over his face, fucking his tongue. I propped myself on one hand and took my dick in the other, jerking myself hard and fast. I gnashed my teeth and snarled and cursed and ejaculated all over him, marking his body with warm, white ribbons of cum. The sight of it splashing onto his stomach, his cock, his thighs, was so deliciously obscene, my orgasm seemed to go on forever.

The second I could control my body again, I grabbed his dick with one hand and licked it clean like an ice cream cone, swirling my tongue around the tip. He moaned, and the sound reverberated through my entire body. I lowered and lifted my head, taking him to the back of my throat again and again and again, until he warned me with a trembling voice that he was going to come and I took him even deeper. A second later, his fingers dug into my flesh and his entire body stiffened beneath me as his cock throbbed repeatedly inside my mouth.

Good fucking God, it was *insane* how much I liked it. And him. And this little arrangement we had.

At this rate, we were never going to leave the house.

TWENTY-SIX

MAXIM

ON OUR WAY to the mall, Derek said he wanted to drive by a certain house that was for sale.

"Why?" I asked. "Are you thinking about moving?"

"No. I'm thinking about fixing and flipping it."

"Flipping it?" I looked over at him, confused.

"It's where you buy a house that needs work, do the work, and then sell it at a profit."

"Ah. I see. Have you done this before?"

"No. It was an idea I had while working on my house. I really enjoyed the work, and missed it when I was done."

"You definitely have a talent for it. And a good eye for design. Your house is so beautiful."

"Thanks." He was quiet for a minute, one hand at the top of the steering wheel, one finger absently rubbing just beneath his lower lip. "I'd have to cut back my hours at work, probably. If I wanted to be really hands on, which I do."

180 MELANIE HARLOW & DAVID ROMANOV

"Would that be a problem?"

He frowned, dropping his hand to his lap. "Probably. I think my dad wants to retire and he's looking at me to take over."

"But he would want you to do what would make you happy, right?"

"Not necessarily."

I wasn't sure how to respond to that.

"The thing is," he went on, "I've been thinking. Ever since you asked me if my job was my passion, it's been bothering me that it isn't. There's nothing about it that inspires me. Nothing creative or meaningful. I make good money, and I'm good at making deals, but it's not fulfilling in a way that working on my house was. And I see you coming here all fired up about chasing a dream and kind of wish I had something like that. It's inspiring."

The idea that anything about me inspired him was beyond crazy. "And I look at you and everything you've done, all the beautiful things you have, your home, your car, all your success, and I think, 'That's what I aspire to be.'"

"There's more to life than a home and a nice car. Those are only *things*. I feel like..." He shook his head. "I don't even know what the fuck I'm trying to say. I guess I feel like I've lived a very safe life. It's comfortable for sure, and I'm grateful for everything I have, but I haven't taken very many risks. I'm starting to think that matters."

"So take one now. It's not too late."

He slowed down and leaned toward me to peer out the passenger side window. "It's that one. With the Spanish Revival architecture."

I looked at the white house with the red tile roof. "It's nice."

"It was built in 1925 and still has a lot of the original features. But it's in pretty rough shape."

It was? Other than an overgrown lawn and some missing roof tiles, I didn't think it was that bad, but Derek's standards were different than mine. "Can we go inside?"

"Not today. I didn't make an appointment." He glanced in the rearview mirror. "Traffic coming. Gotta move."

With one last glance at the house, he pulled forward. "I wanted to be an architect once upon a time."

"You did?" I looked at him in surprise.

"Yeah. But my dad said there was way more money in property development and I should go to business school."

"So you went to business school."

"Yes."

"If you could go back, would you do it differently?"

He took a deep breath and exhaled slowly as he thought. "Hard to say."

"Is it too late?"

He laughed a little. "Yes. I'm not going back to school now. But if there's a way I can flex that creative muscle a little and turn a profit at the same time, I'd jump in. Maybe."

"Do you think you can turn a profit on that house?"

"Yes," he said confidently. "They're asking too much, but I could get the price down. It will still be expensive as fuck, but I have experience in financing real estate, a lot of knowledge about property in this area, and I'm not in a rush. I'd take my time and do it right."

"It sounds like you've given this a lot of thought, and not just in the past few days."

"It's something I've thought about for a while," he admitted as we turned into the parking lot at the mall. "I guess you reminded me of it."

"Why do you think you haven't done it yet?"

"Well, fear, for one thing. Making money isn't guaranteed. And houses around here aren't cheap, even the shitty ones. I didn't want to get in over my head. I've seen it happen where guys tried to move too fast or hired the wrong people or made bad decisions or totally underestimated costs, and before they knew it, the project was completely out of control and they lost everything." He pulled into a parking space and turned off the car. "I don't want to be that guy. I don't want to fail."

"Derek. Trust me. You are not that guy." I wish I had more words to convince him to take the risk, because it was obviously something that would make him happy. "I know we haven't known each other that long, but I truly believe that anything you did, you'd do it right. Go see the house, and see what your gut tells you."

He looked over at me and smiled. "Because your gut is never wrong."

"Exactly. Your gut is like the universe telling you what to do."

"Oh, Jesus." He opened his door. "Come on, let's go."

I decided not to tell him *my* gut was saying he needed to buy that house. For whatever reason, Derek had been holding himself back from things he really wanted his entire life. Maybe it was a fear of failure or of disappointing his father, but I felt like he'd never allowed himself to be the person he was meant to be. And if he didn't listen to his heart and his gut, the real risk was that he could wind up unhappy, always wondering what if, regretting the choices he'd made.

The more I learned about Derek, the more I wanted to help him.

I felt like he'd just shown me the way.

"THIS CAN'T BE RIGHT. One hundred-twenty-five dollars for a pair of *shorts*?"

Derek gritted his teeth. "Okay, will you please stop looking at price tags? Just stop."

I felt bad for being such a pain. We'd been at Nordstrom for an hour already and I hadn't even tried anything on. "But I—"

"Look, it's necessary. Clothing is necessary."

"But not clothing this expensive. Ellen was telling me about this store with nice things for not much money called T.J. Maxx?"

"That would be cheaper, yes, but the quality won't be as good. Things will wear out faster, and you'll spend more money in the long run. Look at it as an investment in yourself."

I shook my head. "My butt is not worth hundred-dollar shorts."

"I disagree. You're going to try those on, and if they fit, I'm going to purchase them for you, along with a few other things to get you through summer. Then we're going to get lunch, because I'm hungry and if you keep freaking out over price tags, I might actually starve to death."

An argument was on the tip of my tongue, but I stopped myself. Derek had said that it made him feel good to do things for me, and I knew what he meant, because I liked doing things for him, too. I wished there were more of them I could do. I nodded, but I felt really uncomfortable that someone else had to pay for my clothes, and didn't know where to look when he was swiping his credit card.

Derek understood. "Here," he said, handing me the bag.

"And don't say a word. I know how you feel, okay? I'd feel the same way. But this is an investment in the future."

When he phrased it that way, I felt better. "Thank you."

We went to lunch, where I ordered something called mac and cheese, which I'd never heard of but Derek assured me was delicious. He was right. I could have licked the plate.

While we ate, I made him practice his Russian words and taught him two more: *pozhaluysta*, which meant please, and *spasibo*, which meant thank you.

The best part was paying for lunch. I insisted on doing it, and although Derek put up a fight at first, he eventually relented. It cost me almost forty dollars, but I'd never been happier to spend money in my life.

"You didn't have to do that," he said as we walked to the car. "You should be saving your money. You saw how much that laptop costs." He was referring to the computer I'd drooled over in the Apple store.

"I saw. And I'll get there, because I do plan to be very careful with money. But there are so few things I can do for you, and you're doing so much for me, I really wanted to treat you."

A couple minutes later, we got in the car and he put a hand on my leg. "You're doing a lot for me, Maxim. More than you know."

No words could have made me happier.

TWENTY-SEVEN

DEREK

THE REST of the week went by way too fast. I went to the gym early each morning before work and Maxim worked late at the bar every night. We didn't even see each other. By the time he got home, I was already asleep, and I woke up so early, he was still in bed when I left. By Friday morning I was tempted to wake him, but I didn't want to be an asshole. *Hey, I know you just got home like three hours ago, but could you roll over and blow me? Thanks. Appreciate it.*

Instead I got myself off in the shower to the memories of us, but it wasn't even close to the real thing. I wanted more of the real thing.

In fact, it was a little disturbing how much I wanted more, and how quickly the days were zooming toward the two-week cut-off. Because we weren't even *doing* anything! What good was letting yourself be gay at home for two weeks if the person you wanted to be gay with was never there?

By Friday evening, I was frustrated beyond measure. After work, I'd taken a run (even though I'd already worked out that morning), washed my car, vacuumed all the carpets, and taken the rugs outside to beat them. None of it relieved the tension.

I realized I hadn't eaten dinner—my appetite had been strange lately, I was either ravenous or so distracted I forgot to eat—so I showered, shaved, and dressed, then went to The Blind Pig for dinner. I had to see him.

Maxim lit up when he noticed me sitting at a high-top table, and I probably did the same, judging from the way my heart started to pound. God, were we too obvious? I dropped my attention to the menu.

He came by a little while later.

"Hey," he said, sliding onto the chair across from me. "I have a quick break. How's your dinner?"

"Good." I set down my burger. "Maybe not as *vkusnyy* as your *syrniki,* but good."

He laughed, his eyes lighting up. "You remembered."

"Yes, but I haven't had much occasion to use them. The only Russian I know isn't around much." Fuck, did that sound needy?

"I'm sorry. I've been working so late." He lowered his voice so only I could hear it. "But I've missed you."

He's missed me. He's missed me. I wanted to let it show how much I liked hearing that, but I couldn't. I wanted to say it back, but I couldn't. I took a drink of my beer, set the bottle down, and looked over my shoulder to make sure no one was close enough to overhear. "Wake me tonight. When you get home."

His eyebrows went up. "You're sure?"

Fuck yes, I am. Even sitting across the table from him was driving me nuts. I wanted to reach over, grab a fistful of his shirt, and yank him toward me so I could devour his mouth. "Yeah. I'm sure."

"Hey, you!" Ellen appeared at my table. "Someone said you were here. Twice in one week, I'm honored!"

"Good." I picked up my beer again, tried to play it cool, but my pulse was racing. Had she heard what I said?

She tilted her head. "No Carolyn tonight?"

Maxim and I exchanged a glance. "Uh, no. Actually, Carolyn and I decided we're better as friends."

Ellen clucked her tongue. "Oh, really? That's too bad. She's really nice."

"She is."

"Well, you'll meet someone else." She perked up. "Hey, want me to introduce you to—"

"No," I said firmly. The dates Ellen set up for me were always disasters. "Do not introduce me to anyone."

She pouted. "You're no fun. You're like a grumpy old man who's all set in his ways and doesn't want to do anything new or different. But you're never going to meet anyone if you keep going to the same places and hanging out with the same people."

"I'm fun," I said, jerking my chin at her. "I'm just busy right now. There's a lot going on." *And I only have eyes for one person. He's sitting right across from me right this second, and I'm having trouble breathing because of it.*

She sighed as if I was a lost cause. Maybe I was. "Fine, fine. Enjoy your dinner. I gotta get back to work. You're okay, Maxim, take your break," she said when Maxim got off his chair. Then she turned to me. "Did he tell you he's been taking the bus the last couple days?"

I looked at him. "No. You are?"

He nodded. "I felt much too guilty needing to be driven all around."

"It's a long walk to a bus station from the house."

He shrugged. "I don't mind. And I like the independence."

"But after work, I make him take an Uber home," said Ellen.

Uber? He didn't even have a credit card yet. "But how do—"

"I call it for him." She giggled. "I told him it was part of his benefits package."

"I told her to take it out of my pay," Maxim said.

"And I'm totally doing that." My sister gave me a look that said *I'm not doing that.* "Okay, I'm going. Bye."

"Bye." I watched her go and looked at Maxim again. "Think she heard?"

He looked blank. "Heard what?"

"Me saying the thing about waking me up."

"Oh. No, I don't think she did." He looked like he might say something else, but didn't.

"What?" I prodded. If there were thoughts about me in his head, I wanted to hear them. Actually, I wanted to hear all the thoughts in his head, whether they were about me or not.

"Nothing." He dropped his eyes to my plate. "I was just thinking that if you ever wanted to talk to a family member about...*things*, Ellen would be a good choice. I think she would understand."

I considered it for less than a second. "Impossible. It would be way too weird. And she'd never keep it a secret. She has the biggest mouth in the world."

"Okay. You know her better than I do. I should get back

to work." He gave me a look that heated my insides. "I'll see you later."

I nodded and lowered my face in case anyone was close enough to see it flush. But I couldn't resist peeking at him as he walked away. His butt looked *so good* in the new jeans.

It would look even better naked in my bed tonight.

THE CREAK of the stairs woke me. *He's home.* Immediately, I started to get hard. *Jesus, give him a minute.*

I'd left my bedroom door open tonight, and I waited for him to walk through it, to shed his clothes and climb in beside me. To offer himself.

A couple minutes went by, and I began to get worried he wasn't coming. Had he changed his mind? Fallen asleep? Did he think I hadn't meant what I said?

A moment later, I heard the bathroom door close and the shower come on. *Aha.* I tried to relax and be patient. Brought a hand to my aching cock and stroked myself slowly. I didn't want to go off like a canon the second he walked in here. But every second was an eternity, and the more I thought about him in the shower, naked and wet and maybe even hard like me, the more agitated I became.

Every sound I heard made the tension in me pull tighter —the water going off, the shower door closing, the bathroom door opening.

Footsteps in the hall.

The creak of my bedroom door.

Hey. A whisper in the dark.

Come here. My own voice, low and commanding.

He slid under the covers and we reached for each other, our bodies coming together like fingers clasped in prayer, arms and legs and tongues intertwined. We lay on our sides, kissing and stroking and clinging, until Maxim pushed me onto my back. He buried his face in my neck and inhaled deeply. "God, I missed you."

I missed you, too. I wanted to tell him, but he was kissing his way down my chest, licking my nipples, sucking them, teasing them with the tip of his tongue, and it felt so good I couldn't speak. My hips thrust beneath him, my cock grinding against his torso. *Oh, fuck. I'm too close. Too close.* If he kept doing that, I was going to come all over us within seconds. I could feel it starting already.

I wanted to be inside him again. No—I *needed* it. Needed to be surrounded that way, accepted that way, embraced that way. Physically, I craved the heat and aggression of it, but some other part of me ached for the connection, to him and to myself.

Mustering my strength, I flipped him onto his back and began to kiss him everywhere, seeking out tender, hidden places on his body. Beneath his jaw. The side of his ribs. Behind his knees. I licked my way up his inner thigh, along his shaft, over his crown. I traced those veins on his lower abs with my tongue like I'd wanted to before.

He rewarded me with soft moans and sharp breaths and his fingers in my hair. He groaned and cursed and growled my name when he came in my mouth. He panted raggedly as I poured warm, slick lubricant into my hand and breathed deeply when I penetrated him with my fingers.

But none of it compared to the way he held me as I buried myself endlessly in his body, the way he took my head in his hands as I dangled over the edge, the way he whispered *baby* as I fell to pieces inside him.

And it was crazy and backward and illogical—I was a full-grown man, twelve years older than he was—yet nothing had ever felt more true. Because I no longer knew where he stopped and I began, who was moving and who was still, whose breath was on my lips, whose taste was in my mouth, or whose heart beat relentlessly inside my chest.

It was just ours. All of it was ours.

"Don't go." My voice sounded needy and desperate, and I hated it, but I didn't stop. "Don't go back to your room tonight. Stay with me."

"Okay," he whispered, touching his lips to mine. "I'll stay."

TWENTY-EIGHT

MAXIM

HE FELL ONTO MY CHEST, and I wrapped my arms around him. Neither of us spoke as our breathing slowed, steadied, and synced, both of us inhaling and exhaling at the same time. The moment was peaceful, the calm after a storm.

And it had been a particularly intense storm.

Had he missed me like I'd missed him? Had he thought about me? Our schedules were so opposite, we'd gone days without even seeing each other. When he'd walked into the bar last night, it was like seeing a movie star come through the door. Actually, it was better than that. There was no movie star who excited me the way he did. He'd looked happy to see me too, but I hadn't missed the careful way he guarded himself around Ellen. He was so afraid of what people would think if they knew about us, about him. I wished he could see himself the way I did.

He kissed my shoulder and lifted himself off me, separating our bodies. "Be right back."

While he was in the bathroom, I stretched out in his bed, sore and tired but happy. *He wants me to sleep next to him tonight.* I could count on one hand the number of nights I'd slept in someone else's bed, and those times had simply been a matter of falling asleep before I remembered to get up and go home. This was different. This was on purpose.

I wondered what had prompted him to ask me, but didn't want to read too much into it. Maybe it meant nothing. Maybe he just wanted to have sex again in the morning. But I was tempted to see it as one more barrier broken.

The bathroom door opened and he joined me in bed again, immediately pulling me close. Surprised but glad, I tucked myself along his side, my head on his shoulder, my arm around his waist.

"Are you okay?" he asked. "I feel like I was pretty rough on you."

"A little sore," I admitted. "But not too much."

"Good." He was silent a moment. "This is nice. I'm not usually a cuddler."

I smiled. "Me either. And it is nice."

A minute ticked by, then he spoke again.

"I can't sleep. Will you sing the Russian song for me?" He couldn't even get through the question without laughing.

I kicked him gently. "Be nice or I'll go back to the guest room."

"No." He squeezed me. "I like you here. I'll be nice —for now."

"You're always nice." I kissed his chest.

He sighed. "My sister thinks I'm a grumpy old man."

"No, she doesn't, not really. She wants you to be happy. And she thinks you'd be happy if you found someone."

"She's talked about me to you?" His tone was slightly defensive.

Careful. "Not too much. She said what you said—that you'd like a family."

"Oh. Right."

"She thinks you'll make a great dad."

Another sigh. Then, "Do you ever think about having kids?"

"Not really."

"Yeah. I didn't either when I was your age. Forty seemed light years away. Fuck, thirty seemed light years away. But time flies. Priorities change. We get old."

"You're not old, Derek."

"I'm old*er*."

"I like that about you."

He made a noise. "Why?"

"Because it makes you wiser and more mature and more experienced. You've done things. You've made mistakes and learned from them. You're not some stupid twenty-year-old who doesn't know shit about life and doesn't care because he just wants to get through the day, get drunk, get laid, whatever."

"You're not like that either," he said.

"No, I'm not. But I don't think I'm a typical twenty-four-year-old. Another reason I came here was because I felt like I'd outgrown my friends. They didn't seem to have any ambition. It's not entirely their fault, because there isn't opportunity there like there is here, but I found myself bored and restless a lot of the time. I wanted something better."

"You're going to get it. It might take some time, but you'll be a success story here. I know it."

I gave him a squeeze. "Hush. You'll jinx me. But thank you."

We fell asleep just like that.

———————————

WHEN I WOKE up the next morning, Derek was gone. For a moment, I was nervous he regretted asking me to stay the night in his bed and was off somewhere punishing himself for it. But then I saw the note on his nightstand, written in black ink on a white notepad. His handwriting made me smile—perfectly formed, angular letters, all caps. The paper had no lines, but his words didn't slant in any direction.

At the gym. Didn't want to wake you. Breakfast when I get back?

P.S. You're cute when you're sleeping.

My heart thumped happily, and I smiled as I stretched out in his bed again. The sheets smelled like him, like us, and I loved it. I loved the memory of last night, how passionate and powerful he'd been—and how vulnerable, too. He'd shown me he'd missed me, even if he hadn't said it. I loved that he'd asked me to stay with him and the way we'd held each other as we'd gone to sleep.

I really hoped he felt the same. At the same time, I also thought it was important to stick to the plan—I would rent my own apartment as soon as possible. In fact, I had appointments to visit two complexes this afternoon before work. The sooner I wasn't dependent on Derek for things, the better. I wanted to stand on equal footing—well, as equal as possible. I wasn't sure I'd ever be equal to someone like him. But I had to try.

After a shower, I got dressed and went downstairs as Derek was coming in the back door. In the kitchen, our eyes met, and we both smiled. Relief—he wasn't sorry. And God, he looked good, even sweaty and windblown.

"Morning," he said. "How did you sleep?"

"Like a baby. You?"

"Great."

"How was your workout?"

He groaned. "Tough. But good. I need to clean up."

"Okay. I could make breakfast if you'd like."

"*Syrniki?*" His face lit up like a kid about to blow out the candles on his birthday cake.

I laughed. "Sure."

As he passed me on his way to the stairs, he gave me a quick kiss. "Sorry, I'm sweaty."

"I like you sweaty."

He grinned and left me alone in the kitchen, where I put on some coffee and got started on the pancakes. It was ridiculous how much I enjoyed cooking for him. After I moved out, I would invite him to my new apartment so I could continue to do it.

He came down about thirty minutes later, inhaling deeply. "God, that smells so good."

I poured him a cup of coffee. "Perfect timing," I said, handing him the mug. "Everything is almost ready."

He sipped the coffee and sat down at the table, which I'd already set. When I put his plate in front of him a moment later, he moaned. "Good thing I did a few extra sets this morning at the gym. How the hell do you eat like this and stay in such good shape?"

"I don't eat like this all the time," I explained, taking the seat across from him. "And I do like to work out, I just haven't had time here yet. But I've always had a fast..." The word wasn't coming to me, and I looked at him for help. "You know, what your body does to burn what you eat."

"Metabolism," he supplied.

"Yes. A fast metabolism."

"I probably had a fast metabolism at your age, too."

"If I can look half as good as you in ten years, I would be thrilled," I told him honestly.

He rolled his eyes. "I don't think you need to worry. So tell me what you've been up to this week, besides taking the bus. We haven't had a chance to talk for days."

As we ate, I filled him in on what I'd been doing the last three days. Jake had gotten in touch when he returned from the mountains, and he felt so bad about what had happened to me that he volunteered to get my four hundred dollars back.

"And did he?" Derek's expression was shocked.

"He did." I shrugged. "I have no idea how, but he gave me the cash yesterday morning."

"That's awesome."

"It is. It means I can pay you the rent we agreed on, which makes me happy. And with what I'm making at the bar plus what I have saved already, I am confident I can afford an apartment. I'm looking at two places this afternoon."

Two lines appeared between his eyebrows. "Are you? I didn't know that."

"I didn't want to bother you. But I called two of the complexes we found the other day when we were looking, and they both have availability."

"Oh." He poked at some fruit on his plate. "When would you move out?"

"Both places start leases on either the first or the fifteenth. The first is a week from Monday, so that's what I asked for."

He nodded slowly. "Want me to go with you today?"

"That would be great, but you don't have to. I understand if you're busy."

"I'm not busy. What time?"

"One is at two, and one is at three. I have to be at work by five-thirty."

He nodded and continued eating. "What about screenwriting classes? Have you looked into those? Don't you want to save for those?"

"I did a little research, yes. Classes are very expensive, so it will be quite a while before I can enroll. And I might want to take some English classes first, to make sure I know what I'm doing when I write. Speaking is one thing, but writing is another. It's much harder."

"What about a laptop? Don't you want a new one?"

"I do, but the old one you gave me works great. If you're okay with me using that for now, I will save for a new laptop in the future."

"I'm fine with that. I just don't want you to think you have to rush out of here and pay rent somewhere if there are things you need to save for."

"I don't think that at all. It's tempting to go buy a shiny new laptop with the money I'm making, which is more than I've ever made before, but it wouldn't be a very good decision. I *need* a place to live. A new computer and screenwriting classes are just things I *want*. They can wait." I grinned at him. "This is me being practical and making a smart decision."

He smiled, a little grudgingly. "Yeah. I guess it is."

We finished breakfast, mostly in silence. It seemed like

Derek's mood had deteriorated a bit since he'd come down-stairs, and I wondered if it was something I'd said. Could he be upset that I'd made appointments to check out apart-ments? Maybe he was offended I wanted to leave? Maybe he wished I'd told him about it first? But that had always been the plan, and as far as I knew, the plan hadn't changed just because we were...whatever we were. *Involved.*

And I wasn't an idiot. Equal footing aside, the longer I stayed here, the harder it was going to be to leave. Already I was thinking ahead to tonight, wondering if he was going to ask me to wake him again and hoping that he would. Maybe he'd even want me to sleep in his bed again, too. And maybe tomorrow morning, he'd sleep in and we'd wake up next to each other. It was the kind of romantic thing I'd never thought about before, but wanted to experience with Derek.

Everything was different now.

TWENTY-NINE

DEREK

HE WANTED TO MOVE OUT.

I knew it was the right decision, but I hated the thought of it. A week from Monday, he'd be gone. Nine days. That's all I had left.

Shouldn't I have been glad? After all, this had been my plan from the start. He was making this easy for me, leaving of his own accord and not forcing me to ask him to go. Because whatever this was, it had to end soon. I'd never been in denial about that, never once considered that anything more could come of this. As good as it was, nothing could.

But still—I didn't want to let him go. I wasn't ready yet. He wasn't out of my system.

I couldn't say that to him, of course. But what I *could* do was be a dick about the apartments we saw that after-noon. And I was. Both of them were perfectly fine and either would have suited him, but I shot down his enthusiasm by finding things wrong at every possible opportunity.

Sure it's close to public transportation, but not much else. God, this place is noisy—listen to that traffic!

The kitchen is okay, but the tiles in the bathroom are all cracked.

See that stain on the ceiling? That means a leak.

This carpet looks like it hasn't been replaced since the fall of the Berlin Wall.

Definitely better in the photos online.

Even so, Maxim liked the second place well enough to leave a deposit in cash and sign a lease. It was mostly furnished, since the previous owner had left suddenly for a job out of the country, so he could move right in on Monday. All he'd really need were some new sheets and towels, which he planned to buy this week.

Inside the dingy little office of the complex manager, I watched him sign the lease with a panicky sense of dread. He was really going. I'd be alone again. Alone and drifting and scared I'd never find this kind of connection with anyone else. My throat was so dry. I wanted to speak, but couldn't. Wanted to tell him not to sign, not to go, not to leave me. I wanted him to need me, because who else would?

Are you fucking crazy? You can't say any of those things! You shouldn't even be feeling them. What the fuck is wrong with you? He wants to leave, and you need to let him live his life. He didn't come here for you, asshole. Now pull yourself together!

Summoning every ounce of strength, I pressed my lips together to keep myself from saying anything stupid. I co-signed the lease. I pushed back at the feelings trying to surface, feelings of inevitable loss and loneliness. Feelings of warmth and affection. Feelings of *what if* and *I wish* and *maybe we could*. I drowned them without mercy at the bottom of my heart.

I couldn't let myself hope. I just couldn't.

"YOU LIKE IT, RIGHT?" Maxim asked as we walked back to the car.

"It's fine."

"I think it's perfect. I know the carpet is pretty worn and the appliances aren't new, but it's good enough for me."

It's not. It's not.

"And I'm glad you came, because I needed to hear the other side to make a good decision."

"Yeah."

"God, I can't believe it." He stopped walking in the middle of the sidewalk and shook his head. "I signed a lease on an apartment here. It doesn't seem real!"

"Congratulations," I said shortly.

"How far from the ocean are we?" He looked around as if he might be able to spot it.

"Maybe five, ten miles."

"Really? That's it?" He smiled, his cheeks flushing. "It's probably no big deal to you, but I grew up so far from the water, the ocean has always been something exotic and incredible to me. As a kid, I used to dream about living on a coast, even before I knew what I wanted to do. And when I learned that there was a place near the ocean called City of Angels, and it was where stories were brought to life for people to watch all over the world, I knew that's where I wanted to live. At the time, it seemed impossible."

"Well, you did it." I wanted so badly to be happy for

him, but all I could think of was myself. *God, I'm such an asshole.*

"I did it. I'm doing it."

By the time we got in the car, I'd made up my mind to say something supportive. "You should be really proud of yourself, Maxim. Plenty of people talk about dreams and never do anything about it."

"Well, they should. Because it feels really good." He looked at me. "Did you make an appointment to see that house?"

"Not yet." I started the car, focusing my attention on the rearview mirror as I backed out.

"Derek," he admonished. "Why not?"

I shrugged. "I was busy at work this week." It was an excuse. The truth was that I'd broached the subject with my father, and he'd told me I was crazy, I'd lose my shirt, and I had no time for side projects, anyway. In fact, he wanted me to take on *more* responsibility in the next six months, not less.

"Call now."

"I'm driving. And I don't have the number."

"Do it when you get home after dropping me at work."

I gave him a look. "That apartment made you bossy."

He grinned sheepishly. "Sorry. But I know you'd do such a great job on it. And I think it's like your dream."

"Maybe. I'll give it some more thought." But it was hard to think about anything that might happen after the next nine days. I didn't want to do it.

When I pulled up to The Blind Pig, he looked at me. "What will you do tonight?"

"Nothing much." *Think about you. Feel sorry for myself. Wallow.*

He opened the door but didn't get out. "Is everything okay?"

"Why wouldn't it be?"

"I don't know."

I refused to look at him. "It's fine. Go to work."

"Okay." Another pause.

I gripped the steering wheel hard, staring straight ahead. *Get the fuck out, Maxim, before I say something I shouldn't.*

"Well, thanks for the ride."

"No problem."

He got out, and I took off the moment the door was shut. In the rearview mirror, I could see him linger there on the sidewalk, watching me. I couldn't get away quick enough, and I wished I could hit the accelerator hard. *Fuck this traffic! Why can't there be an open road when you need to blow off steam?*

I decided to go for a run instead. I went home, changed clothes, grabbed my headphones and took off, my feet pounding the pavement in long, angry strides. I ran fast, too fast, sweat pouring and heart pumping and muscles aching. I ran like something was chasing me, like my life was in peril, like I could escape danger if only I could stay ahead of it.

But it wouldn't let me be. It wouldn't give up. It wouldn't release me.

His arms and legs around me like vines. His head on my shoulder. His breath on my chest. His skin against mine.

After my five mile loop, I ended up in my backyard, hunched over, breathing hard, hands braced on my knees. I wasn't at all sure I wouldn't be sick or pass out. After a minute, I collapsed onto the grass and lay on my back, eyes closed.

Fuck. What was I doing? Trying to outrun a feeling? Trying to punish my body for what it had done? For what it wanted to do? Or was I trying to replace emotional anguish with physical duress? Maybe I thought I could distract myself from unwanted feelings by pushing my body so far it gave out. Then the ache would reside in my muscles, and not in my heart.

Because fuck my heart. It had no business here. This was about one thing, and one thing only—pleasure.

And its days were numbered.

I WOKE AGAIN to footsteps on the stairs. As if my body remembered what followed last time I'd heard the sound, my dick started to get hard, heat rushing my lower body. Would he come to me again? Maybe not, after the way I'd acted this afternoon. Maybe he thought I didn't want him to. Or maybe he knew I did, and he wouldn't just to punish me. Fuck that.

When I heard the shower come on, I decided not to wait. I got out of bed and shoved off my underwear, my erection springing free and twitching with impatience. The hallway was dark, the bathroom door closed.

I didn't knock. Because fuck manners too.

The sight of his naked body, even blurry through the wet glass, ratcheted up the tension inside me. And the hunger—I felt almost predatory as he turned in surprise and saw me there.

I opened the shower door and stepped in beside him. Without waiting for him to say a word, I grabbed him and crushed my mouth to his, pushing him back against the tiles and pressing myself against his hot, wet body. He didn't fight me, but I was rough with him, fisting my hands tight in his hair, shoving my tongue inside his mouth, thrusting my cock against his hip. I felt the need to subdue something or someone, to dominate. To take control and impose my will. I wasn't a fucking idiot, I knew it was myself I wanted to over-power, but I was a failure there. And Maxim, with his unsettling ability to show me who I really was, to make me feel as if I couldn't extricate myself from him, to reflect back at me everything I desired, was the perfect substitute.

I tore my mouth from his and shoved down on his shoul-ders. "Get on your knees."

He dropped willingly, and it pleased me. Hot water sprayed my back as the steam rose around us. I braced myself against the wall as he took my cock in his hand and brought the tip to his mouth.

"Yes," I hissed through clenched teeth. The muscles in my legs tightened as he licked and sucked and stroked. He didn't tease me, wasn't coy or playful, didn't try to wrest control away and make my orgasm his toy. It was as if he knew what I needed and wanted to give it to me. His fingers slid between my legs and rubbed with steady, firm pressure as he took me to the back of his throat again and again. My lower body began to tremble, like the earth quaking and shuddering before a volcanic eruption. I grabbed the back of his neck with one hand and held his head still, plunging into his sleek, hot mouth with hard, deep thrusts. "Fuck!" I yelled, my voice echoing off the tiles as I exploded inside him without even giving a warning.

He didn't care. He kept stroking and sucking and swal-lowing until I was empty and shaking and tingling all over. *Oh God, he's perfect. He's perfect and beautiful and brave and so full of life and why can't this feeling be mine forever? Why can't he be mine forever?*

I dropped to my knees in front of him. Took his head in my hands. Kissed him passionately, protectively, possessively. *Mine. Mine. Mine.* His arms came around me and I was melting at his feet. At that moment, there was nothing I wouldn't have done for him.

"Stand up," I said, sliding my lips down the warm, wet arc of his neck. "Let me."

"Let you what?" His voice was low, a little playful.

Let me make your heart beat faster. Let me make you come. Let me make you feel so good you never want to leave me. Because I don't want you to go, but I can't ask you to stay. "Let me do what I want."

He rose to his feet and tipped my chin up, forcing me to look at him. "I'm all yours."

THIRTY

MAXIM

WHATEVER HAD BEEN BOTHERING Derek the afternoon he co-signed the lease at my new apartment appeared to have worked itself out. We spent the next five nights together in his bed, and every morning, he kissed me goodbye before leaving for work. Twice he came to eat dinner at the bar, and Thursday night he even stayed until closing so he'd be able to drive me home, even though he had to get up early the next morning. We didn't have sex that night because he was so tired, but I didn't care. Falling asleep with his body curled around mine felt as good as an orgasm in a way—a softer, more tender intimacy that made me feel closer to him than ever before.

My notebook, which had turned into more of a journal than a place for ideas, was full of page after page of my feelings for him, which were growing deeper by the day. We didn't talk about them, but I wanted to. I wanted to tell him I was falling for him. I wanted to hear him say the same to me. I wanted to know if he saw anything more than hiding at home in our future. We'd sort of left things open-ended when we'd agreed to see where things went, but on Monday, I was moving into my apartment, and we wouldn't be able to see each other in the middle of the night anymore. What would happen to us? What did he want? I was dying to know all the answers, but I was too nervous to ask the questions. Derek wasn't someone who liked being pushed. And maybe he didn't even *know* what he wanted yet.

I knew what I wanted—more. I'd gotten to the point where I wanted to *be* with Derek, not only at home, but out in the open. I wanted to make him happy, make him proud of me, make him see we had nothing to be ashamed of. I wanted him to include me in his life. Openly gay relationships were possible here—I saw them all the time. I knew how hard it would be for him, and I didn't for one second think I deserved it enough to ask for it, but some part of me had begun to hope he might offer.

Another part of me said *don't be ridiculous, he told you flat out he wants a family, not a boyfriend.* Even if he accepted me, I couldn't give him that. I couldn't work here legally, and if I overstayed my visa and got caught, I could be deported. Who in his right mind would look at a guy like me and see solid parenting material? Certainly not Derek. Half the time, I had no idea what he was doing with me.

But it was the best time I'd ever had, an unexpected gift. I didn't want it to end.

ON FRIDAY MORNING, I woke to find a series of texts from Derek on my phone.

You work too hard. You deserve a break.

I'm taking you away this weekend. Pack a bag with your swimsuit, a nice outfit for a dinner, and something cool for today and tomorrow. We'll get you sunglasses on the way. (I don't know how you're living without them in L.A.) Be ready by 3:00.

And yes, I talked to Ellen and she gave you the weekend off. Consider it a paid vacation.

Yes, a paid vacation. Welcome to America.

I sat down on the guest room bed in a daze, my thoughts jumbled, my heart racing. Was this for real? He was taking me on a trip this weekend? Out in public? Where people would see us together? Where were we going?

And he'd told Ellen about it! What was she thinking? How had he described it? Did she suspect anything?

And what was this about a paid vacation? Was there really such a thing?

Confusion swirled, but more than anything, I was happy. Going away together seemed like a big step. He wouldn't be doing it if he didn't want things to continue, would he?

Maybe this weekend would be a turning point for us.

Packing a bag didn't take long, and I was ready long before three. Not that I didn't trust Derek, but I sent a quick message to Ellen making sure it was okay to take three days off. I didn't want anything to jeopardize my job.

Her reply put my mind at ease. **Yes, of course!! I'm so happy Derek is doing this. Don't let him work while you're gone. He needs a break too!**

He does, I wrote back. **He's too hard on himself.**

She replied with a bunch of emojis—the sun, a pair of

sunglasses, a bathing suit, a tropical drink, a beach umbrella, a big wave—and told me to have fun.

I grinned. The beach. It had to be the beach. He remembered what I'd said about the ocean, and he was taking me to see it. My chest tightened as my heart drummed with excitement. God, he was perfect. He was everything.

"KNOW WHERE WE'RE GOING?" he asked once our bags were loaded and we'd hit the road.

"Not for sure." I couldn't stop smiling.

"No guessing," he ordered. "I want it to be a surprise."

"How long does it take to get there?"

"You sound like my niece and nephew. Not that long," he promised, placing a hand on my leg. "One or two hours, maybe."

A couple hours later, we were still on the road, stuck in traffic. But I didn't care—we'd rolled down the windows, and I could smell the ocean. I kept inhaling deeply, unable to get enough of the warm, salty air.

"Sorry we're not there yet. I wish we could have come during the week. Everybody wants to be at the beach on the weekend. Oh, fuck!" He realized he'd given away the surprise and clapped a hand over his mouth.

"It's okay," I told him, patting his leg. "I had a feeling it was the beach when you said to pack a swimsuit, and then Ellen sent me a bunch of emojis that sort of gave it away."

He groaned. "See? Fucking Ellen and her big mouth. I don't know why I told her the truth. I should have told her I was taking you camping or something."

"No, this is perfect! It will still be a surprise to see it and swim in it and hear the waves. I can't wait."

In a move that shocked me, he took my hand from his leg and kissed my fingers. "Good. I love seeing you so excited."

As we turned from the freeway onto a beautiful road shaded with palm trees on either side, I thought my heart might burst right out of my chest. We drove past a gate that said Ritz Carlton, and I stared at Derek. "Is this... Are we...*staying* here?" There was a Ritz in Moscow, but it was so expensive and luxurious, I'd never even crossed its doorstep.

"Yes. I've driven by this place and always wanted to come here. You gave me a reason. So thank you."

I couldn't even speak.

We checked in, and the ocean beckoned to me through big glass windows in the lobby. "It's so beautiful," I said, my voice full of awe.

Derek smiled. "I asked for a room with an ocean view, so you can see it any time you want."

As soon as we got into our room, I dropped my bag to race out onto the balcony, which overlooked the ocean, as promised. I drew in deep breaths as I drank in the sight of so much blue. "I can't get enough," I said when Derek joined me. "It's even more incredible than I thought."

Pressed close behind me, he wrapped his arms around my waist and rested his chin on my shoulder. "Want to take a walk on the beach?"

"Yes. Although this is nice, too. Being alone here with you." I covered his arms with mine.

"I promise you'll have plenty of both the beach and being alone with me."

I sighed, closing my eyes. "Is this real? Don't tell me if it isn't."

"It's real." He kissed my shoulder, my neck, my jaw. Rested his forehead against my temple. "It's real."

———

LATER, after we'd walked on the beach and swum in the ocean and drunk colorful cocktails as we watched the sun go down, we went back to the room to clean up. As thrilling as it had been to get in the ocean for the first time, I was even happier watching Derek get dressed for dinner. It seemed ridiculous that something mundane like watching him iron a shirt or shave, or style his hair or button his shirt could have such an effect on me, but it did. I could still hear his voice in my head. *It's real. It's real.*

I felt like it was. The more time we spent together, the more willing I was to do whatever it took to keep it. I hadn't moved here expecting to meet someone, but life was strange and wonderful, and I had to believe that this feeling had a purpose. It was too strong, too good, too unlikely for it to be random. Everything inside me, every instinct I had, was telling me to fight for him.

But what weapons did I have? What could I give him in return for changing his life for me? Sex didn't seem like enough. What else did he want?

"So tell me more about what you would do with that house. And did you make the appointment to see it yet?" We were at dinner, sitting on the hotel restaurant patio overlooking the ocean.

He turned his head to look at the water. "Not yet. I don't know that I want to see it."

"What? Why not?"

The waiter appeared with our drinks, and asked if we were ready to order. Once he'd left us alone, I asked again. "Why don't you want to see the house?"

"Because what's the use? I can't buy it. My dad was right—I don't have the time for a project like that. I probably never will." He picked up his wine and drank.

"You asked your dad about it?"

"Yeah. It didn't go well. He wants me to take on more work, not less. I'll get more money too."

"But what about all the things you told me about creativity and risk and passion?"

He shrugged. "It was just an idea, and not a very practical one. There are other things I want more. And you know what?" He drank again and set down his glass before leaning toward me. "Let's not talk about that stuff. We're here to have fun, and I don't want to think about anything beyond that. All that matters is *now*."

But I don't want to be just fun to you. I want to matter. I want to mean something. I want to talk about where we can go, what we can be.

I want you to let me in.

I was beginning to worry it wasn't going to happen.

THIRTY-ONE

DEREK

DENIAL WAS a game I played well.

The field was familiar, I had all the strategies memorized, and the uniform fit like a glove. I'd worn it practically my entire life. Don't want to feel something? Refuse to feel it. Don't like the thoughts in your head? Reject them. Don't like the person you really are? Pretend he doesn't exist. You're only lying to yourself—and what does that matter? Thanks to years of practice, I was an expert at keeping the outside neat and tidy, even if the inside was a fucking wreck. *Especially* if the inside was a fucking wreck.

And it was.

I kept waiting to be sated, to feel as if I'd had my fill of him, so I could walk away from this experiment and get on with my real life. But it didn't happen.

Every day my feelings for Maxim grew stronger. Every night we spent together brought us closer. Every moment we were apart was spent thinking about the next time we could be together. What was supposed to be a quick, indulgent fuck fling was trying to be something else entirely.

I refused to let it. My limit had been reached. After that night in the shower, I'd folded up my feelings like a sweater and packed them away. Told myself it wasn't love; it was infatuation. Novelty. The kick of eating forbidden fruit. The rush of being *bad*. It was just his presence in my house that was making it seem so intense. Once he was gone, I'd be fine.

I'd be fine.

But for our last weekend together, I would be greedy. I wanted him all to myself, no distractions. I wanted more than just a few stolen hours in the dark—I wanted his days *and* his nights, his full attention, a taste of what it would be like to belong to him, to call him mine. I would gorge on him and on us until I was fully and utterly gratified.

Then I'd be able to let him go.

LIKE ALL MY plans where Maxim was concerned, the get-my-fill vacation was not working.

"I never want to leave this place." He looked out at the ocean from where we sat on the restaurant patio Saturday night. "The water, the warmth, the palm trees. It's paradise."

Maybe it was, but I couldn't take my eyes off him. His skin burnished from the sun, his hair neatly styled but tousled by the breeze, the white dress shirt cuffed to show off strong wrists and beautiful hands. *God*, those hands and what they did to me. The way they moved over my body like molten gold, slow and sensuous and fiery hot. They could be gentle or rough, kind or cruel, tender or savage.

They could tease and torture, stroke and sheath, bring me to my knees or send me soaring above clouds. I loved and hated their power over me. Last night I'd bound them with a belt, as if rendering them useless would lessen their effect, but somehow the sight of them restrained by the leather strap had only heightened it. Tonight he wore a watch with a leather band, and every time I looked at it, my pulse quickened. But I tried not to look because I hated thinking about time—it was moving too quickly. Every hour that elapsed brought us closer to Monday. Every minute that passed made it more difficult to keep my feelings buried. They were rising toward the surface like tar seeps from the ocean floor, thick and dark and threatening.

"Derek?"

I raised my eyes to his and realized he'd asked me a question I'd been too distracted to answer. "What?"

He smiled, and my pulse quickened. "Don't you think it's paradise?"

"Yes." I picked up my wine glass and took a big drink.

"What was your favorite part?"

"Hmmm." *Walking into this room with you, because you were brave and reached for my hand and didn't let go until we reached our table.* It was the way I should have felt walking in somewhere with Carolyn...proud, grateful, happy. It was also the most openly affectionate we'd been all weekend, and I'd loved it—but this was a room full of strangers. Would I have felt the same in a room full of friends?

The answer was no, and I hated myself for it.

"I can't choose," I said.

The last twenty-four hours had been perfect. We hadn't left each other's sides once. We'd lain on the beach sharing stories about our childhoods. We'd gotten tipsy on overpriced drinks at the pool, laughing at my attempts to say things in Russian and his insane superstitions. We'd come back to the room, sunburned and sandy and half-drunk on mojitos and each other, falling into bed almost immediately. His skin had tasted like sun and ocean and salt and rum and everything warm and youthful and carefree. Afterward, we'd fallen asleep, wrapped in each other's arms, and I'd prayed for time to stop and let us be like that forever—lost in our own little beach-flavored world where we belonged only to one another. Answered only to one another. Loved one another without shame.

"How's your steak?" he asked.

"Good." I put another bite in my mouth, barely tasting it.

"Mine, too. Although my favorite steak will always be the one you cooked for me the night we met."

I returned his smile without feeling it.

"I remember sitting across from you and feeling like I wanted to stay up all night talking."

I picked up my wine again.

"Derek." Maxim's tone was hesitant. "Is something wrong?"

Yes. I think I'm in love with you. "No."

"You seem...a little quiet."

Because I'm afraid if I start talking, I won't stop. "Oh."

He took a breath, moved some potatoes around on his plate. "I was wondering..."

Oh fuck.

"What Ellen said when you told her we were taking a trip together."

My thighs unclenched. "Nothing much. She was envious but glad."

"Oh." He poked at his green beans. "She didn't think it was odd, the two of us going away for the weekend?"

"Not that I noticed. I...I told her I had to look at some property over here and figured I'd take you along since you really wanted to see the ocean."

"Ah. I see." He looked a little downhearted about the lie. "Well, that's good."

Don't do that, Maxim. Don't be sad that we can't be together. Don't show me or tell me you care. I can't handle it.

We finished dinner and dessert in relative silence, and went back to our room. As always, Maxim went right onto the balcony, as if the ocean drew him by some physical force. I followed, and we stood at the railing next to each other in the dark, listening to the crash of the waves and breathing the balmy night air.

"You let me hold your hand." His words startled me.

"What?" I looked at him, but he kept his eyes on the water.

"Tonight. Walking through the restaurant. You let me hold your hand."

I swallowed hard. "Yes."

"Why?"

"Because..." I looked out over the ocean again, boundless and deep, and felt myself drowning. "Because I wanted to know what it would be like to be yours. To belong to you."

It took him a moment to respond. "And what was it like?"

I closed my eyes, sinking fast. "Heaven. It was like heaven."

"Derek, I—"

But I didn't let him finish. I couldn't. Instead I pulled him to me and crushed my mouth to his, clinging to him as if he could save me from the bottomless depths of my feel-ings. Somehow we made it into the room, where we pulled and shoved at clothing with fumbling hands, reluctant to break the kiss.

We fell upon the bed, twisted up in each other that way I loved, that made me feel so close to him, so completely understood. I wanted every part of him, wanted to climb inside his mind, get lost beneath his skin, reside in the hidden spaces between muscle and bone. And I wanted him inside me, wanted him to fill my body with his own, wanted to surrender to him in a way I'd never done before.

I groped blindly for the lube on the nightstand behind me, and he leaned over me to grab it. "Here," he said, breathing hard as he handed it to me.

I gave it back. "No—you this time."

He paused. "You want that?"

"Yes," I said, reaching between us to take his cock in my hand. Fuck. He was big and thick and hard, and it was going to hurt. But I wanted it to. I wanted to suffer for him. My pain would be an unspoken gift, something honest I could offer up to him in place of the truths I couldn't utter, the promises I couldn't bring myself to make. "Please."

He kissed me hard, turning me onto my back, pinning me beneath him. His voice was low in my ear. "I want to make this so good for you."

Fear and excitement rattled my spine.

He snaked down my body so he knelt between my thighs, pushing them apart. Bending my knees, feet flat on the bed, I closed my eyes and braced for an unfamiliar intru-sion, but he took my cock into his mouth instead. I groaned as his tongue swept over my crown, my body eager and trembling. His mouth was hot and wet and tight and *fuck*, he took me so deep. At the same time, he slipped his lube-slick fingers between my legs, massaging and circling and teasing and oh fuck—

"Maxim." A warning.

He released my cock from his lips and licked a line up my abdomen. "Shhh. Trust me."

I did trust him. But a few minutes later, as he eased one warm, slick finger—and then another—inside me, I wondered if I'd overestimated both my tolerance for discomfort and my ability to handle the psychological difficulty of letting another man breach my body this way. My mind kept trying to run away from it, telling me I wasn't *like that*.

I was. I was like that. And I wanted it, but Christ. *Christ.*

The feeling was strange to me. Foreign. Tight. I willed my body to yield, but my brain was getting mixed signals. One moment, my ass was involuntarily contracting around his fingers, pulling them in like I wanted more, and the next I was terrified I was going to embarrass myself because I felt like I had to pee.

Alarms began to sound.

I don't have control of my body.

I started to panic, my hands fisting in the sheets, my legs shaking.

"Breathe," he whispered, his lips hovering over mine. "Slow and deep."

I inhaled and exhaled, consciously trying to relax all of my muscles. Eventually, I felt the tension start to give. The burn start to fade. Pleasure start to murmur deep within.

My hips began to move.

"That's it, baby."

Fuck. I love when he says that to me.

He kissed his way down my chest, and it was while his tongue was stroking my nipple that something he was doing with his fingers made my entire body start to tingle. A moan escaped me as the sensation slowly but surely intensified. I wanted more, but I couldn't speak.

He added a third finger.

Something is happening to me.

It felt like an orgasm building, but its point of origin wasn't my cock. He wasn't even touching me there. It was deeper, slower, a gradual tightening inside me that sent electric pulses shooting through my entire body, as if my circuitry was being rewired, my body transformed for him.

He took his fingers from me, and immediately I wanted them back. I watched as he put on a condom and covered himself in lube. He'd never looked so beautiful or so fearsome to me. I'd never felt so powerless and vulnerable. My insides quaked as he hooked his arms beneath my thighs and pulled me closer. Pushed my legs farther apart. Positioned the head of his cock.

His eyes closed as he slid inside me in a long, slow, exquisite plunge. I breathed through the stretch and burn of it, glad for the way it hurt, for the way his body would change mine.

When he was buried deep inside me, he tipped forward, bracing his elbows above my shoulders, forcing my knees closer to my chest. He opened his eyes, and I put my hands at the back of his neck.

For a moment, we were still. Our eyes locked. I couldn't breathe. He was everywhere inside me—everywhere. My mind, my heart, my body, my soul. I gave everything over to him. I was his, exactly the way I'd wanted to be, and it was perfect.

He put his lips on mine as he began to move, his body undulating over mine in sinuous waves. I loved the solidity of his body, his weight, the press of his chest. I loved the stroke of his cock against that place inside me, the one that made my entire body come alive. I loved the abandonment of everything but him—of right and wrong, of good and evil, of rules and religion.

Nothing mattered but us. No one existed but us. Time itself was irrelevant.

Maxim's breathing grew labored, and he buried his face in my neck as he drove into me, as if he had to get closer to me any way he could. It felt so good, to be wanted that way, without pretense or inhibition or shame, and I slipped my arms around his back, holding him tight. All I could think was *stay with me, stay with me, stay with me.*

A moment later he sat up and leaned back on his heels, grabbing my thighs to pull me onto his legs. *Fuck yes*—the angle was unbelievable, and I felt that intense internal pull almost immediately. With my feet flat on the bed, I lifted my hips, and he slid his hands beneath my ass, grabbed on, and fucked me hard and fast and deep. My dick was thrusting through my own fist before I even realized I'd wrapped my fingers around it. I was so close to orgasm, so close, so close, so close, the pressure inside me building and building, intense heat radiating throughout my entire lower body, my ass my thighs my back my stomach, everything *tighter hotter yes more oh my God* until I exploded all over my chest and heard Maxim yell *fuck!* and he was throbbing inside me, my ass clenching hard around his cock in what was the longest, most intense orgasm I'd ever experienced. I couldn't stop coming. My hair stood on end. My skin was on fire. My body convulsed. If it hadn't felt so good, I might have thought I was in some sort of physical distress. Cardiac arrest. A stroke. Electrocution.

When I came out of it, I looked up at Maxim in disbelief. He was sweaty and disheveled and so fucking beautiful, it hurt. For one insane second, I was actually afraid I might *cry*.

"Are you okay?" he asked.

Would I ever be okay again? "No."

Confusion and concern rippled across his face. "No?"

"Is there a hole in the ceiling? Because I think I've been struck by lightning."

He laughed. "I know the feeling."

"My legs. I can't feel them."

"Wait till you try to walk."

I groaned. "I have to get up?"

"No. Just a minute." He carefully disengaged his body from mine and went into the bathroom. A moment later he was back with a wet washcloth. I went to take it from him, but he shook his head. "Let me."

I watched his face as he cleaned up my chest, and the tender look on his face nearly broke me. *This. This is what I want. I can't lose him.*

But what could I do? There were no good options, and time was running out. This trip hadn't done what I was hoping it would—in fact, I wanted him more now than ever before. How was that even possible?

He went back into the bathroom, and I closed my eyes.

Punishment. This is punishment for what you've done, and the only thing to do is suffer through it.

THIRTY-TWO

MAXIM

WHEN I CAME out of the bathroom, Derek was already asleep, facing away from me on his side. Poor guy. I'd worn him out. He was going to be pretty sore tomorrow. Hopefully, he'd think it was worth it.

I climbed into bed and curled my body around his, slinging an arm around his waist. His skin was warm and smelled so good, I put my face at the side of his neck and inhaled deeply. Ocean and sex. Nothing better.

This weekend had been incredible. There wasn't one moment I'd trade for anything, and there were some—like the way he'd held my hand tonight, the way his voice had trembled when he said he'd wanted to know what it was like to be mine, the way he'd offered himself to me in the most intimate and deeply personal way he could—those moments would stay with me forever. I'd felt so cherished and trusted and close to him.

Was it enough? Was I enough? He still refused to talk

about the future. I'd been about to tell him how I felt when he derailed the conversation with sex. I couldn't resist him when he got like that—hot and demanding—but where did that leave us? The sex was beyond amazing, but I wanted to hear him tell me what we had was worth more than that. That I was worth more than that.

Tonight when I was cleaning him up, I'd seen the look in his eyes. Surprise and gratitude and affection. With my hands on his chest, I'd felt the way his heart was beating. He'd liked being taken care of—it made him happy. He was always the one who rescued and protected and put others first, whether it was family or friends or even the animals he said Ellen was always foisting on him. What a relief it must have been to let himself be cared for that way, especially after what we'd done. I knew he hadn't taken it lightly, and some part of him probably wondered if I'd look at him the same way I did before. If I'd see him as something less then perfect now that I'd seen him at his most vulnerable, his most honest, stripped down to nothing but his deepest needs.

The realization made me snuggle closer. Underneath his perfect exterior, Derek was human and wanted to be loved for who he was. He wanted to feel worthy of being loved. *I wanted to know what it would be like to be yours. To belong to you*, he'd said.

Acceptance.

He wanted to be accepted. The trouble was, it wasn't my acceptance he needed.

It was his own.

DEREK WAS quiet the next morning—and sore. I had to smile when he groaned getting out of bed.

"You okay?" I asked.

"No. Muscles I didn't even know I had are screaming." He limped toward the bathroom.

"Need help?"

"No. If I don't come out, I'm dead and you killed me."

"But was it worth it?"

At the bathroom door, he looked over his shoulder, his expression serious. "Fuck yes, it was."

My grin widened. "Good."

He didn't die, and we went down to breakfast, during which he was mostly silent and distracted. I didn't push him to talk, because I understood there were things he had to work out in his head, and he wasn't the kind of guy to trust his gut, like I was. It was going to take some time.

"WANT TO WATCH A MOVIE OR SOMETHING?" he asked later that evening, opening a bottle of wine. He'd gone to the gym when we got back from the beach, and it seemed to have improved his mood. We'd ordered pizza, and he'd even let me pay for it with my new credit card.

"Sure. What's your favorite?"

He frowned. "I don't know if you'll like it. It's not that well-known."

"I don't mind. I like all movies. What is it?"

"It's this Woody Allen movie called Sweet and Lowdown about this guitar player in the 1930s. He's kind of a mess. Super cocky because he's so good, but haunted by the one guy in the world that's better than he is. Then he falls in love with this girl who doesn't speak." He laughed. "I'm not describing it very well. But there's something about it I love. It's a great story, and it was cast perfectly."

"I love great stories," I told him, getting plates from the cupboard. "And Woody Allen is a fantastic writer. Let's watch it."

We ate dinner and watched the movie, pausing it only to take our dishes to the kitchen and put away the extra food when we were done eating. Returning to the couch, Derek turned off all the lights, pulled the ottoman close, and stretched out his legs. I sat next to him, giving him more space than I wanted to.

"Hey." He put an arm around me. "Come over here."

I gladly moved closer and melted into the curve of his body. Hope began to bubble through my concern.

We finished the movie, and I absolutely loved it. For one thing, one of the characters couldn't speak, so her thoughts and feelings were communicated entirely by expression and gesture and nuance. As someone who struggles occasionally with language, I appreciated the brilliance of her performance.

And it gave me even more insight into Derek too. The film ended with the main character admitting he'd made a mistake about something—a critical decision that had caused his life to take a certain path, and there was no going back. He was going to suffer the consequences of that mistake forever. But there was an upside—his playing grew more beautiful, more emotional, every bit as good as his rival's.

I wondered if something about that spoke to Derek, the idea of coming to a crossroads and making a choice, and even if you chose the path that caused you to suffer, you could find beauty or nobility in it.

Don't let your mind run away from you. Maybe he just likes the movie.

I was still pondering it as the credits rolled. He turned the television and stereo off, but didn't move.

And then, "Don't go."

Silence. Then I spoke.

"What?" Although I'd heard him fine.

"Don't go. Tomorrow. Don't move out." His tone was one of quiet desperation.

"Why?"

"Because I don't want you to."

It wasn't that his words didn't make me happy, but my gut said something was slightly off. "You don't want me to?"

"No." Both his arms came around me. "I like you here."

"Does that mean you're ready to—"

"It means I like you here. It means I loved being with you this weekend. I want to hold on to it."

I so wanted this to mean he was arriving at a place of acceptance. But I wasn't sure. I sat up and faced him, wishing I could see better in the dark. "So you want to...be together?"

"Like we have been. Yes."

Like we have been. In secret. "You still want to hide?"

"Yes." He said it like it was obvious. "And if you move out, we'll never see each other."

"So you want me to live here so that we can see each other in private, in the middle of the night?"

"You don't enjoy our time together in the middle of the night?"

"Derek, it's not that." Fuck, arguing in my second language was hard. "It's...it's that it feels like a step backward. This weekend was so nice, being out in the open."

"We can do that sometimes. Take trips." He sat up too,

and I could see the tension in his body by the way he fidgeted. "It just has to be somewhere people won't know us."

I shook my head. "How long do you think we could go on like that? Me living here, us taking trips...it will be obvious what's going on within a short amount of time. Ellen isn't stupid."

Derek struggled to reply, and something occurred to me.

"You're not planning on it lasting that long."

"I didn't say that."

I scooted back, needing a little distance. "You're still intent on a wife and kids. I'm just for fun?"

He didn't answer fast enough, and I stood up.

"No, Derek. I don't want that. You might think I'm just a kid, or a poor-ass immigrant, or someone just looking for a good time, but I'm not. And I don't want to be your temporary toy while you keep looking for a woman."

"What do you want?" He stood too. "A fucking ring?"

"No!" I took a deep breath. Getting angry at him wouldn't help. "Look. I wasn't looking for a relationship when I moved here. It was the furthest thing from my mind. I was prepared work really hard, as many hours as I had to every single day to make it in this country. And that's what I'm doing. I don't want to go backward."

"I'm not asking you to," he snapped.

"But you are." I struggled with how to explain what I wanted to say. "I moved here for me. Because I have a dream for myself. Then I met you, and that dream changed."

He moved toward me, but stopped, hands fisted at his sides. "How?"

"Now I find myself thinking about you and us as part of my dream. I came here to make a new life, and I want you to be part of it. Not in secret, like we're ashamed of each other. Out in the open."

He flinched. "I can't."

"Then I can't, either. I don't want to live two lives, Derek. One in public and one in private, neither of them one hundred percent *me*. And I don't want to hide." I lowered my voice even more. "I've lived that way already. It doesn't feel good."

He was silent.

"If you want to be somebody else for the rest of your life, go ahead. I don't."

"You don't understand how hard this is for me," he said through clenched teeth. "It's not about you."

"Is that what you think?" I moved a step closer. I wanted him to see my face. "I've never felt like I was good enough for you. This feels like you're agreeing with me. And that hurts."

"It's not that at all!" he burst out. "You're everything to me. And the way you make me feel—no one has ever, ever made me feel those things before. I've never wanted anyone the way I want you."

"But you're willing to give that up?"

"No! That's why I'm asking you to stay." He grabbed my head and sealed his mouth over mine, and the temptation to say *fuck it, I'll stay for this feeling* nearly overwhelmed me. He pulled back a little. "Please don't leave. You're the only one who understands me."

I hesitated, feeling like I was being ripped in two. "Then that should be worth something more than this." Gently, I pushed his arms down and walked out of the room.

He didn't come after me.

Upstairs, I got into bed, wishing I didn't have to sleep

here. It would be hard knowing Derek was right across the hall and hurting, especially when I knew I could take away the pain. But that would only be on the surface. Deep down, he'd never be at peace with himself if he didn't live the way he felt. If I gave in, if I stayed, he'd only keep putting that off. He'd never let me love him the way I wanted to. He'd never really let me in, even if he loved me too.

Then he would leave me.

No. It would be foolish to stay. I had to walk away, for both of us. My only hope was that he'd miss what we had enough to change the way he thought. If he didn't, I'd have to deal with the loss and move on.

But at least I'd have given us a real chance.

AFTER A SLEEPLESS NIGHT, I waited until I heard Derek leave for work, then I packed up my meager belongings and ordered an Uber. I left the clothing he'd loaned me folded on the stripped guest room bed, his old laptop on the kitchen table, and the house key he'd given me on the counter next to a note.

Thank you for everything. I will always be grateful.

Maxim

My head felt cloudy from the lack of sleep, but I didn't want to make coffee in his kitchen. I would get some breakfast somewhere eventually. Right now, I just wanted to leave. The memories were getting to me.

Right there is where he kissed me for the first time.

Right there is where I dropped to my knees.

Right there is the door he knocked on in the middle of the night.

Right there is where we argued and tumbled to the ground.

Right there is where he first tasted me.

Right there is where he said *I want to fuck you.*

Right there is where he asked me to stay the night in his bed.

Right there is where he left me a note that said *you're cute when you're sleeping.*

And right there...right there is where he stood when I walked away.

I went out to wait on the front porch, too restless and upset to stay inside, pulling the door shut behind me. It locked with a heartless click, and that was that.

THIRTY-THREE

DEREK

I DIDN'T SLEEP at all.

All night I lay there, my body still sore, my mind a jumble of anger and frustration and hurt, my heart splintered into bits.

He said no. He was leaving. He didn't want me enough to stay.

How could he do this to me? How could he make me fall for him this way, turn my life upside down, make me doubt everything I believed in and wanted and worked for, and then walk away?

He was acting like a child, wanting all or nothing. It wasn't that simple. He didn't get it. He didn't know how hard it had been for me to ask him not to go. He didn't know what it had cost me. I'd had to admit to myself that I wasn't strong enough to bear the punishment I'd brought on myself, that I was *weak weak weak*, that I wanted what he made me feel more than I wanted to be straight.

Part of me knew I was being a selfish prick. That asking him to stay was a short-term fix to a long-term problem, a Band-Aid over a gaping wound. It would make me feel good temporarily, but what about the future? What if I never got him out of my system? What if things between us only got better? Or what if I met the right woman, the one who could make me fall for her, the one who could do for me what Maxim could? That was still a possibility, wasn't it? So I should be glad Maxim had left. He'd saved me the trouble of breaking things off later.

Because all the reasons we couldn't be together still existed. I didn't want to be gay. I wasn't. It was just him. This was simply a roadblock on the way to the right kind of future. A test. I'd always been good at tests, and there was no reason I couldn't pass this one. I'd had my fun, my fling, my side trip, and now it was done.

But I punched my pillow a few times and buried my face in it, full of rage. I wished I could scream. I wished I could tear myself limb from limb. I wished I could drink myself into a stupor so that I wouldn't feel this hopelessness, this loss, this fear that I'd never be happy no matter what I did.

It was fucking hell. But I deserved it.

I DRAGGED my ass out of bed around five the next morning, skipped the gym, and got ready for work. I was bleary-eyed and exhausted and still sore as fuck. But the memory was worth it—I hadn't changed my mind about that.

My anger from the night before had mellowed somewhat, but the despair remained. I figured I'd throw myself into work and try not to think about him leaving my house for the last time. Try not to remember all the things he'd said last night. Try not to see his point of view. But it was impossible.

You're still intent on a wife and kids.

I don't want to be your temporary toy.

I don't want to live two lives.

I'm not going backward.

I've never felt like I was good enough for you. I know that I'm not. This feels like you're agreeing with me. And that hurts.

Sitting at my desk behind my closed office door, I closed my eyes and slouched in my chair. Fuck. I'd hurt him. It wasn't true, what he'd said, but I knew it looked that way. Of course he was good enough—more than good enough. Too good. He deserved someone who could accept him, who could share one life with him, who could love him the way I wanted to, but couldn't. Openly, fully, unconditionally.

It killed me to think of him with someone else. Those hands on someone else's skin. That laugh in someone else's ear. That endless enthusiasm for life brightening someone else's day.

I kept looking at my phone, hoping he'd text me something, anything. A question about his new place. A request for help. Even if he just needed a ride somewhere, I'd have run out to pick him up.

But he didn't reach out.

What do you expect? You insulted him. It's better this way.

Still, when I got home later that night and saw his note, my chest tightened painfully. Before I could help it, I was wandering into his room. It smelled like him. He'd stripped the bed, or I'd probably have gotten in it and wrapped myself up in the sheets he'd slept in last night. I missed him already. His clothes were gone from the closet and dresser—I checked all the drawers—and his phone wasn't on the nightstand. I sat on the bed and opened the drawer.

My heart kicked up. He'd left his notebook.

Don't do it.

But I did it. Of course I did. It was the one piece of him I had access to, the one thing that might ease some of this loneliness.

I opened to a random page, glad to see it was in English, then started flipping through, as if skimming it would make it less of an invasion of privacy. Phrases jumped out at me.

So unexpected...this thing between us...wants to deny it... a truth about him no one else knows...never wanted someone like this...love his arms around me while we sleep...can't stop thinking about him...wish I could be what he wants...it's so good...a turning point for us...know what I want...include me in his life...never imagined myself with children, but...I'm in love with him...

In love with him?

My eyes scanned every word on the last page before I could stop them, my insides churning. He must have penned them last night.

He asked me not to move out tomorrow, but not because he wants to be with me for real. I'd hoped that after this weekend, he might think I was worth taking a risk for, worth coming out for, but he doesn't. He still wants to hide. It would be so easy to give in, to stay and be with him on any terms. But I can't. I want more. I want to share my life. I want him to be proud of me. I want to make him happy, and I think I could if he'd let me. But not in secret.

I'm done hiding. I'm in love with him, and walking away tonight was one of the hardest things I've ever done, but I did it for him as well as for me. He'll never be happy if he doesn't face the truth.

I clapped the notebook shut and dropped it onto the bed as if it had bitten me. I shouldn't have read it. Now I had his words in my head. *I'm in love with him.* Was he? Did he feel that way? Why hadn't he ever said it?

Same reason you didn't, asshole. He's scared.

Groaning, I flopped back on the bed and threw an arm over my eyes. I was a selfish prick. I wanted to hear him say it. I needed to hear him say it. I was sick and that was the cure. If I could just hear him admit he felt the way I did, then I wasn't alone.

I took my phone from my pocket.

Stop it, you self-serving fuck.

I didn't. I texted him. **I miss you already. Call me?**

Five minutes went by. Then ten. Then twenty.

I frowned. But he was at work, right? Maybe he hadn't seen my message yet.

I went downstairs and ate leftovers for dinner without tasting anything. I loosened my tie. I poured some whiskey.

An hour passed. Then another.

He had to have seen it by then! Was he ignoring me? How could he! If he loved me, he'd at least respond to my text.

Maybe he didn't have his phone. That had to be it. He didn't have his phone and he was as miserable as I was, thinking I didn't care about him. I had to fix it.

I left my glass of whiskey half-finished on the counter, raced upstairs to grab the notebook, and jumped into my car.

I parked in the garage down the street and rushed down the sidewalk to the bar, then burst through the door like an angry cowboy in an old western. I must have looked ridiculous, but I didn't care.

Ellen saw me right away and came over, her face concerned. "Hey. You okay?"

"Where's Maxim? I need to see him."

"I think he's in the basement pulling some liquor. You know where it is?"

"I'll find it." I took off, leaving her blinking after me and probably totally confused, but I didn't stop. Through the kitchen. Down the stairs. Around the corner.

He was alone among the shelves, squinting at a list in the dim light.

I went at him hard, backing him against the brick wall, crushing my mouth against his, wanting to say what I came here to say but terrified to end the kiss, because what if it was the last one I ever got?

Finally he pushed me away. "Derek, what the hell? You can't do this."

"I have to. I'm in love with you."

"What?"

"I'm in love with you. And you're in love with me." I held up the notebook.

His eyes went wide. "You read my notebook?"

Fuck. "Just the last page," I said, squirming. "And I'm sorry, okay? I know it was wrong, and I'm sorry, but—I had to know how you felt."

He grabbed the notebook from me. "You knew how I felt. I told you last night."

"You didn't tell me you loved me." My heart was racing so hard. "Do you?"

"Would it have made a difference?"

"Yes!" I yelled, although I wasn't at all sure I meant it.

"Oh, really? What difference? Are you ready to love each other for real? Or do you want to keep it hidden?"

"I'm—I'm protecting it! If we put it out there in the open, it will be ruined, Maxim. Right now it's something beautiful and extraordinary and special. It belongs to us. If other people know, they'll fucking vilify it. They'll make it ugly. They'll say it's crazy and wrong. If we keep it for ourselves, it stays safe."

He shook his head. "No, it doesn't. You're the one making it ugly, Derek. Not anyone else. And I won't be part of it."

"But—"

"You should go now. You said what you came here to say."

Frustrated and helpless, I ran a hand through my hair, feeling my eyes go damp. "I don't know what to fucking do. I'm being torn apart from the inside out. I don't want to live without you in my life, but I can't bring myself to change my mind."

"Then this is goodbye." His voice shook. "I want nothing more than to be with you, to take care of you and let you take care of me. I'd even begun to imagine a future for us—a *family*. To me, *that's* what's crazy about this. You're turning away a chance at your dream because it doesn't look exactly like you wanted it to. But I can't make it into anything else."

He was right. And he was so much smarter and perceptive and stronger than I'd given him credit for.

"Go," he said firmly. "I have work to do."

But I couldn't leave. "Tell me first. I want to hear the words." I'd never hated myself more than I did at that moment. But I needed him to love me.

"I love you." His eyes held mine, his voice was calm. "Now go punish yourself for it."

With a sob caught in the back of my throat, I turned away and stormed up the stairs, back through the kitchen and restaurant and out the door.

He knew me too well. He *saw* me.

It was painful, like the desert sun on skin already burned and blistered.

I didn't sleep at all.

THIRTY-FOUR

MAXIM

DAYS WENT BY.

I fixed up my apartment. I worked long hours. I invested in an old laptop I found for sale on Craigslist. I researched immigration law.

I enrolled in an online English class I could afford. I inherited a bicycle that needed work from a regular at The Blind Pig and repaired it, so I wouldn't have to pay for the bus all the time.

And I missed Derek every fucking minute.

I tried to put on a smile at work, but it was hard. Finally, a week after Derek had left me in pieces in the basement at work, Ellen approached me toward the end of a shift.

"Come on, my friend. We're checking out early and we're going to get a drink somewhere. I've had all I can take of this miserable silence."

I didn't have it in me to argue. And I needed a friend.

We walked down the street to another bar, and slid onto

stools next to each other. She ordered a glass of wine, and I asked for a beer, and while we waited for it, she propped an elbow on the bar and he chin in her hand.

"Spill it."

"Spill it?"

She nodded. "Spill it. It means talk. Tell me what's bothering you."

I shook my head. "I can't. It would mean betraying a confidence."

"Okay, then I'll guess." She put her hands in her lap and sat up taller. "This is about you and my brother. You have feelings for each other. He's being stubborn and won't admit it, so you had to walk away."

My eyes went wide. "That's a little creepy, even for me."

She smiled briefly. "I'm good." Then she sobered again. "But this is not good. Tell me how you feel about it."

I struggled with the decision. If I was honest with her, it meant outing Derek, and that wasn't my place.

"If you're worried about telling me Derek is gay, or at least gay where you're concerned, you can forget it. He's made that really fucking obvious all by himself."

"He has?"

She rolled her eyes. "Yes! You know I had my suspicions anyway, and then that night at dinner at his house, there was just this...vibe in the room. I could see it between you. Then he broke it off with Carolyn. Then he's coming up here all the time, and it sure as heck wasn't to see his sister." She laughed, shaking her head. "The way his face lit up when he saw you made it pretty obvious. His aura was totally changed. Then there was the romantic weekend in Laguna Beach. I'm not sure what about that plan he thought said 'I'm totally straight, nothing to see here,' but that pretty much confirmed it, if I'd had any remaining doubt."

All I could do was stare at her.

"Maxim, I think it's wonderful." She smiled, putting a hand on my arm. "Really."

Our drinks arrived, and I took a long pull on my beer. "He doesn't."

"What happened? Can I ask?"

I was in desperate need of a sympathetic ear but wanted to be careful. "After the weekend away, I was ready to be more open. He wasn't."

"Give him time. He's so stubborn, Maxim, always has been. And this is a huge thing for him. I told you how we grew up—he's fighting all those demons."

I nodded. "I get it. But I don't think he really wants to win that fight. He's hoping it goes away."

She sighed and took a sip of her wine. "It isn't going to."

I lifted the bottle to my lips again rather than answer.

"So now what? Have you even spoken since you moved into your apartment? What about that night he came barging in here needing to see you?"

"That was the day I moved out. He...didn't want me to go."

"But he didn't want you to stay?"

"No, he did. But in secret. I couldn't do that to myself." The rest of what we'd said, I kept to myself. Some things were too private and painful to share.

"No, nor should you. God, he drives me crazy sometimes. Is he worried about our parents?"

I nodded. "Among other things."

"I hope he's not worried about me." She touched her chest. "I think it's fucking perfect. And our brother David would too. We never bought into all that sin bullshit."

"I think Derek did," I said quietly.

She nodded and drank more wine. "In a way, yes. But part of me thinks it was more about pleasing the adults in his life. He bought in because it was expected of him."

"Maybe."

"I mean, there's a lot of things wrong in this world. Terrible, cruel people. Abuse and injustice. For God's sake, this is *love*. Some part of Derek must see that."

"I wish he did."

"And my dad is tough on him, even to this day, but part of me thinks my dad would appreciate that he'd raised a man strong enough to stand up for himself and what he wanted."

I shrugged. I'd never met their dad, and I probably never would, so what did I know?

She put her hand on my arm again. "I'm sorry, Maxim. I wish I knew how to make it better."

"It's okay. There's nothing either of us can do. It's Derek's choice."

"Maybe he'll still make the right one," she said hopefully.

"I don't know. I think his beliefs are too deeply ingrained. And please don't say anything to him." Suddenly I remembered what Derek had said about her inability to keep a secret.

"I won't," she assured me. "Even if he comes to me, I won't tell him we talked. You're safe."

"Thank you. And thanks for listening."

"Thank you for trusting me." She tipped her head onto my shoulder. "I'll be praying for you. To the gods, the goddesses, the universe, and anyone else who will listen."

I laughed a little, but deep in my heart, I felt it was

hopeless. The longer we went without talking, the more convinced I became that Derek had been able to move on.

"Have you seen him?" I asked, trying not to sound too emotional.

"No, I haven't." She picked up her head and looked at me. "I think he's holed up at home, alone and miserable. He hasn't even called me."

It only made me feel worse.

THIRTY-FIVE

DEREK

I WASN'T SLEEPING. I barely ate. I skipped the gym practically every other day. I had no energy, and everything depressed me.

My house was too quiet. My bed too empty. My life too lonely.

What was he thinking? How was he doing? Was he working a lot? Did he like his new apartment? Did he miss me at night the way I missed him?

After ten days of this torture, I found myself talking to strangers at the grocery store just for human connection. I knew I could have called Gage or Ellen, but I didn't trust myself not to blurt the truth and melt into a pathetic puddle of shame and humiliation for what I'd done.

Finally, I broke down and went into The Blind Pig on my way home from work one Friday night. I hadn't seen Maxim in almost two weeks, and my hands shook as I pushed open the door. Had it really only been a month since I'd come in here to pick him up? So much had changed since then. I wasn't the same person at all.

So why are you trying to act like it?

I pushed the voice aside and walked to the bar, careful to appear cool and casual. I didn't look around for him until I'd ordered a beer and counted to twenty. Then I let myself glance around, as if I wanted to see what was new here.

He was wiping down a high-top table behind me, and I couldn't tell if he'd seen me yet. I whipped my head around and focused on my beer again. My heart thundered in my chest, and I felt short of breath.

"Hey, stranger." Ellen appeared behind the bar and grinned at me. "Haven't seen you in forever. Been busy?"

"Yeah." I ran a hand through my hair. "Work stuff. Lots of work stuff."

"Dad running you ragged?"

"Something like that." I dragged on the beer bottle, sucking it down.

"Well, it's good to see you. Can I get you something to eat?"

I wasn't hungry in the slightest, but it would give me a reason to sit there. "Sure. Bring me whatever."

She sighed. "One whatever, coming right up."

As soon as she disappeared behind the kitchen door, I looked for Maxim again, but he wasn't behind me anymore. Scanning the room again, I found him in a far corner, loading empty glasses onto a tray. When he brought them behind the bar, he spotted me.

I smiled before I could help myself. My throat was dry. My chest was tight. He'd gotten a haircut, and it looked fantastic. And those eyes—how could I have forgotten how blue they were? His hands, fuck I missed his hands. I missed everything.

By contrast, he did not look happy to see me. He washed the glasses with a stony look on his face, and then came over to me. "Derek."

"Maxim." I held out my hand, and he shook it across the bar. "Good to see you."

He nodded shortly. "You too."

"Got a minute to talk outside?" Fuck. What was I doing?

"Not really."

"Oh. Well, how are things going?"

"Fine."

"Like your new place?"

"Yeah."

"And the job is still good?"

"Yeah."

This was not going smoothly. *If I could just get him alone...* "What time are you off tonight? I thought maybe we could catch up a little. Want to come by the house?" I didn't even care if anyone heard me.

"Sorry. I can't."

I frowned. It had taken a lot for me to come in here tonight, and to ask him to come over when any number of people around me could have heard. Why did he have to be so stubborn?

We stared at each other for a long, tense moment before he spoke. "I have to get back to work."

"Okay. See you." I gripped the beer bottle so hard I was surprised it didn't shatter.

When Ellen brought my food a little later, I asked how he'd seemed the last couple weeks.

"Fine, just fine," she said airily before walking away.

It pissed me off. How could he be fine? Out of the corner of my eye, I saw him smiling at someone at the end of the bar. Leaning *way* out of my seat to see who it was, I felt fire shoot through my veins when I saw it was another guy. Tall, dark hair, bearded, thin but muscular. Obviously attracted to Maxim, judging by the way he touched his arm and laughed at something he'd said.

I fumed, my nostrils flaring. It was one thing to watch women flirt with him, but it was another thing altogether when a man did it. I wanted to break that guy's hand for touching Maxim.

I turned my attention back to my plate and ate, but I couldn't have even told you what it was.

I'd never been so miserable. Had I fucked everything up? What if I'd made a mistake?

I needed to talk to someone, but who?

THE NEXT DAY WAS SATURDAY, and after a grueling workout at the gym, I came home, showered, and went out for breakfast. I hated eating alone in my kitchen now. Sitting by myself at a table for two, I ordered eggs, bacon, and potatoes, and tried not to feel sad about the empty chair across from me. Two women passed by my table on their way to the door, and one of them stopped.

"Hey, Derek."

I looked up and saw Carolyn. "Oh, hi."

"Here by yourself?"

"Yeah." I must have looked pretty downhearted about it, because her brow wrinkled with concern.

"Want some company?"

I shrugged. "Sure."

"Give me one second. I was just leaving, so let me say goodbye to my friend." She patted my arm. "Be right back."

A moment later, she returned and ordered a cup of coffee. "So catch me up with you. What's going on?"

I studied her for a moment. She looked pretty, no makeup on, hair in a ponytail, relaxed and happy. I envied her. "Let's talk about you first. What's new?"

She chatted about her marathon training, her new niece, her job, and then she blushed, a girlish smile brightening her face. "And I met someone."

"You did?" My food had arrived and I paused with my fork halfway to my eggs. "That's great."

"He *is* great," she gushed. "He's a runner too, and we met at the shoe store. He just moved down from San Francisco. We have such a good time together."

"Wow." I poked at my potatoes. "I'm really glad to hear that."

"Thanks. I have a good feeling about him. But enough about me." She waved a hand in the air. "What about you? How's work? How's life? You look a little down."

I lifted my shoulders, terrified of opening my mouth.

"Derek, what is it?" She took a sip from her coffee, then set down the mug and touched my hand. "Look, I know things didn't go the right way for us, but I'd like to be friends. And I'm a really good listener. If you—"

"You were right," I blurted. "About me. And Maxim. You were right."

Her mouth fell open. "I was?"

"Yes."

She took it in, eventually nodding. "Okay. Well. That explains some things."

I closed my eyes and exhaled, then felt her hand on my wrist. "Hey, I don't mean that in a bad way. It's more of a relief for me. I could not figure out what I was doing wrong."

"You didn't do anything wrong."

"I knew that, rationally." She gave me a shy smile. "But women fret about these things. I'm very happy to hear it wasn't something I did or didn't do."

"It wasn't," I assured her.

"So what's the problem?" She picked up her coffee again. "He doesn't have the same feelings?"

"No. He does," I said glumly.

She blinked at me. "So...you should be together. Try it out."

"It's not that simple," I said irritably. "I can't just suddenly be gay. What would people think?"

"Fuck people!" The outburst was surprising, coming from her. "If they're not happy for you, then fuck them! Maybe they don't realize how hard it is to meet someone you like that likes you back the same way."

I thought about that, shoved food around on my plate. "People will talk about me."

"Let them talk. You know who you are."

"They'll say mean things. They'll turn what he and I feel into something ugly."

"Who. Cares." She set her cup down hard. "I'm serious, Derek. You can't live your entire life trying to please other people. You'll go crazy. You'll never be happy. And you know in your heart it's not ugly."

"But it's...it's how I was raised. To think of it as wrong. To think of it as a defect. To think of myself as *off* in some way. It made me work that much harder to be right."

She leaned forward in her chair, her arms folded on the table. "So what do you want? To be *right* in some meaningless, outdated, unfair, inhuman way? Or to be *happy*?"

"But I want a family," I said. "I want to be a father."

"So have a family. Be a father."

She sounded like Gage, like it was so easy. "I don't know if I could do that to my kids. Raise them in such a—"

"Loving home? Look, even if Maxim isn't the one, there is no reason why you can't have children. You'd be a great dad, Derek." She reached out and touched my arm again. "You're *going* to be a great dad. You could do it on your own. You're a caretaker. You're kind and sensitive and strong."

"I'm not." I shook my head. "I'm not strong at all. Maxim's the strong one. He told me he loved me, but he had to walk away if I wouldn't come out about us."

She bit her lip. "Do you love him?"

I nodded, my throat going tight.

"Then you know what to do. Trust me, Derek. This doesn't happen every day. When you feel that for someone, you grab onto it. And you don't let go."

Swallowing hard, I shoved a bite of breakfast in my mouth. I wanted to do what she said. But I wasn't there yet.

ANOTHER WEEK WENT BY, during which I went over and over what Carolyn had said. What Maxim had said. What I felt in my heart. What I wanted for the future. I'd thought I would feel better, more righteous as time went on, but I didn't. All I felt was sad and confused and sorry and lonely—so, so lonely.

I couldn't go on like this. I either had to fucking be a man and get over it, or be a man and own up to it.

Around five P.M., I got a text from Gage. **Hey, just a reminder about Will's 6th bday party on Sunday. 3:00.**

I texted him back. **Sounds good. You free for a beer tonight?**

He replied after ten minutes. **The ball and chain shall release me for two hours between seven and nine. Does that work?**

I replied that it did and we made plans to meet. My stomach was not okay, and my brain said this was crazy, but for once, I felt like maybe I'd breathe easier tonight when I tried to sleep.

I'd come to a decision.

THIRTY-SIX

DEREK

"SO I HAVE to tell you something." I wasn't in the mood to put it off. I'd waited until our beers arrived, and that was long enough.

"Okay." Gage looked at me a little funny.

"I'm in love with someone."

His jaw dropped. "Seriously? That's great, man. Who is she?"

I shook my head, closed my eyes, and braced myself. When I opened them again, I spoke the truth. "It's not a she, it's a he. It's Maxim."

I'd thought it would nauseate me. I'd thought it would feel wrong. I'd thought it would be the hardest thing I'd ever done. But it wasn't. Actually, the truth had skated pretty easily off my tongue.

Gage squinted at me like he might have heard wrong, mouth agape. "What?"

"It's Maxim," I said, my confidence growing. Fuck, this

felt good. How had I not guessed how good this would feel? "I'm in love with Maxim."

"Goddammit!" He closed his eyes and pressed his lips together. "Do you know what this means? I lost the bet."

"The bet?"

"Yeah." Gage took a long swallow of his beer. "Lanie bet me after that night at your house, when we all had dinner, that you guys had a thing. I didn't see it *at all*."

I blinked in surprise. "Fuck. Really? Carolyn said the same thing."

Gage nearly choked on his beer. "Are you kidding me? How am I so dense?"

"Don't feel bad. I worked really hard not to let it show. I worked really hard not to feel it at all."

"Did you?" He looked at me sympathetically. "That's got to be hard."

"Yeah." I shook my head. "But it didn't work. I still feel it."

"Does he?"

"He did a couple weeks ago. But I fucked it up."

"How?"

"I told him we had to stay a secret. It hurt him."

"I get it. That would hurt."

It felt like he punched me. "Yeah. But I wasn't ready to accept it yet—the fact that I wanted to be with a guy."

Gage thought for a moment, took another drink. "Have you always felt like that? Attracted to guys?"

The back of my neck got hot. "Sort of. From the time I was young, I had the occasional feeling for someone. But I was always able to ignore it."

His expression turned guilty. "I feel kind of bad that I never knew or guessed this about you. We've been best friends forever."

"Don't feel bad. I did everything I could to hide it. And I liked girls too. It wasn't really that big of an issue."

"I was just going to ask that. If you'd been faking it with women."

"Not necessarily. But it's been a really long time since I've had good chemistry with a woman. And I've never had chemistry with anyone like I do with Maxim."

"Wow. So what now?"

I took a deep breath. "Now I try to figure out where to go from here, I guess. How to be honest about my feelings. How to accept this about myself. How to convince Maxim to give me another chance."

"Tell me what to do to help you," he said seriously, setting his beer bottle down. "Lanie and I will do everything we can."

"Can I bring a guest to the birthday party Sunday?"

He grinned. "Absolutely."

I WAS TEMPTED to go right from there to The Blind Pig, but I didn't want to say what I had to say to Maxim in public. I texted my sister.

Need to talk. Can you meet me for breakfast tomorrow?

She replied within ten minutes. **Sure!**

We set the time and place, and I drove home, feeling hopeful for the first time in weeks. I'd done it—I'd told the truth about myself to someone, and he'd been supportive.

I could breathe.

"SO WHAT'S UP?" Ellen pulled her hair into a ponytail, then picked up her coffee cup.

My stomach was jittery. Telling Gage had felt easier, for some reason. I opened my mouth to speak, closed it, took a sip of coffee, fussed with my napkin in my lap. "I have to tell you something, but it's difficult to say."

"Let me help. You and Maxim."

I stared at her. "Yeah. How'd you know?"

She rolled her eyes. "Because I'm your sister and sisters know everything. But really, anyone with two eyes and half a brain could have guessed it."

"Really?"

"Really. You weren't fooling anyone. Not very well, anyway."

"Huh." I scratched my head.

"But I get why you tried to. This isn't easy for you."

"No." I frowned. "It isn't. And Mom and Dad—"

"Are not part of this. These are *your* feelings and you have to own them. I know what Mom and Dad think, but if they love you, and they do, they will want you to be happy."

"They might never accept this, or him."

She shrugged. "Then it will be their loss. Maxim is amazing."

"He is."

"So give them a chance to accept it. This is a big change, and it might take some getting used to. But it's okay." She leaned forward and ruffled my hair. "You're okay."

"Stop it." Laughing, I pushed her hand away and tried to fix my hair.

She grinned and sat back, picking up her coffee cup again. "Have you talked to Maxim yet?"

"No. Is he working tonight?"

"He's supposed to."

"Maybe I can catch him before he goes in. I don't really want to do it in public."

"Isn't that the point?"

I frowned. "Yes and no. He's still Russian. Just because he wants to be open about the relationship doesn't mean he'd be comfortable with a big scene at work."

"True. But I still think you should talk to him as soon as possible. He's been really sad about this."

My heart squeezed. "He's talked about it?"

"Not much. But I'm good at reading people. Don't drag this out. You guys deserve to be happy, and life is short."

"You're right. I don't want to live this way anymore. I suddenly feel like I've wasted so much time pretending to be someone else."

"Does your real self still have the thing about paper napkins?"

I glared at her. "Yes."

She laughed. "Good. You can't totally take away my big brother. I kind of like him."

"Thanks. Hey, can he have tomorrow off? I want to bring him to Gage's son's birthday party."

She smiled back. "That's a great idea. Absolutely."

AFTER BREAKFAST, I went to the mall to pick out a gift for Will. I roamed the aisles of the toy store aimlessly, trying to think of what a six-year-old boy would like, but coming up empty. When I noticed a kid who looked about that age standing with his father in the Lego section, I decided to ask for advice.

"Excuse me. I have to buy a present for someone who's

turning six. Can you maybe point me in the right direction?"

"Oh, I bet Mason can. He's six, too." The guy ruffled his son's hair. "Which one do you like best, Mase?"

"This one." He pointed to a box with a big Lego helicopter on it.

"We did like that one," his father agreed, pushing his glasses up his nose.

"Perfect. Sold." I took the box off the shelf and tucked it under my arm.

"There you are." Another man holding a shopping bag and the hand of a little girl maybe two or three years old walked toward us. "We thought we lost you. We're all set."

"Mason wanted to look at the Legos," explained the man in the glasses.

"Dad, can I get one please?" the kid asked the guy holding the hand of the girl.

"No," the men answered together.

"Let's go." The guy with the glasses smiled at me. "Have a good one."

I nodded and watched in awe as the perfect little family walked away from me.

Ellen would have called it fate. Maxim might have called it a sign from the universe. A month ago, I'd have rolled my eyes and called it a coincidence. Today, I saw it as something more—proof.

With love, anything was possible.

THIRTY-SEVEN

MAXIM

I SPENT the entire week after rejecting Derek's offer to talk outside at The Blind Pig wondering if I'd made the wrong decision. But every time I thought it through, I came to the same conclusion—I couldn't give in just because I missed him or because he looked as miserable as I felt or because it would feel so good to be in his arms again. I might not have had much in the way of material wealth, but I had pride.

So when he called me the following Saturday afternoon, I almost didn't pick up. But something in my gut told me to answer.

"Hello?"

"Hey, it's me. How are you?"

"Good. You?"

"Good. Hey, I've got something to show you. Can I give you a ride to work?"

I stiffened. "I don't know."

"Please, Maxim. Give me one hour, as a favor. That's all I need."

The thought of saying no to a favor for Derek was unthinkable. He'd done way more than one favor for me. Maybe he needed help with something. "But I have to be at work by five-thirty."

"No problem. I'll pick you up at three, okay?"

"Okay. See you then."

I WAS NERVOUS, waiting for Derek to arrive. I'd gone down to the parking lot so he wouldn't have to get out of his car and come get me, and I was sort of pacing back and forth on the sidewalk when he pulled up. At the sight of him behind the wheel, my stomach muscles clenched. I got in the passenger side and shut the door, my heart beating erratically.

"Hey," he said, smiling sideways at me. A little apprehensive, maybe, but much more relaxed than he'd been the last few times I'd seen him.

"Hey," I echoed warily.

"You look a little scared." He wore sunglasses, so I couldn't read his eyes, but his tone was light, teasing.

"Not scared. Just curious, I guess. Wondering what this is about."

"Let me show you." He pulled away from my complex. "It's a short drive. Twenty minutes or so."

I tried to think of where he might be taking me, but I couldn't.

"So tell me what's going on with you."

I miss you every day. "I've been working a lot."

"Ellen told me. That's great."

I'm lonely at night. "I bought a used laptop, and I'm taking an English course online. Mechanics and grammar, things like that."

"Good for you."

Nothing feels good without you. "And I met someone who works at Paramount as a screen writer."

"Really? Where?"

"He's a regular at the bar. Ellen introduced me. And he offered to let me shadow him at work a little bit, to get a feel for the job. I won't get paid, of course, it would be more as a favor, but I don't mind. Everyone has to start somewhere."

"Of course they do. That's fantastic, Maxim. I'm so happy for you."

"I wanted to tell you about it right away," I admitted. "But I wasn't sure I should call you."

"I understand." He didn't say anything else, and I wondered again where he could possibly be taking me.

A few minutes later, I recognized the neighborhood we were in, and I sat up taller in my seat. "The house."

He grinned. "The house."

"You bought it?"

"Not yet. I thought I should see it first. And I wanted you with me."

My pulse galloped away from me, taking my thoughts with it. What did this mean? Had he changed his mind about us?

He parked in the house's driveway, behind a small white Toyota. "That's probably the agent's car. She must be inside already. Before we go in..." He shifted in his seat to face me, removing his sunglasses and laying them in his lap. Then he reached over and took my hand. "I need to apologize. You were right. If we're going to be together, it should be out in the open. I'm so tired of feeling ashamed of myself. I don't want to pretend I don't feel this way anymore. It's not worth it."

I couldn't find words, so I squeezed his hand.

"And I hurt you," he went on. "I made you feel like you weren't enough, and that isn't true. I've never felt this way about anyone before, never trusted anyone so deeply. I've never wanted to change my life so drastically to be with someone, but I know it's the right decision." He took a breath. "Because you make me happy. You make me believe. You make me better. And none of my dreams matter if I can't share them with you." He pressed his lips to my fingers. "Say it's not too late."

"It's not too late," I managed, but my throat was so tight.

"Say you still want to be with me, even though I'm a grumpy old man who can't see the truth right in front of his face."

"Don't be ridiculous. Of course I do." I leaned forward and pressed my lips to his, and he took my head in his hands, deepening the kiss. It was the kind of thing he'd never have done in broad daylight before, even in his car. It filled me with hope.

He rested his forehead against mine, eyes closed, his thumbs brushing over my cheeks. "I was scared I'd lost you."

"Never. I've missed you so much."

"I missed you too. And we have some time to make up for." His meaning was unmistakable.

"We do," I agreed. "But maybe not right here. I don't want to be *that* open."

He grinned and let me go, slipping his sunglasses back on. "Me neither. Come look at this house with me. If the inside is what I'm hoping for, I'm going to buy it. From now on, I'm going to do more things that make me happy, and I won't care what anyone says."

We got out of the car and walked toward the porch. "I'm so glad you brought me here. And I'm proud of you."

His smile lit me up inside. "I'm proud of you, too."

WHEN WE WERE DONE at the house—it was exactly what Derek wanted, and he was going to put together an offer—he came into work with me. Ellen saw us walk in together, and watched us approach the bar with her eyebrows raised.

"Does this mean what I think it means?" she asked. "Detente?"

"Detente," Derek confirmed, sliding onto a chair.

"Can I stop pretending I don't know now?" She jumped up and down like a puppy.

He groaned. "You can stop. But don't—"

She squealed and came running around the bar to throw her arms around me.

"—make a big deal about it," Derek managed to finish before Ellen let go of me and strangle-hugged him so hard he choked. "Ellen. I can't breathe. Let go."

"Sorry," she said. "I'm just really, really emotional about this. It's so right." She grabbed both our hands and seemed to peer into the air around us. "Your auras are in perfect harmony."

I laughed as Derek rolled his eyes at his sister. "Oh, Jesus. Can I get a beer, please?"

"You got it." She beamed at the two of us. "Maxim, you want the night off?"

"Thank you, but no," I said. "I need all the shifts I can get."

"So responsible." She shook her head admiringly. "Okay, go get me some ice, please? I'll grab Derek's beer." Practically skipping back around the bar, she teased over her shoulder, "*Told* you it was fate!"

———

LATER, when Derek had eaten dinner and was ready to go, he caught my eye and motioned me over to where he stood by the door.

"Can I see you later?" he asked quietly.

My heart jumped. "I was hoping you'd ask."

He took my hand and pressed a key into my palm, then closed my fingers around it. "This is yours. Wake me up." Then he kissed me quickly on the lips, and walked out.

I tucked the key in my pocket and went back behind the bar, heat flushing my cheeks. A sink full of dirty glasses waited to be washed, but I stood there staring into space. *He kissed me. In public.*

"I saw that." Next to me, Ellen giggled. "I totally saw that, and so did a lot of people in here."

"It's kind of crazy, the change of heart," I said, smiling in disbelief. "It's like day and night or something."

She lifted her shoulders. "He knew what he wanted all along. He just needed a little push."

"Well, you gave it to him."

She shook her head. "Nope. You did. He saw the way you stood up for yourself and realized he could learn something from you."

"You think so?" I loved that idea.

"Believe me." Her grin was smug. "Sisters know everything."

I USED the key to let myself into Derek's house, a familiar rush moving through me as I climbed the stairs. After a quick shower in the guest room bath, I entered his room, my cock already rising in anticipation. It had only been a couple weeks, but it felt like forever.

I crawled under the covers and he reached for me, moaning deep and low as our bodies and mouths came together. Pressed skin to skin, we kissed and touched and murmured about all the places on each other's bodies we'd missed. We explored those places with hands and lips and tongues. We panted and groaned and fought off release until neither of us could stand it any longer.

"I want you inside me again. I need it." His voice was low and intense. "But I want to be on top this time."

A few minutes later he was lowering himself slowly onto my cock, the muscles in his abs flexed tight, his thighs clenching under my palms. I sat with my back propped against the headboard, watching in aroused disbelief as he took me deeper and deeper, until my entire shaft was buried within him.

His eyes were locked on mine as he struggled past the pain, his hands gripping my shoulders.

"Breathe," I whispered.

After a few tense moments, he began to move, rocking his hips over mine, slowly at first, in sensual rippling motions that made my jaw drop. "You're so beautiful," I whispered.

He leaned back a little, changing the angle, moving

faster, and then it was me who had to breathe deep, because the sight of him fucking me so expertly, using my body for his own pleasure, was enough to push me right over the edge. I fought back, trying to sustain this state of pure ecstasy, but his hands traveled down over my chest, and his fingertips brushed my nipples, and his body was so hard and male and muscular, from the thick flesh of his thighs to the ridges of his stomach to the bulge of his shoulders, and his cock was bouncing between us and I grasped it tight so he could fuck my hand too, and it was all too much, too hot, too hard, too tight, too impossible to hold on. A second later he was groaning and gasping and coming all over my hand and my chest and I let everything go, bursting wide open inside him in wild, uncontrollable spasms.

He shifted forward, kissing and kissing and kissing me like he'd never stop. "I love you," he said against my lips. "I'm so fucking in love with you. This is so much more than I ever knew I wanted. But God, I want it. I want everything. And I want to give you everything."

"You do. You have. This means everything to me—being with you."

He kissed me again, his hands tight around the back of my neck. "You might have to be patient with me."

"I'll do anything for you."

"Stay the night." He buried his face in my neck. "I can't let you go yet."

"Okay, baby."

"And tomorrow, will you come with me to Gage and Lanie's for their son's birthday party? Ellen said you could have the day off."

A shiver moved through me. "Are you serious? You're ready for that?"

"I'm ready. I want to be with you, Maxim. I love you, and fuck anyone who says it's not right."

"What about your parents?"

He sat back and looked at me. It was dark, but I could see his serious expression. "Fuck anyone who says it's not right," he repeated. "No matter who it is. *This* is who I am. *You* are who I love. It's *right*."

My throat got tight, and I nodded, swallowing hard. "It's right."

THIRTY-EIGHT

DEREK

I PARKED along the street as close to Gage and Lanie's house as I could get and turned off the car. My heart was beating a little quicker than usual, but I had no qualms about this decision.

"Ready?" I looked over at Maxim, who seemed much more nervous about it. His hands were fidgety, and he kept chewing his bottom lip.

But he nodded. "Ready."

We got out, and I grabbed the gift from the back seat. It was a perfect summer afternoon, sunny but not sweaty hot, a breeze coming from the hills. As we made our way down the sidewalk toward the house, I heard music and splashing and shouting.

"The kids can be a little crazy," I said apologetically.

"I'm used to kids. I've got a little sister."

"That's right, sometimes I forget that. I'd like to meet her."

He laughed. "She'd love that. Maybe she can come visit me. Stay in my fancy apartment."

"I meant to ask you about that last night, but I kept getting distracted by your body." I elbowed him playfully. "Do you want to keep your apartment?" We turned up the driveway, and the noise got louder. "It's totally up to you. I loved having you live with me, and you could save money, but I know you like your independence too."

"Let me think about it," he said. "I appreciate the invitation, but it might be good to have our own places for a while."

It would mean we would have to work harder to see each other, but I didn't want to push. I knew he didn't want to go backward, and I was willing to work for him. I took his hand and led him around the house toward the yard.

He squeezed my fingers. "You okay? You seem so calm, but I know this can't be easy."

God, he was so fucking sweet. I paused in the shade on the side of the house and gave him a quick kiss. "I'm a little nervous, yes. But it's the good kind of nervous. I'm excited. And proud. This morning, I woke up and felt completely happy. It almost feels like a new life. *Our* life. And this is just the beginning."

He smiled at me, the same warm, grateful smile he'd melted my heart with the night we'd met. "I love you."

I'd never grow tired of hearing that. "I love you, too."

We moved out of the shadows and into the sunlit yard hand in hand.

EPILOGUE

DEREK

"WANT to sit here for a few minutes?" I asked, glancing at two Adirondack chairs on the lawn at the Laguna Beach Ritz Carlton, as if I hadn't already chosen it as the perfect spot. "Watch the sun set before we go to dinner?"

"Sure." Maxim smiled, and my heart beat faster, the way it always did. But tonight was different.

We were celebrating six months together, the sale of the house I'd fixed up, and the completion of his first course in screenwriting.

We were also about to get engaged, but he didn't know that.

We sat down side by side, and I took a drink from the glass of champagne in my hand before setting it on the table between us. Maxim set his down too, and pulled out his phone to take a few pictures of the pink and orange sky as the sun sank beneath the hazy blue horizon. It was a pleasantly cool fall evening, wind rustling the palm trees overhead, the temperature hovering around sixty, but my skin felt warm beneath my jeans and gray sports jacket. I was glad I hadn't worn a tie.

"I almost forgot how beautiful it is here." He shook his head as he put his phone back into his jacket pocket. "A photo could never capture it."

I reached over and took his hand. "No. It couldn't."

He looked over at me, his blue eyes appearing even deeper in the fading light. "I'm remembering when we were here last time."

I smiled. "We've come a long way since then."

"We have." He looked out over the ocean again. "Every morning I wake up and wonder if it's all just a dream."

"I do the same. But then I open my eyes and you're there next to me, and I know it's real." Waking up next to him every morning was a gift I'd never take for granted. He'd kept his own apartment for a couple months, but after that I'd begged him to move in with me. We spent almost every night together anyway, and the nights we didn't, I missed him too much. I'd wasted enough time, and I didn't want to squander any more of it.

Not that the road here had been easy. My friends and siblings had accepted our relationship without question, but my parents were still struggling. At first they'd been mostly confused, then they'd ignored it, as if by refusing to acknowledge the truth it might simply go away. My father thought it was part of the "lunacy" that had caused me to cut back my hours at work so I'd have more time to devote to the house I'd bought, and told me I needed to go talk to a priest, like the devil had possessed me or something. But I stood my ground, stating that Maxim was part of my life now, and if they wanted a relationship with me, they had to accept him, too.

They were slowly coming around—we'd been invited to Thanksgiving dinner and it had gone well, if a little awkwardly—and it was Maxim who always reminded me to have patience with them. *Give them time*, he'd say whenever I got frustrated with their reluctant support. *Remember, it was hard for you too at first.*

He had the biggest heart of anyone I'd ever known.

We finished our champagne as the sun disappeared, bathing the lawn in twilight. "Should we go?" he asked, squeezing my hand.

"Yes." But once we stood, I turned to face him and slid my arms around his waist. "Just a second. There's something I want to say."

"Of course."

My legs trembled slightly as I took a deep breath. "Before you came into my life, I didn't know who I was. I had this idea about who I wanted to be, and I tried hard to fit that mold, but I never felt right in my skin. I think one of the reasons I was so concerned about neatness and order in my life on the outside was because I had no control over the inside. I didn't trust myself to feel the right things, so instead I focused on being perfect in other people's eyes, because I could never be perfect in my own. And I never let anyone see the real me."

Maxim put both arms around me, pressing his lips to my shoulder.

"Then I met you. For the first time, I trusted someone with all of me. I let someone in. And I did it because I looked at you and saw the part of myself I'd never understood and thought was wrong, but it was beautiful. Finally, with you, because of you, the pieces of me all made sense." My chest and throat grew tight. "I fell in love with you that very moment, and it happens all over again every time I look at you." I released him and reached into my pocket for the ring. My shaking fingers closed around the box, and I pulled it out as I dropped to one knee.

His eyes widened. "Oh my God."

"Every single day, I thank God you got on that plane. And your bag was stolen. And my sister called me. I don't know if I believe in fate, but I believe we were meant to be together, and I want to spend the rest of my life with you." I opened the box, revealing a thick platinum Cartier band. "Marry me."

"Oh my God," he repeated, his eyes tearing up. "Are you serious?"

"I'm serious."

He closed his hands over mine, leaned forward and kissed me, and I thought my heart was going to explode. "Yes. *Yes.*"

I stood up and slid the ring onto his finger, my sight going blurry with tears. He threw his arms around me and we held each other tightly. *"Ya lublu tebya,"* he whispered, which I knew now meant I love you. "Never in a million years did I think I could be this happy," he went on, his voice cracking. "You are everything to me. *Navsegda.*"

"What's that one again?"

"Forever."

The lump in my throat grew, and I swallowed hard as we let go. Then I turned him to face the hotel behind us, where Ellen was crouched about a hundred feet away on our second floor balcony, filming the entire episode on her phone. Next to her stood my brother and sister-in-law, and Gage and Lanie, and they all started cheering. "Say hi."

"Oh my God." Maxim put his hands to his face and burst out laughing before embracing me again, burying his face in my neck. "This is the best day of my life."

I laughed too. "This is only the beginning, babe. The best is yet to come."

A FEW MINUTES LATER, everyone met us out on the lawn with tears and hugs and smiles and more champagne. Ellen made a toast.

"To my big brother Derek, whom we all thought was being too picky all those years, but who knew all along that perfection was only six thousand miles and one stolen bag away. And to Maxim, for chasing the dream that brought him here and never giving up. I can't wait to call you my brother."

"Cheers!" shouted Gage, prompting a chorus of them.

"*Na zdorovie!*" I added, then looked at Maxim. "How did I do?"

"Perfect," he said, eyes shining. "You're perfect."

Later, after we'd celebrated at dinner and then some more in the bar, everyone went back to their rooms, and we discovered that ours had been decorated with rose petals and candles, courtesy of the hotel.

We lit the candles and appreciated it all for approximately one-point-five seconds before falling onto the bed and tearing at clothes. With the last of my psychological barriers broken, sex with Maxim was even more intense, unclouded by thoughts of guilt or shame. My desire for him was something I loved about myself rather than something I hated, and I reveled in all the ways I wanted to express it, whether it was getting inside his body or welcoming him into my own.

That night we took turns, flip fucking each other in hot, sweaty madness until we couldn't hold back anymore and watched one another fall apart in the most achingly beautiful moment two people could share.

Afterward, we lay wrapped in each other's arms, the balcony door open so we could hear the waves, the candlelight flickering, the air scented with rose petals and sex.

"I can't stop looking at the ring on your finger," I told him, lacing his fingers with mine above my chest.

"I want to put one on yours."

I smiled. "When do you want to get married?"

"Is tomorrow too soon?"

Laughing a little, I kissed his forehead. "Probably. But we don't have to put it off."

"Good. I don't want to wait." He pressed his lips to my chest for a moment. "I want to be your husband. I want to have a family with you. I want to belong to each other, now and forever."

My throat felt thick when I tried to swallow. "I want all of that too."

He looked up at me. "And years from now, we can tell our kids the story of the night we met."

"We were not a very likely love story," I said.

"We were better than that." He kissed my lips, and I felt it in my soul. "We were a *real* love story, and those never end."

I kissed him back, my heart swelling like the ocean, vast and full and deep.

THE END

ACKNOWLEDGMENTS

I am so grateful to the following people:

To David, co-author and friend, thank you for taking this journey with me, for creating characters I fell in love with, and for lessons in Russian, birthday cake, and gardening. I could never have told this story without you. *Ya lublu tebya!* (How did I do?)

To Kayti, Laurelin, and Sierra, thank you for reading my words, laughing at my jokes, and understanding every single one of my multiple personalities. Noir Mel doesn't have feelings, but if she did, they'd all be for you.

To Crimson, LeAnn, Margaret, Melissa, and Melanie, thank you for the constant support, encouragement, and inspiration (oh, the inspiration). You're the best crew ever. #gayngsters

To Jenn, Nina, Sarah, Shannon and the entire team at Social Butterfly, you're amazing at what you do! Thanks for helping me get noticed in a crowded room.

To Nancy, thanks for quick and fantastic editing. Someday I will give you more time. (This is probably not true, but I feel like I should say it.)

To Rebecca, for endless cheerleading no matter what I do.

To Flavia, for being the magical unicorn of foreign rights.

To Letitia, for another gorgeous cover and putting up with my requests.

To the incredible authors who found time to read early and offered such generous support: Sierra, Sarina, Ella, Brooke—you inspire me!

To Melissa Gaston, for taking this ride with me and driving this train when I can't. None of this would be possible without what you do for me every single day.

To my husband and kids, I love you more than bacon. That's a lot.

To my readers, who see beauty and worth in every kind of love story. I promise to keep them coming.

M.H.

Thank you to Melanie Harlow for being my friend and my partner in crime, and for bringing out the best in every love story.

D.R.

ABOUT THE AUTHORS

Melanie Harlow writes sexy, emotional romance about strong, stubborn characters who can't help falling in love. She's addicted to bacon, gin martinis, and summer reading on the screened-in porch. If she's not buried in a book or binging on Netflix, you might find her running, putting a bun in someone's hair, or driving to and from the dance studio. She lives outside Detroit with her husband and two daughters.

For David Romanov, STRONG ENOUGH is to a great extent autobiographical. Born in Russia and raised in Europe, he landed in the United States at the age of 24, where he learned a lot about cultural differences between East and West. David firmly believes in *the one* and learning through love. When he isn't traveling or educating Melanie in Russian culture, he enjoys books and the company of his husband and dog in Los Angeles.

Melanie, how did this co-writing project come about?

M: David came up with the idea and pitched it to me, and I loved the premise so much I knew I wanted to write it, but I didn't want to do it alone. I felt like his perspective was critical, since much of the story was autobiographical for him, and I'd never written M/M before. I was nervous! Having him along for the journey made me feel more confident. I was also looking to branch out, write something different, challenge myself. So it was perfect timing.

David, had you ever thought about writing a romance before? Will you write again?

D: I'd never thought of it before. In fact, I am not even a fiction kind of guy. But Melanie changed that—her books are more than just a story. I admire what she does and being a part of her book is an honor for me. So never say never!

Melanie, you've never co-authored before. What was the collaborative process like?

M: It was fantastic. I had a feeling it might be a challenge for me, since I had never co-written and really like control, but because he and I brought such different things to the table, our process was easy once we got the hang of it. David was the creative force behind the characters, the plot, many ideas for scenes and conversations, and of course all things Russian! I was more comfortable on the sentence level, since I had writing experience (and English is my first language, LOL), so he would send scenes or ideas to me and I'd flesh them out into chapters. There was a lot of back and forth to ensure we were depicting the characters authentically.

David, what was it like working with Melanie on this book?

D: Incredibly inspiring. Not a single time did she tell me I was wrong, but her own example always made me want to be better. She is a terrific writer, real friend, and the best partner in crime ever. To be completely honest, I didn't think she was serious when she suggested we co-write the book, and I had no idea how we were going to complete it on time. We actually finished it two days before the deadline. I have infinite respect for her as an author.

For both of you, what was the best part of co-writing?

M: We laughed a lot! And I loved having a partner to come up with ideas when I got stuck. Sometimes he would suggest something and at first I'd be like, "No, that won't work." But then after giving it some thought, I'd realize he was totally right! David might not have writing experience, but he has great instincts when it comes to character and story. I also learned a LOT writing this book.

D: On top of rolling on the floor laughing my butt off most of the time? Reading my ideas in Melanie's flawless execution. Somehow she knew exactly what I was trying to say and several times a thought crossed my mind that she's a telepathist. Teaching her about the in-and-out of gay things and Russian lifestyle was a lot of fun.

M: I repeat. I learned A LOT.

Melanie, were there specific things you had to teach one another about?

M: Yes! I think we could teach a class on cultural differences between a Russian and an American trying to write a romance together! It was a challenge to keep Maxim from sounding or acting too American sometimes. And of course, I had to write love scenes that were *very* different from what I'd written before. I wanted to be as authentic as possible, and getting inside the head of a gay man, Russian or not, was another challenge. But by the time the book was finished, David said, "I think you were a gay Russian in a former life." I was so happy.

David, what did you learn writing this book?

D: As an author, about developing the characters. See, I like nice people in real life and I wanted all the characters in the book to be perfectly good. But it just wasn't real. Every coin has two sides, and I had to learn to accept and love both sides of our characters.

M: I'm butting in even though this question wasn't for

me. I loved that he realized this once we started writing. At first, he was reluctant to let Derek act like a jerk or Maxim say anything too defensive. Gradually he came to see that good characters can be nice people who make bad decisions. It creates good tension!

Melanie, were you nervous about branching out into M/M?

M: Not really. I know M/M isn't every reader's thing, and that's fine. A lot of people like pineapple on pizza, and I think it's the weirdest thing ever. Response in my fan group when we announced the project was so fantastic, I was even more excited to release something different. I want to write all kinds of love stories. They're all beautiful to me! And I will definitely write M/M again.

D: How come you don't love pineapple on pizza? It's my favorite.

M: Fruit does not belong on pizza!

David, to what extent is STRONG ENOUGH autobiographical for you?

D: At least two thirds of the Russian character is based on me. I don't have a wild imagination so most of the things I wrote were inspired by my own experiences in real life. It was fun to play with the facts, change a couple of details, shape it into an independent character and watch his life unfold before our eyes. I don't use *Russkiy* words when I'm talking in English and I'm not as principled as Maxim, but we do have a lot in common. I do have a younger sister living back home, and when I moved to L.A. at Maxim's age, I had a similar story at the airport—that was real.

Melanie, what was your favorite part of the book David wrote?

M: The first kiss scene in the kitchen--I love how that went down. And I love the Russian stuff! I cracked up when I read this line: "I forgot my entire English." It was so perfect.

David, what was your favorite part of the book Melanie wrote?

D: The relationship between Derek and his sister, Ellen. I was laughing so hard every time they interacted. Melanie has a great sense of humor.

For both of you, which scene in the book is your very favorite and why?

M: Such a hard question! I guess if I had to choose, I love the scene where Maxim comes home and Derek says, "Fight me." Maxim really stands up for himself, and Derek is so tortured--it was fun to write. I also loved the scene where they're in the car and Derek is trying to help Maxim plan ahead and Maxim tells Derek about all the Russian superstitions. You can see how different they are, but how good they'd be together. And those superstitions kill me.

D: I love the Woody-Allen-turns in the book. Those make my heart beat faster. For example, when Derek accidentally runs into Carolyn. I love Carolyn's character and I asked Melanie to have her in the story as much as we could, even though the book was not about her. The part where Derek and Maxim meet for the first time left me very happy, too.

Some of the scenes can get pretty steamy.

Was there ever a time that you felt you needed to have a cigarette afterwards?

M: Hell. Yes. Those two together were hot.

D: I was on fire most of the book. I was pretty clear about what would happen in those scenes, but to describe them on paper was easier said than done. A couple of times, I had to send Melanie a literal outline of what they'd do, some pictures to illustrate it and said: "Please do it. I can't."

M: Totally true, he did. And I sympathized, because writing sex scenes is (for me) the hardest thing about writing a romance. But he made it easier by sending links to these unbelievably hot gifs. He'd be like "this, and then this, and then this." I'd start fanning myself and then hammer out the scene.

When and where do you write? Do you play music?

M: I write at my desk in my office mostly, but I move around the house sometimes. If I'm stuck, often a change of venue will help me look at things differently! I write during school hours, generally 8:30 AM to 3:30 PM. And I can't write with music--I need silence.

D: I feel like I'm doing the exact same thing, locked in the office with no music between the gym in the morning and my dog's walk in the evening. Actually, I wrote a couple of chapters on my phone while traveling.

Melanie, how do you decide what to put on the cover of a book? Who chose the cover of STRONG ENOUGH?

M: I like to have my cover photo before I even write the book. It's good inspiration! But that didn't happen with

STRONG ENOUGH. We actually didn't have a cover until right before release! It took a while to find the perfect photo. We both wanted a couple and a certain mood. David found the photo, and I'm so happy he did!

David, how did you find the photo? What did you like about it?

D: Tumblr. I spent days looking for a photo that would be STRONG ENOUGH and reflect a *feeling* rather than being simply sexual. And out of all photographers in the world we both liked only one, Vitaly Dorokhov, who turned out to be Russian. Some things are meant to be.

M: Totally agree!

What did you learn about yourselves while writing this book?

M: I learned that I'm capable of collaboration! I definitely want to co-write again. Sierra Simone, Laurelin Paige, Kayti McGee, and Helena Hunting are at the top of my list.

D: For the first time since moving to the United States, I was able to look at myself from a different perspective and observe the differences between a Russian and an American. I deeply love both and it's fascinating how distinct we are in the way we talk, act, think and even feel. I feel happy the readers of the book will learn the truth about what's really in the heart of a seemingly cold Russian personality.

If you were given the opportunity to start your lives over, what's one thing you would make sure you were strong enough to walk away from? What's one thing you would make sure you were strong enough to hold on to?

M: I think all my experiences, even the mistakes, have led me to where I am today, so I don't know that I'd change anything. But something I try to stay away from is engaging in negativity--sometimes that takes strength. And I always want to be strong enough to hold onto my family!

D: Every moment of my life I would hold onto things that in our world are often considered weaknesses: kindness and love. You must be really strong inside to act with kindness and from love. I believe evil and violence always come from a place of weakness.

Do you feel like you were destined to meet and become friends?

M: Absolutely. I think that all the time. And I know I never would have written this book without him. It's one of my favorite stories I've ever written!

D: From the moment I first saw Melanie at the hotel in Chicago. She is the reflection of every single quality I adore and admire in people.

M: I'm going to weep. That is the sweetest thing ever. There is something I truly admire about David, too, and I not only felt it but see it over and over when he meets my readers. When he's talking to you, he is fully focused on you. He sees you. He listens. He makes you feel like you are the most important person in the universe at that moment. I don't even know how he does it! But it's incredible. I tried to give Maxim that same quality.

Thank you to all the Harlots who submitted questions to us! We love you!

CONNECT WITH US!

Sign up here to be included on Melanie Harlow's mailing list! Once a month, you'll receive new release alerts, get access to bonus materials and exclusive giveaways, and hear about sales and freebies first!

http://subscribe.melanieharlow.com/g5d6y6

Are you a Harlot yet?

To stay up to date on all things Harlow (and Harlow/Romanov), get exclusive access to ARCs and giveaways, and be part of a fun, sexy and drama-free zone, become a Harlot!

https://www.facebook.com/groups/351191341756563/

Connect with Melanie:

Facebook: https://www.facebook.com/AuthorMelanieHarlow/

Amazon: http://amzn.to/1NPkYKs

Twitter: @MelanieHarlow2

Website: http://www.melanieharlow.com

Connect with David:

GoodReads: https://goo.gl/2Bekxz

Facebook: https://www.facebook.com/David-Romanov-Author-1487479804635708/

Amazon: http://amzn.to/2rWkfUO

ALSO BY MELANIE HARLOW

The Speak Easy Duet

Frenched

Yanked

Forked

Floored

The Tango Lesson (A Standalone Novella)

Some Sort of Happy

Some Sort of Crazy

Some Sort of Love

Man Candy

After We Fall

If You Were Mine

Made in the USA
Middletown, DE
23 June 2017